The Year
of the Intern
by
Robin Cook, M.D.

A SIGNET BOOK

SIGNET
Published by the Penguin Group
Penguin Books USA Inc., 375 Hudson Street,
New York, New York 10014, U.S.A.
Penguin Books Ltd, 27 Wrights Lane,
London W8 5TZ, England
Penguin Books Australia Ltd, Ringwood,
Victoria, Australia
Penguin Books Canada Ltd, 10 Alcorn Avenue,
Toronto, Ontario, Canada M4V 3B2
Penguin Books (N.Z.) Ltd, 182–190 Wairau Road,
Auckland 10, New Zealand

Penguin Books Ltd, Registered Offices:
Harmondsworth, Middlesex, England

Published by Signet, an imprint of New American Library,
a division of Penguin Books USA Inc.

This is an authorized reprint of a hardcover edition published by
Harcourt Brace Jovanovich, Inc.

First Signet Printing, September, 1973
20   19   18   17   16   15   14   13

REGISTERED TRADEMARK—MARCA REGISTRADA

Printed in the United States of America

*This book is dedicated to the ideal of medicine
we all held the year we entered medical school.*

Contents

Contents

Acknowledgments

This book was written under the Pacific Ocean, while the author was on Polaris submarine patrol in the U.S.S. *Kamehameha,* and it could not have been written without the kindness and understanding of the *Kamehameha*'s commanding officer, Commander James Sagerholm. To him I acknowledge a debt of thanks.

Thanks, also, to Craig Van Dyke, M.D., a psychiatrist in the making, who practiced before he started and thereby sustained the author through many a dark night of doubt and revision.

The First Word

Americans cling to their myths. Nowhere is this more evident than in the emotion-charged realm of medicine and medical care. People believe what they want to believe, what they have always believed, and either ignore or dismiss as false anything that threatens their comforting confidence in their own doctors or the kind of medical treatment they may be receiving.

Only recently, and with reluctance, has the public at large begun to stir out of its smug assumption that medical personnel and care in the United States are the best in the world. And even this unwelcome awakening has been accomplished more by economics than by reason, more by the rising costs for medical care than by the quality of that care. Although Mrs. Brown may concede that a few things are wrong, nevertheless she clings firmly to the belief that her own dear doctor down the street is the best doctor in town—such a wonderful man! And all those young interns, bless their souls—so dedicated and wholesome!

The basis for this adoration of the medical world lies deep in the psyche of the modern American. His romance with medicine is demonstrated daily by the hours he spends transfixed in front of the television set watching the diagnostic and therapeutic triumphs of omniscient physicians.

Such romanticism, with its directed credibility and, hence, its tolerance so narrow, makes the presentation of contradictory ideas extremely difficult. Nevertheless, that is the goal of the present book—to strip the contemporary mythology and mystique from the year of internship and to convey it in all its hard reality. The psychological effects of internship on the doctor are profound. (That being so, imagine the effects on an endless parade of patients!)

I fervently ask the reader to set forth with an open mind, putting aside that almost irresistible urge to glorify medicine and the people involved in it, and to try to understand the actual effects of an internship on a real person. The people involved in medicine *are* real people, beset by a complete array of hang-ups—anger, anxiety, hostility, egocentrism. When placed in an adverse environment, they respond like people, not superhuman healers. And, television dramas notwithstanding, internship as it exists today *is* an adverse environment. (The lack of sleep alone is sufficient to explain a host of aberrant behavior patterns; recent studies have shown that an individual will quickly become schizophrenic if deprived of enough sleep.)

All the events described here are real. They constitute typical—not unusual—days in the life of an intern. Dr. Peters himself represents a synthesis of my own experiences and those of my intern colleagues. He is therefore a composite of several real people. While he does not display the aberrations of a particular psychosocial personality, he nonetheless stands for every intern to a greater or lesser degree. That he emerges as an often whining and complaining individual who fails socially as he develops professionally should not be surprising. True, during his internship Dr. Peters gains greatly in medical knowledge and experience; he also develops a more objective attitude toward death. At the same time, however, there is a concomitant intensity in his repressed anger and hostility that leads toward greater isolation, more autistic behavior, stronger feelings of self-pity, and an inability to establish significant interpersonal relationships.

Other aspects of medical practice as presented here will also grate upon accepted beliefs. Again the reader is implored to keep an open mind, to remember that much of the impersonality and anonymity directed toward patients is simply the inevitable result of familiarity with human illness.

Such impersonality can, of course, be taken to extremes where the patient ceases altogether to be an individual and becomes merely an object to be treated. This is definitely pathological. The potential of reaching this pathological state does exist for an intern. In fact, the potential is virtually forced on him, to cope with—usually without guidance—as his nature dictates.

One word to anticipate a specific criticism: since Dr. Peters interned in a community teaching hospital, rather than in a university medical center, some will object that any conclusions may apply only to that environment. Perhaps such a comment has a certain merit, but I do not believe it reduces the validity of my central argument. On the contrary, Peters's experiences might well have been intensified if set within a university center. The competition there among interns—the game of keeping ahead of the next guy—is almost always more severe, and, in such a context, chart work and searches of the medical literature are likely to receive more concern than the patient in the daily value system. I believe that Dr. Peters's experiences apply essentially to both the university and the community teaching programs. What happened to him is substantiated by a convincing similarity of incidents related to me by a number of doctors from each type of internship.

The hospital environment that is not represented here is the nonteaching, nonuniversity hospital. It is possible the criticism does apply to internships in such institutions.

The manuscript of this book was read by eight doctors, none more than three years past his internship. All but one agreed that the content is authentic, bluntly realistic, and completely representative of his own situation. The dissident stated that the attending physicians in the hospital at which he interned had been more readily available for teaching, more sensitive to his needs, than they are depicted here. This doctor had interned at a West Coast university medical center. Perhaps the lesson to be drawn from this is that all medical novices should intern where he did.

I repeat that this book is true. If it does not represent all internships in all hospitals, it represents most in many. It reflects honestly a pervasive condition, disheartening at the least and dangerous at the worst. That is sufficient reason for *The Year of the Intern.*

Day 15

General Surgery

I was already out stone-cold when the telephone rang again, half an hour later. I got it on the end of the first ring, reaching instinctively, almost in a panic, as the surgery book that had put me to sleep crashed off the bed onto the floor. God, what now? The nurse was desperate: "Dr. Peters, the patient you saw earlier has stopped breathing and he doesn't have any pulse."

"I'm on my way."

Fumbling down the phone, I went into my routine: pants, shirt, shoes, a dash down the hall to the elevator as I zipped my fly. I pushed the button and heard the high-pitched whine of the electric motor. Waiting impatiently, I suddenly realized I didn't know which patient she meant. There were so many. Mental pictures of those I had seen that night raced through my head. Mrs. Takura, Roso, Sperry, the new one, an old man with stomach cancer. It must be he. He was a private patient, and the first time I had seen him was when I'd been called away from dealing with the new admissions because he had developed a sudden severe abdominal pain. He had turned out to be emaciated and so weak he couldn't move, could hardly answer questions. . . .

Frustrated at the slowness of the elevator, I slapped my hand against the door.

My information on the old man was meager. The nurse on the case didn't know much. There was no case history on the chart, just a brief note saying he was seventy-one and had been suffering from gastric cancer for three years; his stomach had been removed by surgery about two months earlier. According to the chart, he had entered the hospital this time because of pain, dizziness, and general malaise.

Grinding to the end of its mechanical deliberations, the elevator arrived and the maroon door folded into the wall. I

4

stepped in, pushed the button, and waited impatiently again for the clumsy beast to take me to the ground floor.

My examination of the old man had not revealed anything unexpected. Clearly, he was in great pain, and with good reason—the cancer had undoubtedly spread inside his abdomen. After trying vainly to reach his private physician by phone, I had simply started a new intravenous drip and ordered some Demerol to help him sleep. Nothing else had occurred to me.

The elevator delivered me to the ground floor at last. I quickly crossed the courtyard, entered the main hospital building, and used the back stairs to get to the patient's floor. As I stepped into his room, I saw the nurse standing helplessly in the soft glow of the bed lamp. The man was so thin that each individual rib poked out on the sides of his chest; his abdomen dropped into a pit below the rib cage. He lay perfectly still; his eyes were closed. I looked closely at his chest. I was so accustomed to seeing chests move in steady respiration that my eyes tricked me into thinking this one rose and fell a little, but it didn't. I tried for a pulse. Nothing. But some people have very faint pulses. I checked to make sure I was on the correct side of the wrist, the side with the thumb, and then I held the other wrist. Nothing.

"No cardiac arrest, Doctor. I was told by the attending that we shouldn't call a cardiac arrest." The nurse sounded defensive.

Shut up, I thought, irritated and relieved at the same instant. I wasn't worried about calling an arrest. I just wanted to be absolutely certain, because this was the first time I had been faced with the sole responsibility for pronouncing death. Sure, there had been deaths in medical school, plenty of them, but always back then—only last year, in fact, yet so long ago—always then the house staff had been there to help, an intern or a resident; it wasn't a student's job. Now *I* was the house staff, and I had to make the decision alone; a judgment call, I thought wryly, like baseball, safe or out and no appeal to the umpire. He was dead. Or . . . was he? Demerol, thin old man, deep anesthesia—the combination could produce suspended animation.

I took out my stethoscope slowly, postponing the decision, and finally settled the pieces into my ears while I held the diaphragm on the old man's heart. A series of brittle crackling sounds came up to me as his hairs moved under the stethoscope tip in response to my own trembling. I couldn't hear the heart—yet couldn't I, almost? Muffled and far away? . . . My

overheated imagination kept giving me the vital, normal beat
of life. And then I realized it was my own heart echoing in my
ears. Pulling the stethoscope away, I tried again for pulses, at
the wrists, groin, and neck. All was quiet, yet an eerie feeling
said he was alive, that he was going to wake up and I was
going to be a fool. How could he be dead when I had talked
with him a few hours ago? I hated being where I was. Who
was I to say whether he was alive or dead? Who was I?

The nurse and I looked at each other in the half-light. I had
been so absorbed in my own thoughts that I was almost surprised to see her still there. Holding open the man's eyelids, I
peered down into a pair of brown eyes, normal looking except
that the enlarged pupils did not contract as my penlight beam
passed over the aged cornea. I felt sure he was dead; I hoped
he was dead, because I was about to pronounce him so. "He's
dead, I guess," I said, looking at the nurse again, but she
turned away. Probably thought I was an ass.

"He's the first patient directly under my care to die," she
said, turning back to me suddenly. Her hands hung limply at
her sides. It took me a moment to realize she was pleading for
me to say something about the Demerol, that it hadn't been
the Demerol she had given. But how was I to know what
killed him? A scene from an old horror movie kept flashing in
my head, the one in which the corpse rises slowly from a cement slab in the morgue. I was becoming angry with myself,
but I simply had to listen again. The stethoscope went back in
my ears. In the still night my own breathing crashed in my
head. Dead, death, cold, silent, whispered the rational centers
of my brain. I should say something nice to the nurse. "It must
have been very smooth and effortless—he died with dignity.
I'm sure he's grateful to you for the Demerol." Grateful?
What a bizarre thing to say. There I was wrestling with my
own uncertainties, barely keeping ahead, and still trying to
persuade someone else to be calm. Fighting an urge to feel for
the pulses again, I pulled the sheet up over his head. "We'd
better call his doctor," I said as we left the room.

The private M.D. answered the phone so quickly his voice
was like a cold washcloth on my face. I told him who I was
and why I was calling.

"Fine, fine. Tell the family, and get an autopsy for sure. I
want to see what happened to that connection I made between
the stomach pouch and the small intestine. It was an anastomosis made with only a single layer of sutures. I really think
the single-layer technique is the best; it's so much faster. Any-

way, the old man has been a curious case, especially since he lived so much longer than we expected. So get an autopsy, okay, Peters?"

"Okay, I'll try."

Plunging back into the silence of my mind after this jovial one-sided conversation, I tried to organize my thoughts. The private doctor wanted an autopsy. Fine. Great. Where was the family's number? A female arm came over my shoulder, pointing to a line on the chart: "Next of kin—son." Really a lousy situation. Unknown stupid intern calling in the night. I tried to think of some neutral word, one to convey the fact without the meaning. "Dead," "demise" . . . no, "passed away." The ring of the phone was interrupted by a cheerful hello.

"My name is Dr. Peters, and . . . I'm sorry to inform you that your father has passed away."

At the other end there was a long silence; perhaps he hadn't understood me. Then the voice returned.

"It was expected."

"There's something else." The word "autopsy" was on the tip of my tongue.

"Yes?"

"Well . . . never mind. We'll discuss that later, but I must ask you to come to the hospital tonight." The nurse had been telling me that in frantic pantomime.

"All right, we'll be there. Thank you."

"I'm terribly sorry, and thank you."

An older nurse materialized from the darkness of the corridor and pushed a number of official papers under my nose, indicating where I was to sign my name and write the time of death. I wondered when he had died; I really didn't know.

"What time did he die?" I asked, looking at the new arrival, who was standing on my right.

"He died when you pronounced him dead, Doctor." This nurse, a night supervisor, was known for pithy rhetoric and a jaundiced view of interns. But not even her acid tone and her obvious scorn for my naïveté could erase the scene of the dead man rising from the slab.

"Call me when the family arrives," I said.

"Yes, Doctor, and thank you."

"Well, thank you," I returned. Everybody thanking everybody. In my tiredness small things loomed huge and absurd. The urge to go in and feel again for a pulse was still with me, but with an effort I went rapidly by the dead man's room; the nurses might be watching. Why did I keep worrying about him waking up? What about the man as a person, didn't that matter? Yes, of course, but I didn't know him. I stopped on the landing of the stairway. True, I didn't know him, but he was a person. An old man, seventy-one, sure—but still a man, a father, a person. I continued down the stairs. I couldn't fool myself. If he woke up now I'd be the joke of the hospital. Confidence in being a doctor was coming slowly enough; that would kill it.

Back in the elevator, I tried to remember when I had changed, but I could only recall scenes, possible small turning points, such as my first visit to the ward during medical school, and the eleven-year-old girl who lay on the bed looking hopefully up at us. She had cystic fibrosis, which is usually terminal. Listening to the house staff discuss the cases, I had melted, unable to look the youngster in the face. "Perhaps there's a chance we can keep her alive until her late teens," the attending physician had said as we walked away. At that instant I almost became a plumber.

The elevator door opened. Somehow, sometime, my responses had changed. Now I was worrying that someone would wake up in the morgue and ruin my image, make me look ridiculous. All right, I had changed, clearly for the worse, but what could I do about it?

Back in my room, the bed squeaked as it took my weight. In the semidarkness, my mind's eye called up every detail of that skinny dead body. Did other interns brood like this? I couldn't imagine it, but then, I couldn't imagine what they would think. They seemed so self-possessed, so certain even when they had no right to be. Before med school, I had imagined an intern's crises in a different way, as somehow more noble. Always the problem had revolved around the loss of my own patient after a long struggle, the anguish of a life lost. But here I was sweating over whether someone else's patient would start breathing again, and it bugged me that I could dismiss the person part. It was nine-forty-five. I rolled over, picked up the phone, and called the nurses' quarters. At that moment I needed someone to be with, someone to prove that life went on. "Miss Stevens, please. Jan, can you come over? No, nothing's wrong. Sure, bring the mangoes. That's right, I'm on call."

Through the curtains I could pick out a few stars. For two weeks I had been an intern, the longest two weeks of my twenty-five years, the culmination of everything, high school, college, medical school. How I had dreamed of it! Now nearly everybody I knew was in this blessed state of internship, and it was a crappy job, and when it wasn't crappy it was a confusing mess. "Well, Peters, you've really done it now. I just want you to remember that it's easy to drop out of the big leagues but almost impossible to get back in." That is a direct quote from my surgery professor when he learned that I had decided to intern at a nonuniversity center, away from the ivory-tower medical circuit, out in the boondocks. And to the eastern medical establishment there is no boondock like Hawaii.

In terms of the immutable intern computer-matching system, I had been destined for any Ivy League internship. On that score, it was true enough that I had dropped out. But in the end I couldn't help myself. As med school wore on I began to see that becoming a doctor meant giving yourself over to the system, like a piece of wood on a chipping machine. At the end of the machine I would be smooth and probably salable, full of knowledge. But as the chips flew away, so would those "nonproductive" personality traits—empathy, humanity, the instinct to care. I had to prevent that if I could, if it wasn't too late. So at the last minute I had jumped off the machine. "Well, Peters, you've really done it now."

Losing the skinny old man had me up tight, and I leaped off the bed even before Jan knocked. Thank God it wasn't the phone. I was afraid of the phone. "Jan, it's good to see you, mangoes and all." Mangoes, just what I needed. "Sure, you can turn on the light. I was just sitting here thinking. All right, leave it off. Knives and a dish? You want to eat those mangoes now?" I didn't want mangoes, but it wasn't worth an argument, and, anyway, she looked delicious with the soft light shining on her hair, and she smelled as if she'd just stepped out of the shower, sweeter than any perfume. But the prettiest thing about Jan was her voice. Maybe she'd sing a little for me.

I got a dish and two knives, and we sat on the floor and started eating mangoes. At first, we didn't talk, and that was one reason I liked her, for her reticence. She was good to look at, too, very much so, yet awfully young, I suspected. Before tonight we had gone out twice, yet we weren't at all close. It didn't matter. Well, it did matter, because I wanted to know her, especially right then. There was something poetic about her blond hair and small features; just then I needed us to be close.

The mango was sticky. I peeled the whole thing and went over to the sink to rinse my hands. When I turned back to her, she was facing away from me, and the light from the window

was throwing areas of silver sheen on her hair. She was leaning on one arm, with her legs tucked along her other side. I almost asked her to sing "Try To Remember," but I didn't,
probably because she would have—she did almost anything I
asked in the way of song. If she started singing now, though,
everybody in the quarters would hear it. In fact, they probably
could hear us eating the mangoes. As I sat down next to her,
she tilted her face and I could see her eyes.

"Something happened tonight," I offered.

"I know," she said.

That almost stopped me right there. *I know.* Like hell she
knew, and I not only knew that she didn't know, but also that
I wasn't going to be able to explain it to her. I went on anyway.

"I pronounced a skinny old man with cancer dead, and right
now I'm afraid the phone will ring and it'll be the nurse saying
he's alive after all."

She tilted her head the other way, taking her eyes away.
Then she really said the right thing. She said that was funny!
Funny?

"Don't you think it's crazy?"

Well, yes, it was crazy, but it was funny, too.

"You know that a *person* died tonight, and all I can think
about is that he might still be alive and it'll be a big joke. A
big joke on me."

She agreed that it would be a joke. That was the extent of
her analysis on the subject. I persisted: "Don't you think it's
strange for me to think such a stupid thing about the final
event of somebody's life?"

That was too much for her, I guess, because the next thing
she said was to ask if I didn't like mangoes. I like mangoes all
right, but I didn't want any just then; I even offered her some
of mine. Despite the misfirings, I somehow felt better, as if
trying to communicate my thoughts had removed the skinny
old man from the front of my mind. I wondered if Jan would
sing "Aquarius." This girl made me feel happy in a simple
way.

I put my arm around her, and she popped a piece of mango
into my mouth, ludicrously throwing up a barrier without
meaning to. So, okay, we won't talk about my skinny old man,
I thought. I kissed her, and when I realized she was kissing me
back, I thought how nice it would be to make love with her.
We kissed again, and she pressed against me, so I could feel
her warmth and softness. My hands were still sticky from the

mangoes, but I ran them up and down her back, wondering if she would make love. The thought chased everything else from my mind. It was ridiculous to be on the floor, and I was pondering how to get us both over to the bed when I realized she wasn't wearing anything under her light dress—I had been too busy caressing her back to notice. She sensed my desire to move, and we stood up simultaneously. As I began to lift her dress, she stopped me, clasping my forearms, undid the back, and stepped out of it, so beautiful in the soft light. She might not have understood my problem, but she certainly had cleared my mind. That poetry I had thought about her enlarged to include her breasts. I peeled off my shirt, dropped the stethoscope on the floor, and moved to her quickly, afraid she might disappear.

The telephone rang. The moment was gone, and the skinny old man was back in my life. Jan lay down on the bed while I stood looking at the phone. My mind had been clear and well directed ten seconds before; now it became a jumble again, and with confusion came the terrible thought: He's started breathing. I let the phone ring three times, hoping it would stop. When I answered, it was the nurse.

"Dr. Peters, the family has arrived."

"Thank you. I'll be right there."

A sense of relief flooded over me; it was only the family. The old man was still dead.

I put my hand on the small of Jan's back; her soft warm skin demanded attention, and the graceful curve of her back didn't help me think how to ask the family for an autopsy. Finding my white shirt was easy, but the stethoscope eluded me until I stepped on it as I was putting the shirt on.

"Jan, I've got to run over to the hospital. I'll be right back, I hope."

Blinking, I stepped from the warmth of the room into the fluorescence of the hall, on my way to face the trial of the maroon elevator.

There is something ominous about the darkness and silence of a hospital asleep. By now it was ten-thirty, and the ward had slipped into the night routine, a kind of half life made up of soft lights and muted voices. I walked down the long hall toward the nurses' station, past rooms marked only by the flow of night lights. At the other end, I could see two nurses talking, although no sound reached me. The hall seemed especially long this time, like a tunnel, and the light at the end reminded me of a Rembrandt painting, sharply bright areas surrounded by burnt umber. I knew that the calm could be shattered at any moment, driving me forward to face some new crisis, but for the moment that world stood still.

Autopsy. I had to ask for an autopsy. I remembered my first one, in the second year of medical school at the beginning of our pathology course, when I still thought medicine made everybody well. "File in here, men, and group yourselves around the table." We had all looked the same in our white coats, marching in like well-behaved school children, which I suppose we were. And then I had seen her, not the one we were there to see, but another one, on the next slab, who was next in line to be autopsied. Her skin was a cold yellow gray, with a pox of herpes zoster extending from the right arm over the breast to the midline. Herpes zoster is a very serious and vivid skin disorder characterized by large crusted lesions. Its visual effect had been doubly startling in those surroundings. The woman lay on a cement table amid a thousand foul stains. Water flowed under and around her down longitudinal channels about three inches apart, falling into a drain at the base with an obscene sucking noise. Some scratchy pencil marks had been made on a manila tag tied around her right arm. Her hair looked brittle. But the thing that had bothered me most was the sickly color of her skin. About thirty, not much older than I am, I had thought. The sight had made me feel not physically ill, as a few of the med students did, but somehow mentally bankrupt.

She was undeniably dead, really dead, and yet she looked so alive except for the color. Dead, alive, dead . . . those words, absolute polarities, had seemed to fuse in my mind. The body I had dissected in first-year anatomy hadn't been anything like this. It had been dead and hadn't even suggested being alive. It's the surroundings that make it bad, I had told myself, the crumbling dirty-gray room and the half-light, itself seeming foul and decayed as it struggled through grimy windows. What the hell do you want, Peters? A velvet bier, candles, and roses?

But that woman wasn't the patient we had come to see. I had pressed in among the white coats grouped around another examining table, and had caught glimpses of fleshy organs and heard gurgling noises as the pathology professor cut away, demonstrating his technique. I hadn't been able to see enough to appreciate the lesson, and, anyway, what had interested me was back over my shoulder. Everybody else had been transfixed by those organs; I couldn't stop looking at the wrong body. I hadn't wanted to touch her, but I had, and finding that she wasn't very cold had only made it worse. I hadn't been shocked anymore, just scared, and not because I had touched her but because she was slapping me in the face with the elementary fact that the difference between life and death was a matter of time and luck. Neither meant anything to her now. Scared, too, because she had been a young woman, perhaps desired and full of possibility, and now she was dead and yellow, lying on a stained cement slab in a dirty subterranean room. It was one thing to deal with sex when it hummed with life, warmth, and vigor. But I couldn't deal with this. My jumbled mind had registered a hundred thoughts; sex had undeniably been among them, my own memories of sexual love.

That had been a long time ago and six thousand miles away. Right now, I had to deal with the skinny old man's autopsy. "The family is over there, Doctor, on the couch," said one of the nurses when I reached the ward reception area. Two people seemed to appear suddenly where none had been before. As we approached each other, the word "autopsy" kept bringing back that brittle hair and herpes zoster. Maybe I should call it a "post-mortem"; sounds better.

"I'm sorry."

"It's all right, we expected it."

"We would like an autopsy." The word came quite naturally, after all.

"All right, it's the least we can do."

The least we can do? It puzzled me that they felt they had to do anything at all. I had felt rotten enough being the one to call them so late at night and say that their father was dead, and now I felt even more guilty asking for the autopsy permission. But apparently they felt guilty, too. Since no one can be blamed for death, everyone shares the guilt. The least we can do? I was making too much of a simple comment. What response had I expected from them? Accusations? Tantrums? Most people, I would learn, are simply struck numb by death and carried along by their ordinary, civil, reflexive behavior.

"We'll take care of the rest of the paper work, Doctor," one of the nurses offered.

"Thank you," I said.

"We appreciate what you've done, Doctor," said the son as I stepped away from the nurses' station.

"You're welcome." Nice people, I thought, walking away, and how lucky for me that they can't read my thoughts. Even now I felt an urge to go groping over the dead man's body for a pulse. If they knew my secret fear, would they be angry or just shocked? Shocked at first, probably, and then angry. But what would they think if their father woke up in the morgue? At that I smiled to myself, for of course hardly anybody gets taken to the morgue nowadays. Most go to a funeral home. Too many TV programs and bad movies. I was a fool, I mused, especially when I was tired, and at this point I was exhausted.

"Doctor, the phone is for you." The voice came after me as I was almost to the end of the dark hall. It must be Jan, I thought, and remembered suddenly how good she had looked standing naked in my room. Her image fused with the autopsy room in medical school, with that yellow body and the herpes zoster on the breast. But the call wasn't from Jan; it was from Ward A—another frantic nurse. Something about somebody's venous pressure going to zero. The skinny old man's son was still standing there. I caught his eye one last time, for an instant, and I suddenly felt proud to be there, and then foolish at my pride. Running the other way down the hall, I thought my situation was anything but glorious.

Venous pressure? My knowledge of it consisted of a dutifully memorized definition: "Venous pressure is the resting pressure in the large veins of the body." Other than that I knew almost nothing. Regardless, I rushed headlong, as if I knew everything. That was my job.

What little courage I had fell away when I saw that the nurses were gathered around Marsha Potts's room. Marsha Potts was the tragedy of the hospital. On rounds the very first day of my internship two weeks ago we had stood in her room as the story unfolded. Ulcer symptoms had brought her into the clinic, and there it had been, big as life, right on the X ray. It always made everybody happy when you could see an ulcer. The radiologist was pleased because he had gotten a good film, and the surgeons were ecstatic, complimenting one another on their diagnostic acumen and sharpening their scalpels. It was a fine time. Usually it was fine for the patient, too, but not for Marsha.

The doctors had performed a gastrectomy, taking out most of her stomach and sealing the end of the small intestine that normally leads out of the stomach. Then they had selected a point a few inches farther down the small intestine and, after making a hole, had sewed it to the little pouch made from the remains of the stomach, thus giving Marsha a new, if somewhat smaller, stomach. This operation, known as a Billroth II, entails an enormous amount of cutting and stitching, and is therefore popular with surgeons.

Marsha had sailed smoothly through it all—at least, everybody had thought so—until the third day, when the connection between intestine and stomach pouch broke down. This had allowed her pancreatic and gastric juices to leak out inside her abdomen, and she began to digest herself. The digestive enzymes literally ate their way up through the incision, and her abdomen became an open draining wound about twelve inches in diameter. The nurses kept it covered with baby food, in the attempt to absorb some of the pancreatic juice and neutralize the enzymes. For weeks now the putrid and penetrating smell had turned everybody's stomach. But for me the worst thing about the case was that I knew I couldn't handle it. No way.

When I entered the small room where she was isolated, the situation was as bad as it could be. Her skin was a terrible jaundiced gray, and her hands were flapping feebly by her sides. The nurse seemed relieved that a doctor had come, but, instead of gaining confidence from that, I could only think, Oh, you silly girl, if you could see into my mind you'd see nothing at all, a big void.

Marsha Potts had apparently suffered total body failure. Leafing through the stacks of charts and laboratory results, I tried to get some hint of what was going on and buy a little time to collect my wits. A large black cockroach clung to the wall over the bed, but I didn't bother it; we'd get it later. It was hard to imagine that life in any form depended on my thoughts.

Yet a bit of information was beginning to drift across my mind. The pulse, yes. I felt for it and found it strong and full, about 72 per minute, almost normal. Good. Now, if the venous pressure had gone to zero while the heart seemed to be working okay, it must mean there wasn't enough blood on the venous side. At least I was thinking. The last thing I wanted to do was remove the bulky, sodden dressing from her abdomen. Drops of perspiration rolled down my face. It was damn hot in here. Blood pressure? The nurse said it was 110/90. How the hell could her blood pressure and pulse be so good without venous pressure? With no venous pressure the heart wouldn't fill, and if it wouldn't fill nothing would come out, hence no blood pressure or pulse. That's how it was supposed to work, but obviously in this case it wasn't. Damn those physiology professors. In the medical-school physiology lab, they had a dog with tubes sticking out of his heart, arteries, and veins.

Everything worked perfectly there, as it usually did in the laboratory. When the professors reduced the blood in the dog's heart by dropping the venous pressure, the dog's blood pressure followed suit and fell rapidly. It was automatic and reproducible, as if the dog were a machine.

Marsha Potts was no machine. Still, why couldn't she work like the animals in the laboratory, instead of presenting me with an insoluble, overwhelming mess? I hardly knew where to start my examination. She didn't have any swelling of her skin from fluid retention, except on her backside—the usual place for such edema, as a result of lying in bed too long; Marsha had been flat on her back for about three months. I bent her left hand back, and it jerked forward. Fantastic. She had liver flap. When the liver fails, the patient develops a curious reflex: if you bend the hand back onto the wrist it jerks forward in a flapping movement, like a child waving bye-bye. Experiencing the joy of a positive finding, I looked again at the chart. Liver flap was not listed. I didn't know much about venous pressure, but I could write whole pages about liver flap, which I had found only once before. I tested her other hand, and the reflex worked again. It meant she was in very bad shape. In fact, while I was slipping into an academic appreciation of my diagnosis the woman was dying before my eyes.

In truth, she was already virtually dead; yet, technically, she was still alive. She had friends and a family who thought of her as a living person. But she couldn't talk, and every organ system was failing. Could she think? Probably not. In fact, for just a moment I knew she'd be better off dead, but I pushed the notion roughly away. How can you *know* someone's better off dead? You can't; it's sheer presumption. Marsha Potts's case was getting physically confusing, too. The woman with the herpes on her breast had looked alive but was in fact dead. The one in front of me in that small hot room was alive, but . . . What about the intravenous?

"How much IV fluid has she had over the last twenty-four hours?" I asked the nurse.

"It's all here, Doctor, on the input/output sheet. It's been about 4,000 cc."

"Four thousand!" I tried not to appear surprised, although it seemed a lot to me. "What has it been?"

"Well, mostly saline, but some Isolyte M, too," she answered.

What the hell was Isolyte M? I had never heard of it. Twisting the bottle that was running, I read "Isolyte M" and, twist-

ing it the other way, "Sodium, chloride, potassium, magnesium
. . ." No need to read farther; this was a maintenance solution. The input/output sheet was a jumble of seemingly ran-
dom figures, but I liked that. Right from the beginning of
medical school I had been fascinated by the balance of fluids
and electrolytes, so fascinated that I could sometimes worry
about the sodium and almost forget the patient. This patient's
input seemed to match her output except for what had soaked
into that huge dressing covering the wound. A sump suction
had been set up to pull fluid from the bottom of her abdominal wound, but it didn't seem very effective. Also, the bland
food she was getting probably didn't have much nutritional effect. It was delivered to her stomach by a tube through her
nose; since her own digestive juices had formed a fistula, or
passage, between the stomach and the colon, the food was actually going directly from the stomach to the large bowel and
out the rectum essentially unchanged.

Although she did not appear to be dehydrated, her urine
showed obvious evidence of infection, in the form of blood,
bile, and small bits of organic matter floating around in the
catheter bag. With so much crud in there, the only way to
learn if her urine was too concentrated was to test its specific
gravity.

"I don't suppose we have a hydrometer on the floor, do
we?" The nurse disappeared, only too pleased to be given a
task, regardless of its potential merit. I still had no way to explain Marsha's venous pressure. I continued to examine her,
looking for some sign of cardiac failure to explain it and finding none at all. Apparently the inevitable was closing in: I
would have to look at her wound.

"Is this what you mean, Doctor?" The nurse handed me a
bottle of papers designed to test urine for sugar.

"No, a hydrometer, a little instrument you float in the urine.
It looks like a thermometer." She disappeared again while I
looked at the label on the bottle she had given me. Perhaps I'd
test the urine for sugar anyhow; no reason not to.

"Is this it, Doctor?"

"That's the baby." I took the hydrometer and unhooked the
catheter bag. Holding my breath to avoid the smell, I poured
into a small vial what I guessed would be enough urine to float
the hydrometer. Carefully I lowered the instrument into the
urine, but I couldn't get a reading. The damn thing kept sticking to the side of the flask rather than floating free as it was
supposed to. I held the flask in my left hand and tapped it with

the knuckle of my right index finger, trying to free the instrument. I only succeeded in splashing urine on my arm. By adding more urine to the vial, I finally got the hydrometer to bob up and down. The specific gravity was within normal limits—in fact, was absolutely normal—so Marsha wasn't dehydrated. For some reason, medical people shy away from the word "normal" without its qualifiers; it's always "within normal limits" or "essentially normal."

Marsha groaned again. As I drew in a big breath, I was whacked by a symphony of smells in the room. As far back as I could remember, I'd never been able to cope with bad odors. In grammar school, when one of my classmates vomited I had been sure to follow with a sympathetic reflex once the smell reached me. In medical school, despite three masks and all sorts of mental tricks, I had been known to retch in the middle of pathology lab.

Still trying to think of an explanation for Marsha Potts's condition, I wondered if she might have Gram-negative bacteria in her blood stream, perhaps a bacterial infection like pseudomonas, for instance; pseudomonas sometimes leads to a condition called Gram-negative sepsis, which is one of medicine's most terrifying sights. One minute the patient is all right; then a shiver and everything goes to hell. Maybe that could explain the venous-pressure problem. But I saw no sign of sepsis.

Marsha was moaning regularly now, and each moan was like a new indictment passed down against me. Why couldn't I figure this out? Walking around to the other side of the bed, I directed the nurse's attention to the cockroach, which had moved a few feet, down to shoulder height. She jumped and vanished, returning almost instantly with several yards of toilet paper, which made quick work of the bug. A bug like that didn't bother me much—not like the rats in the hospital in New York. The grounds people there had always said they knew about them and were working on the problem, but I had seen them again and again.

Perhaps something was wrong with the three-way stopcock on the intravenous line. When I opened the stopcock to the position for measuring venous pressure, it didn't budge from zero. Flipping it closed again, I filled the column with the IV solution and then connected the column with the patient. The level stayed up for a few seconds before starting to fall rapidly, then slowly, as the nurse said it would, first to 10 cm. and finally to zero. Confusing, especially those three-way stop-

cocks. I had never quite gotten them straight, never quite
known which knob to turn for what connection.

I asked the nurse for a large syringe full of saline and unhooked the whole tangle of tubing from the catheter going into
the femoral vein, just below the groin. Marsha had been sustained intravenously for so long that her arm veins were useless for IV's, and the doctors had begun using her leg veins.
To my surprise, no blood from the vein came back up into the
catheter tube, even with the pressure of the maintenance solution gone. When I flushed about 10 cc. of saline fluid through
the catheter with the syringe, I felt a definite resistance; then
suddenly the saline fluid went more easily. As I withdrew the
plunger of the syringe, a red streak of blood appeared in the
catheter.

Obviously there had been a plug at the end of the catheter
inside Marsha's vein, probably a small blood clot, which had
acted like a ball valve, allowing the IV maintenance solution
to enter but keeping anything from coming back. A venous-
pressure reading depended on blood being able to rise through
the catheter. All this I told the nurse, but I didn't tell her that
the blood clot was now probably in Marsha's lungs. If so,
though, it had to be small, thank God.

Hooking up the column once more, I filled it and lined it up
with the patient. After I was certain it showed a normal venous pressure and was going to stay there, I restarted the IV.

"I'm sorry, Doctor, I didn't know," the nurse said.

"No need to be sorry, no sweat." I was glad to have solved a
problem, even a miniproblem. Considering that I had started
with a blank mind, the achievement seemed notable, although
the patient was the same. She moaned again, her lips twitching. She was just a shadow of a person, really, and my awareness of her erased the feeling of accomplishment. All I wanted
to do now was get out of there, but it was not to be.

"Doctor, as long as you're here, would you mind looking at
Mr. Roso? His hiccups are keeping the other patients awake."

As the nurse and I walked down the corridor toward Roso's
ward, I thought what an unusual building the hospital was,
something entirely new in my experience. Its halls communi-
cated directly with the outside, at least in the old, low section,
and grass grew right up to the edge of the hallway. A large
monkeypod tree dominated the courtyard, leaning and rustling
in the wind. The grounds were immaculately manicured and
studded with enormous tropical trees. What a difference from
other hospitals I'd worked in. There had been one tree on the

grounds of my medical school in New York, but it was cut down before I left. The rest was cement and brick, all yellow. But the wreck of them all was Bellevue, where I had done my fourth-year clinical clerkship (working essentially as an intern, although I was officially still a medical student). The halls there were covered with depressing brown paint, everywhere peeling away and so disgusting to touch that we had been careful to walk in the middle, away from the walls. My on-call room had a broken window and uncertain plumbing. It stood on the other side of the hospital from the medical wards, which could be reached only by navigating the respiratory center, where all the TB patients were. During the journey, I had sometimes unconsciously held my breath as I passed through the respiratory ward and so arrived breathless at my destination.

If Dante could have seen Bellevue, he would have given it a prominent place in the *Inferno*. How I had hated those two months. I saw a movie once that reminded me of Bellevue; it was Kafka's *The Trial*, and in it characters were forever moving down endless halls. That was Bellevue, endless halls, especially if you were holding your breath. Any window clean enough to see through revealed only another dirty building with more halls. Even an innocent act of nature could be dangerous. I once went into the men's room rather hurriedly, unzipping as I walked through the door, and literally fell into a group of patients who were busily mainlining heroin with hospital syringes. That was the first time patients threatened to kill me, but not the last.

Hawaii was nothing like Bellevue. Here I hadn't been threatened, not yet, anyway, and all the walls were clean and carefully painted, even in the cellar. I had supposed all hospital cellars looked alike, but here they were clean, even bright.

I don't know why TB worried me so much. Part of the irrational in all of us, I suppose, when you decide some things are bad and others won't affect you. After I read about malignant hypertension, I thought I had it every time I got a headache. Maybe TB bothered me because my first patient for physical diagnosis had had TB.

All of us medical students had been listening to each other's chests, which resulted in a lot of laughs and little instruction. Then we had been bussed out to a chronic-disease hospital to listen to patients for the first time. This place was called Goldwater Memorial, and it made Bellevue look like the Waldorf. After drawing a card with someone's name on it, I had approached the man's bed feeling so transparently *new* that I might have had a sign on my forehead reading "2nd Year Medical Student, 1st Attempt." Everything had gone fine until I listened to his left-costophrenic-angle area from the right side of the bed. Leaning across his chest, I had told him to cough, which he did, directly in my ear, and I could feel it dripping down the side of my head, all those drops of yellow phlegm teeming with antibiotic-resistant tuberculous organisms. Not even a shampoo in the men's room, using liquid soap from the dispenser, had made me feel right. When I got back to my apartment I had had to shampoo again and again, like Lady Macbeth.

So far, I hadn't had to deal with any of this hospital's TB patients. Maybe there weren't any in Hawaii.

My reverie ended. I looked at the nurse who was walking with me to see Roso. She was another of Hawaii's assets, very pretty, with a mixture of Chinese and Hawaiian blood, I guessed, a good slim figure, almond eyes, and beautiful teeth.

"Do you like to surf?" I asked, as we arrived at the door to the men's ward.

"I don't know how," she said softly.

"Do you live close to the hospital?"

"No, I live in Manoa Valley with my parents." That was unfortunate. I wanted to hear her talk, but we were nearing Roso's room.

"Has Roso been vomiting?"

"No, not at all, just hiccuping. I never thought hiccuping could be so bad. He's miserable."

Glancing at my watch before stepping into the ward, I saw it was going on midnight. Even so, I didn't mind seeing Roso. In many ways he was my favorite patient. Small night lights near the floor gave off a suffused glow that seemed to mix with the even sounds of breathing and snoring. Suddenly a sharp hiccup pierced the tranquillity, and the snoring went out of phase. I could have found Roso in inky blackness by those hiccups. We had operated on him my second morning as an intern. Actually, "we" is not quite accurate: the chief resident and a second-year resident had done the operating while I stood and held the retractors for three hours. I was the first to admit my ineptitude in the operating room; and the way things were going, my ignorance was secure. Unlike a lot of medical students, who as a rule are eager for surgery, I was short on operating-room experience, mostly because I hadn't wanted it, but also because I had been more interested in the electrolytes and the fluid problems after the operation. This had suited everybody. The other med students didn't dig the chemistry, while I had trouble bringing myself to stand for six hours in the OR watching other people cut and sew. Especially after the scene that took place the second time I had "scrubbed" back in New York.

It was to be a cancer operation, a complete breast removal, or radical mastectomy, as it is called, by the Big Cheese, the World-famous Surgeon himself. Being only a second-year medical student at the time, I had had a lot of misgivings about it, and the fact that everybody seemed a little tense, even the residents, had added to my anxiety. Suddenly the Big Cheese had come striding into the operating room, regally splendid and late as usual. He had fingered a few instruments in the big sterilizer tray, picked the whole thing up, and crashed it to the floor, swearing that they were scratched and bent and totally unacceptable. The noise had scared the anesthesiologist so much that he jumped and knocked the mask right off the patient. I had disappeared, hoping I wouldn't be missed, which was indeed the case.

Eventually, of course, I began to stay through some operations, start to finish, but I have not to this day figured surgeons out. Another of them back there was such a quiet, pleasant fellow until he was in the operating room, where I once saw him hurl a clamp at the resident anesthesiologist because the patient moved. On another occasion, the same man ordered one of the surgical residents out of the OR, claiming he was breathing too heavily. At any rate, so far there hadn't been much incentive for me to spend time in the operating room, and I was pretty green at surgery when my internship started.

Despite my inexperience, I knew the scrub routine, how to wash my hands, holding them just so, how to dry them, and how to put on the gown and gloves; I could even tie a few surgical knots. This had been learned pretty much by trial and error. My first scrub, in third-year med school, had been for a suture job in the emergency-room OR. I had spent the usual ten minutes scrubbing my hands and forearms, and had cleaned my nails with an orange stick before awkwardly donning the gown. I had on the baggy pants, the hat, the mask, the whole works, and the nurse had finally helped me with the rubber gloves. After twenty-five minutes of concentrated effort, at last I was ready to go; my hands were as sterile as a moon rock. Then I had casually picked up a stool and walked over to the patient, thereby contaminating my hands, my gown, everything. The nurse and the resident had laughed hysterically; even the bewildered patient had joined in as I started over from the beginning.

In Roso's case, even from my limited vantage point behind the retractors, I had known that nothing about his ulcer operation was going smoothly. The chief resident kept cursing the poor protoplasm, and I had to agree that Roso's tissue bled easily. Some heavy bleeding started near the pancreas at the bottom of the hole, but the two of them managed to complete the Billroth I, which meant hooking up the stomach and intestine just about the same as they had been before the operation, although minus the ulcer. Then I was supposed to put in Roso's skin sutures. It was no big deal to anyone except me; for me it was everything. I thought about asking one of the residents to put his finger on my first throw of the knot, like tying a Christmas present. It seemed a funny thought for about a second.

Actually, for a procedure so simple, tying that knot had been aggravating as hell. Sutures are often very narrow and difficult to feel through rubber gloves, especially at the tips, where the rubber is thickest and where you need the most sensitivity. I knew I had to tie the knot so that the edges of the wound came together, just kissing, without tension and without causing the skin to roll under. I also felt everyone watching me, judging. Although I knew a lot of things, nothing mattered then except that knot, because the knot is the thing without which an operation falls apart quite literally.

The end of the black silk in my right hand disappeared in the skin on one side of the wound and emerged on the other. I brought it together with the other end of the silk strand, in my left hand, and laid the first throw, tightening it until the edges touched lightly. Now for the next throw. But as soon as I let up on the tension, the wound popped open. I pulled it together again and put down the other throw as fast as I could, hoping somehow to beat the dehiscence—that gapping. The pitiful result left the edges of the wound dangerously far apart. Then, to my dismay, a hand reached out with scissors and cut the knot while partially suppressed giggles bubbled in the background.

Another hand began the suture again, dipping the curved needle easily under the skin to span the incision and come out the other side. I looked up in supplication to heaven; what good was I here when I couldn't even tie a knot?

I had gotten another chance on Roso's second row of stitches, which went in the opposite direction. By the time the second throw went down, the suture was so tight that the skin was bunched up in little ripples and the edges were rolled under from the tension. Out came the scissors again, courtesy of the second-year resident who had snipped through my first knot, and the wound separated with relief. It looked so easy and rhythmical when someone else did it. I had detected a trick here and there, though, a twist after the first throw, for instance. Instead of leaving the suture flat on the first throw, you pulled it back, both strings toward you. But that was only half of it. I tried again, with a little better result, although it was still too tight. At least Roso had been finished, for the time being.

The first suggestion of trouble was the hiccups, which had started about three days after the operation. Coming regularly every eighteen seconds, they were amusing at first. In fact, Roso became a hospital curiosity with his funny, clockwork hiccups. He was only fifty-five, but years in the pineapple fields made him look much older, all stooped and skinny; his pants kept falling off as he plodded through the ward pushing his IV stand. He, too, had run out of arm veins for his IV's and, like Marsha, had a catheter in his right groin. This caused even more trouble. If he tightened the drawstring enough to keep his pants on, his IV stopped. So he had to walk with one hand on the IV pole, the other holding up his pants.

Roso was Filipino, and his English vocabulary was limited to fifty or sixty trenchant words, which he used to convey emotional concepts. "Body no more strong," he would say, and it sufficed, like haiku poetry. I understood him and liked him very much. There was something tremendously noble and courageous about the man. Moreover, I think he liked me, which I realized later was an important part of my effort to keep him alive. When he saw me on morning rounds, Roso would smile broadly despite his hiccups, which made his whole body jump. Anyone could see that he was exhausted. I had tried every remedy I could find in surgical, medical, and pharmacological books, even folk medicine—breathing into a paper bag did not help him. In a more scientific vein, I had had him inhale a jug of 5-per-cent carbon dioxide, with no effect. Amyl nitrite and small doses of Thorazine hadn't worked, either, nor had calcium, which I tried in an attempt to correlate the hiccups with his general hypernervous state; his reflexes were so brisk that when I hit below his knee with my rubber hammer he'd flip his slipper off. My big mistake all along was in not considering the hiccups as symptoms of something deeper. I kept seeing them as an isolated problem, when in sad fact they were just a side effect of the smoldering catastrophe inside.

The next symptomatic hint had occurred when the resident ordered Roso's stomach tube removed and fluids allowed by mouth. Within an hour his stomach blew up to twice its normal size, and he began to vomit. In no way could we have made him more miserable, what with the hiccups, the vomiting, and the lack of sleep; any one of them would have been enough to drive most people crazy, but valiant little Roso would still be there smiling every time I saw him. "Body no more strong," he'd say, always the same words, but carrying a slightly different meaning each time, depending on how he said them. "Body more strong soon"; I began to use his vocabulary in that curious way you do when talking to someone who doesn't speak very good English. You begin to think he'll understand better if you make mistakes, too. During medical school, with Spanish-speaking patients, I'd catch myself saying, "Operation you need inside abdomen." This made no sense, of course, because if the patient understood the words surely he'd understand them in the right order. Mainly we were trying to reach out to these people, to connect.

So poor old Roso had been put on intravenous fluid accompanied by constant gastric suction through the tube that disappeared into his nose en route to his stomach. Racked by constant hiccups, he vomited every time we took the tube out, whether we fed him or not. Just a few days earlier the tube had gotten completely clogged up, so that nothing but food stood between Roso and death. When I irrigated the nose tube to relieve the clogging, out had come a glob of material that looked like coffee grounds. It was old blood. It was lucky that I liked balancing fluid and electrolytes, because several times a day I had to figure out how much sodium and chloride were in those fluids that came out of him and replace them, plus the usual maintenance. I even gave him magnesium, on the chance it might help, after I came across an article in the hospital library on magnesium depletion.

But Roso's big problem was inside, beyond my touch. Like Marsha Potts, he was leaking at the anastomosis site, the connection between the small intestine and the stomach pouch, except that in Roso's case the incision hadn't broken down. It was just leaking steadily all inside him, blocking his stomach and causing the hiccups, keeping him on IV fluids, driving his

weight down every day so that now it was no more than eighty
pounds. Fighting hard against the weight loss, which also
meant loss of strength, I found articles about protein solutions
and high percentage glucose solutions and tried everything they
suggested; still he lost weight, going from merely skinny to the
skeletal appearance of clear starvation. And through all this
hell he smiled and talked his haiku. I liked him. Moreover, he
was my patient, and I'd see him any time he needed me.

"Roso, how you doing?" I asked, looking down at him now.
What a sight he was lying there in the gloom, wearing nothing
but pajama bottoms, with an IV sticking in his right groin and
the tube hanging out his nose. Every eighteen seconds his body
twitched with hiccups.

"Doktoor, no more strong, too weak already." He managed
that much without hiccuping. We had to do something. I had
been plaguing the attending physician, the chief resident, everybody, but to no avail. Wait, they said. I knew we couldn't
wait. Roso still trusted me, but his will was wearing out. "Doktoor, I no wanna live no more—" *hiccup* "—too much." No
one had ever said that to me, and it stopped me cold. Although I could understand how he felt, I wouldn't admit to
myself that he'd reached this point, because I had seen what
happened to patients when they gave up fighting. They died,
just drifted away. Something in the human spirit could hold
everything together, even in the face of utter physiological collapse, until the spirit gave way and carried the body down with
it. Sometimes the despair was so obvious you didn't ask a patient for normal responses, but Roso had spoken it, and that
made his case different. I told myself that he just wanted to let
me know he was near to giving up but actually hadn't yet.

He desperately needed sleep. Although I could give him
that, it was a two-edged sword. Sparine, a potent tranquilizer,
would knock him out, anesthetize even the hiccups. But with
that tube down his throat he was in constant danger of pneumonia, especially if he was unconscious; without the tube he
might vomit, and if he vomited while he was knocked out, he
might aspirate.

The Demerol and the skinny old man upstairs still nagged
me, too. His relatives had been splendid about everything, never sensing the doubt in me, taking my words at face value, not
cringing at the autopsy request. What if I had told them that I
only *thought* their father was dead? How could they know that
the difference between life and death was sometimes not black
and white, but gray and indistinct? Marsha Potts, for instance:

was she alive or someplace in between? I guessed I could call her alive, because if she got better she'd be fine, maybe; on the other hand, she probably wouldn't get better, and at least part of her brain might already be dead. Some of her liver must surely be gone, in order for her to have jaundice and liver flap; her kidneys, too. Again, it wasn't black and white, any more than my decision about Roso and the Sparine. But Roso was in need of a rest, and I had an irresistible urge to do something. That must be a strong human drive, to do something—just as when somebody in a crowd faints, one bystander is sure to run for a glass of water and another always makes a pillow for the head. Both actions are ridiculous in medical terms, but people feel more comfortable to be doing something, even in a situation that calls for a type of action they are not equipped to give.

I had had the same sensation several times. Once, during a high-school football scrimmage, I had been hurled onto a pile-up just as a guy broke his leg with an audible crunch, the leg bending off at an angle below his knee. Although he wasn't in much pain, the rest of us were panic-stricken, and, true to stereotype, I tried to get him to drink some water. I think that at that moment I set out unconsciously on the road to med school. The idea of knowing what to do, of satisfying an urge to act, was overpowering.

So, all right, Peters, now you're a doctor—do something for Roso. Right, the Sparine it would be, and the second I made that decision, the happiness of positive, directed action flooded over me.

"Roso, I make you sleep you feel more strong."

As I sat down at the nurses' station, the almond-eyed nurse slid Roso's chart across to me. She looked even prettier than she had before. "Are you Chinese?" I asked, not looking at her.

"Chinese and Hawaiian. My grandfather on my mother's side was Hawaiian."

I thought it would be fun to get to know her. "How come you live at home?"

No answer to that. Well, the hell with it. I opened the chart to write the Sparine order. Too bad, though. She looked like all the girls I had expected to see under Hawaiian waterfalls. Only I hadn't been outside the hospital long enough at that point to see any waterfalls, and my sex life, if you could call it that, was restricted to Jan. Would she still be there, even at midnight?

I'd better get the hell out of here, I thought, as I wrote "Sparine 100 mg. IM stat," put a marker in the chart to indicate a new order, and tossed it on the counter. Roso would sleep. The last time I gave him 100 mg. he was out for eighteen hours.

"Doctor, as long as you are here"—the fateful, familiar question—"would you mind seeing a man with a cast, and also the quadriplegic?" I knew the quadriplegic, but not the man with the cast.

"What's wrong with the cast?" I asked with some hesitation, fearing a request for a new cast at that hour.

"He says it cuts into his back when he moves."

"And the quadriplegic?"

"He refuses to take his antibiotic."

Actually, I hadn't really wanted an answer to that question. Paralyzed people caused me about as much psychic distress as those with tuberculosis. My mind went back to the most attractive building and the most depressing service in medical school, neurosurgery and neurology. I remembered examining one patient who answered my questions as I stuck him with a pin. He had seemed so normal I almost wondered why he was in the hospital until, when I pricked him again, his eyes suddenly disappeared into his head and the right side of his body stiffened, pushing him onto his left side and nearly rolling him off the bed. All I could see were the whites of his eyes, and I was as paralyzed as he was, not knowing what the hell to do. There wasn't even the satisfaction of running for a glass of water. The patient was only having a convulsion, but I didn't know that then. He could have been dying, and I would have stood there with my mouth hanging open. No one outside the medical world can know what a crisis like that means to a medical student. You get so gun shy that you try not to be around when something goes wrong.

Neurology students were expected to stand with hands in pockets enjoying the professor's elegant diagnosis: "Some of the spinal pathways cross over before running to the brain. Others don't. If you have a lesion effectively cutting off one side of the spinal cord, the tracts that cross will still work. Here, notice how this patient is able to feel this temperature change but cannot have any proprioceptive sense, because I can move the toe in any direction without his being conscious of it." And so it went.

Everybody had a ball discussing those tricky little temperature fibers crossing over in the ventral white commissure and running up the lateral spinothalamic tract to the posterolateral ventral nucleus of the thalamus. Great arguments erupted over whether fibers were unmyelinated or myelinated. No field of medicine can match neurology for high-flown jargon. Meanwhile, nobody thought much about the patient. Well, you hardly had time, trying to remember all those tracts and nuclei, and besides, you couldn't do anything, anyway.

Perhaps it was this lack of possibility that made paralysis cases so hard for me to handle emotionally. I particularly remembered one neurology case in medical school, although it was not unusual; in fact, it was a fairly typical case. The patient had lain before us in a respirator, his facial muscles moving constantly. Nothing else about him moved: he could control nothing else because the rest of him was a pile of immobile, unfeeling tissue and bone, completely helpless and totally dependent on the respirator for life. The professor had been saying, "You will find this an extremely interesting case, gentlemen, a fracture of the odontoid process, which caused the spinal cord to be severed just at the point where it comes out of the head." The professor was loving it. His diagnostic triumph had been accomplished, he proudly told us, only after a delicate X-ray procedure through the mouth. Then he was off, puffed like a pigeon and virtually cooing, into a long discussion of how the atlas had been dislocated from the axis.

I had not been able to take my eyes off the patient, who was staring fixedly into the mirror just over his head. About my age and a hopeless case. To know that his body and mine were essentially the same, that the only difference was a tiny disconnection deep in his neck and that this fractional difference was total, had made me conscious of my body at that moment as never before, and ashamed of it. Just then I had felt hunger, my fingertips, a backache, sensations he would never have again. I was filled with helpless rage and a kind of heartsickness. Movement is so much a part of living, almost life itself, that from day to day normal people deny this kind of death. Yet here in front of me was death in life, and my mind was screaming at me that my own body hung on the same fragile string that lay broken there under the respirator. Many times since, in the dark moments, I had thought that the morbidity in medicine made it the wrong road for me, but I kept at it. Do other doctors have such doubts?

For now, however, the man with the cast came first; I'd see the quadriplegic later. I got a cutter out of the closet and walked down the hall with the nurse. Turning into the room, we came upon a man in a gigantic spica cast extending from his navel all the way down his right leg to the toes. The left leg was free. That morning, he had fractured his femur about midway between groin and knee, and the cast had been put on right away. As usual on the first day in such a constricting mold, the man was excruciatingly uncomfortable. I found the edge that was bothering him and began to cut pieces away. It would have been quicker with the power cutter from the emergency room, but midnight is the wrong time for a tool that sounds like a chain saw. Besides, the vibration always scared the patient half to death, despite all your assurances that the power cutter vibrated very rapidly and therefore would cut only something stiff, not soft like skin. He would seem to understand until the cutter whined into action, knifing easily through the rock-hard plaster. I finished my cutting, and the fractured-femur case lay back with a sigh of relief, gratefully moving from side to side. "Much better, Doctor. Thank you very much."

Simple things like that make you feel good. Of course, anybody off the street could have cut away the offending piece, but no matter. To know that the man would rest easily now somehow justified me and made my being there worth while. I was learning that an intern is not often allowed to make patients more comfortable. He is usually hurting them, sticking needles into them, putting tubes up their noses, coaxing a cough after an operation to force them to fully expand their lungs. That cough is especially hard and painful for chest cases. In chest surgery, it is a common procedure for the surgeon to split the breastbone down the middle, and wire it together again at the end of the operation. Four or five hours later, it was my job to cram a small tube down the patient's windpipe, irritating the membrane to force a full cough. The method was foolproof. Like anyone with something in his trachea, the patient invariably coughed, thinking halfway through that the convulsion would tear him apart, trying to stop but not being able to, and finally subsiding, sweat-soaked and exhausted, as I pulled the tube out. In the long run I had perhaps helped the patient avoid pneumonia or worse, but in the short run I had put him through hell. So making the man with the cast more comfortable was not to be lightly regarded.

My euphoria didn't last long, however, for now I had to face the quadriplegic. Completely paralyzed from the neck down, he lay in a Striker frame on his stomach. A stream of anguished profanity poured out of him. A tube twisting out from underneath his body was connected to a clear plastic bag half full of urine. Urine was always a big problem in these cases. Since a paralyzed patient loses control of his bladder, he requires a catheter; with the catheter comes infection. Most cases of Gram-negative sepsis that I had seen came from urinary-tract infections. Criminal abortions were the not-so-rare exceptions. At the end of my gynecology service in third-year med school, we had so many septic criminal abortions that an epidemic seemed to be sweeping New York. Young girls, mostly, who generally waited until the infection was roaring before they came in, and even then they gave us no help with the diagnosis. Never. Some of them died denying the abortion right up to the end. With the legalization of abortion, I suppose the picture has changed, but many times back then I saw Gram-negative sepsis set in, with the irreversible combination of zero blood pressure, failing kidneys, and dying liver. Those Gram-negative bacteria like the urine, especially after a patient has been taking the usual antibiotics.

Looking at this fellow as he lay there crying and cursing, I knew all those things. Figuratively, I had my hands in my pockets, not knowing what to say or do. What would I want if I were twenty and lying in that contraption with everybody saying take it easy, you'll be all right, and knowing it was a lie? I thought maybe I'd like someone strong, who wasn't trying to fool me, who acknowledged the bald truth. So in an effort to be firm, I told him he had to take the antibiotic, that we knew it was tough, but still he had to take it. He had to take the responsibility of being human.

Sometimes we surprise ourselves, talking out of unknown places inside us. I didn't know whether I believed what I was saying or not, but out it came. While I stood there the boy stopped crying long enough for the nurse to give him the injection. It suddenly became important for me to know whether he was relieved or only furious, but I couldn't see his face, and he didn't say anything. Neither did I. The nurse broke the silence and told him to try to get some sleep. Since I couldn't think of anything to say, I put my hand softly on his shoulder, wondering if he could feel my touch and my sorrow.

I knew I had to get away from the ward now or collapse. At any time, in any hospital, a thousand small chores are there to be done, like looking at someone's drain, checking an incision, responding to a complaint about a stiff neck, restarting an intravenous. Actually, the nurses in Hawaii were pretty good about starting IV's; back in medical school it had been a primary job for the student. Neither rain nor snow could spare us from being called at three-thirty in the morning to trudge off across the deserted New York streets to restart an IV. One winter night I had braved the elements only to be confronted by a veinless man. I had poked and cursed, and finally started an infant scalp-vein needle on the back of his hand. Then back through the rain, eventually sliding into my bed after being up for more than an hour, whereupon the phone rang again. It was the same nurse, half apologetic and half aggressively defensive. While putting on some more tape to reinforce the IV, she had accidentally cut the tubing.

In any case, there is always a lot to be done on any ward. Although the nurses will normally cope, if a doctor is around he's sure to be kept busy, and I was fading fast. There was only one job I wanted to do before going back to my room—to see Mrs. Takura in intensive care. I hoped that Jan had had enough sense to crawl under the covers before going to sleep. It was well after midnight.

We never called the intensive care unit by its full name, just ICU. Of all the names, initials, abbreviations, and jargon an intern hears, none can make him jump like ICU, because this is where the action is, a room in perpetual crisis. The chances of being called to the ICU at least twice a night were very high, and the chances of not knowing what to do were impossibly higher. That the nurses were efficient and knowledgeable only made it worse. You began to wonder what you had learned during those four expensive years of medical school. Schwartzman reaction, that's what we had learned. Two lectures on that, and no one was even sure it existed. Something's screwy when a doctor knows all about a disease that might not exist, but less than the nurse about any ICU situation. Of course, if the patient happened to have a Schwartzman reaction, I'd be an instant success: I could discourse at length on what the distal convoluted tubule of the kidney would look like under a light microscope, among other things. As for practical measures, however, we hadn't had time in medical school, nor had the pathologist cared, a fact that truly bugged me. The nurses had mostly carried bedpans through their three years of training. That's not fair, I realize, but, still, their training was trivial compared to the stacks of mechanism, enzymes, and Schwartzman reactions we had to memorize. Yet in the ICU I might as well have been carrying the bedpans. I often felt I'd better get the hell out of there before something happened that required an intelligent response.

An intern is supposed to pick up the practical stuff as he goes along, but if he got more of it in medical school he'd be a lot better off and so would the patients. In a working hospital nobody cares what you know about the Schwartzman reaction. The surgeon looks at your knots. "Weak," he says, "awfully weak." The nurse wants to know how much isuprel to put into 500 cc. of dextrose and water. "Well, how much have you been using on this patient?" "Usually 0.5 mg." "Hmmm, that should be okay." You don't have the guts to ask whether isuprel is the same as isoproterenol. Would she like to know about the thalamic radiations of the ventral nuclei of the cerebellum? No, and rightly, for it wouldn't help a single person in the ICU. What a way to live.

These thoughts were very much with me as I walked through the swinging doors of the ICU, as usual hesitating in wonderment at this strange mixture of science fiction and stark reality. Weird instruments hung from the walls and ceiling, adorned with their thousand buttons and switches and oscilloscope screens. Sonarlike beeps mingled symphonically with the rhythmic click-clack of the respirators and the muffled sobs of a mother hunched over a bed in one corner. Moving and flickering as they stood guard over life, these machines often seemed more alive than the patients, who lay immobile, covered with bulky mummylike dressings and connected by plastic tubes to clusters of bottles that hung from the tops of poles. The mixture formed an alien and mysterious environment.

Nonmedical people react strongly to the ICU. It is the solid, physical incarnation of their fears about death and of the hospital as a place of death. Cancer, for instance, is certainly the most feared disease of our time, but unless you are the victim or a close relative or friend, it hardly exists outside hospitals. In the ICU, cancer hangs in the air like a sickening, primeval smog. If you work there a lot, you can easily forget that the hospital is a place where life begins as well as ends. But babies are not born in this room, and most people, with reason, associate it with the ominous, the unknown, and the final, where life hangs by its fingertips.

Although the normal human being does not enjoy a visit to the hospital, once he is in the ICU it holds him with its magnetic fascination, despite the morbidity, or perhaps because of it. His eyes dart around absorbing the fantasy, building monuments in imagination to the abstract power of medicine. Medicine must be powerful indeed, with all those machines. Otherwise, why have them? An observer, however, always senses the undercurrent of fear that mingles with the visitor's respectful awe, catching him in the conflict of wanting to be there and wanting to flee at the same time.

I felt the same ambivalence, for a different reason. I knew that most of the machines did almost nothing. Some of the smallest ones, though unimpressive to look at, did all the work. Those little green respirators, for instance, clicking and clacking as they breathed for the people who needed them, were worth all the others put together. The complicated ones, with their screens and electronic blips, were not doing anything unless they were being watched. Medical school *had* taught me how to read these oscilloscopes. I knew that an upward sweep on the screen indicated millions of sodium ions rushing into the muscle cells of the heart. Then came a bump on the screen as the cells contracted while the cytoplasmic organelles worked like crazy to pump the ions back into the extracellular fluid. Fantastic to think about; but this scientific wizardry was only half the job. On the basis of these curves and sweeps, a doctor still had to make the diagnosis and then a prescription. That's what pulled me apart, wanting to be there because I could learn a lot in a short time, yet always terrified that I wouldn't know what to do when total responsibility fell on me because I was the only doctor around.

In fact, my fear had already been justified several times—for instance, during my first night on call as an intern, when I was paged to deal with a hemorrhage in the ICU. Rushing upstairs, I had reassured myself with the fact that localized pressure would stop any bleeding. Then, entering the room, I had seen him and stopped in my tracks. Blood was pouring out of both sides of his mouth, drowning him in a red river, a continual bloody gush. It wasn't vomitus; it was pure blood. Terrified, I had just stood there watching, dumfounded, while his eyes pleaded for help. Later I was told that nothing could have been done. The cancer had eaten through the pulmonary vein. But all that mattered to me was that I had been lost, emptyheaded, and immobilized. For nights afterward I had relived that scene, and now I had an obsession about being able to do something, even if it wouldn't help the patient.

Mrs. Takura was propped up in a corner bed. She was almost eighty, and her head was wreathed with fine white hair. A Sengstaken tube hung out of her left nostril, firmly held by a piece of sponge rubber that wrinkled and distorted her nose. A few drops of blood had dried in one corner of her mouth. The Sengstaken tube is about a quarter of an inch in diameter, and it is a rough one. Inside this large tube are three smaller ones, called "lumens." Two of the lumens have balloons attached, one inside the tube in a short lumen and one on the end in a long lumen. In order for the Sengstaken tube to work, the patient must swallow all this apparatus, never an easy task, and especially hard when the patient is vomiting blood, as is usually the case. Once the tube is down, the balloon on the bottom of the tube, in the stomach, is inflated to roughly the size of a large orange; this anchors everything in place. About halfway up is the second balloon; when inflated it takes the shape of a hot dog nestling inside the lower esophagus. The third lumen, small but long, simply dangles in the stomach for use in evacuating unwanted fluids, like blood. The point of the whole thing is to stop esophageal bleeding through pressure exerted on the walls of the esophagus by the hot-dog balloon.

Only once before, in medical school, had I treated a patient who needed a Sengstaken tube. His problem was alcoholism, which had caused severe cirrhosis and, eventually, liver failure. Mrs. Takura wasn't an alcoholic, of course—her problem sprang from an earlier case of hepatitis, years before—but their cases had a common aspect. A damaged liver impedes the passage of blood, so that pressure gradually rises in the blood vessels leading to the liver and then backs up, causing the veins of the esophagus to dilate and, in extreme cases, to break. At this point the patient vomits copious amounts of blood. Although I had treated the alcoholic for only a day or two, I vividly remembered trying to help him swallow those balloons. When he couldn't do it he had been taken to surgery, and he never made it back to the ward.

Portal hypertension with bleeding esophageal varices was a serious affair, but so far we had been able to stabilize Mrs. Takura's by getting the tube down her. And she was scheduled to be operated on in eight hours or so.

She didn't look Oriental, despite her name and her abundant good cheer and inner calm, traits that I was beginning to see in all Orientals. Every time we talked she was lucid and alert, knowing just what was happening and speaking very quietly. I think she would have calmly discussed her geraniums in the middle of a typhoon. When she asked me how I was, as she always did, the answer seemed important to her. We got along well. Besides, I thought she would recover. You get that feeling with some patients, just an irrational hunch. Sometimes it works out.

Once, a few hours after her admission, the doctors had tried to remove the Sengstaken tube, but this had resulted in recurrent heavy bleeding and sent her into shock before the tube could be replaced. Since I had been off duty that night, I missed the blood and drama; she did scare me badly the next morning, however, when her blood pressure suddenly dropped to 80/50 and her pulse shot up to 130 per minute. Somehow, I had been collected enough to order and administer more blood, realizing that the steady bleeding had finally affected her pressure. When the blood pressure came up again nicely, my spirits rose with it. Cause, effect, cure. This should have given me a bit of lasting confidence, but, curiously, believing that a right decision lay behind every situation only made me more nervous. To give the blood had been a right decision, but a simple one; next time it might be different.

Tonight, Mrs. Takura was pleasant and calm, as usual. I checked her blood pressure and the balloon pressures, and generally messed around trying to justify my being there, although I really only wanted to talk to her.

"So, are you ready for your little operation?"

"Yes, Doctor, if you are ready, I'm ready."

That was a shocker. I felt sure she meant "you" in the collective sense, the whole surgical service. She couldn't have meant me. I was nowhere near being ready, despite the fact that I did know a good bit about the operation, at least the theory of it. I could talk for twenty minutes on portal-pressure gradients, on the various benefits and disadvantages of the surgical approach by forming a portal-vein-to-inferior-vena-cava anastomosis, end to end or end to side. I could even remember the diagrams of the splenorenal union—that was end to side. The whole idea was to relieve the blood pressure in the esophagus by connecting the liver venous system, where the pressure had risen and caused the bleeding, to a vein where the pressure was still normal, like the interior vena cava, or the left renal vein. Also lodged in my memory were the comparative mortality figures for these various procedures, but I didn't want to think about that. How can you look at a patient and think 20-per-cent mortality?

"*We're* ready, Mrs. Takura." I leaned hard on the "we," when in fact I wanted to say "they," for I had never even watched one of these operations, called a portal caval shunt. Theoretically, it was fantastic. Nothing excited the professors so much as talking about those pressure changes and hooking up this with that. Once they got started, they particularly enjoyed rattling on about obscure articles written by Harry By-

plane of Umpdydump University (Harry was always a very
good friend, of course), which showed that some article by
George Littlechump at Dumpdydump University had been
wrong in assuming the intralobular hepatic vein pressure gradients with the portal interlobular plexus weren't important.
That was it right there, the kind of stuff you got a lot of on
medical-school ward rounds. To win the game, you had to
quote the most obscure article about some pressure gradient
(they especially liked pressure or pH gradients) saying that
Bobble Jones had shown conclusively (any doubt was disaster) that in a series of seventy-seven patients (an exact number, even if fictional, was necessary), all seventy-seven died if
they went to the hospital. It didn't much matter what you said
at the end as long as you got in enough numbers and gradients
and personal references to the author; then you were golden,
and rocketed to the front of the class. That was the big
leagues: "Well, Peters, you've really done it now." What about
Mrs. Takura? Forget the patient, man, we're talking about hy-
drogen ions in the blood, that's pH, with a little p and a big H.

I can remember a time we were all clustered around this
one bed during medical-school teaching rounds. The short
white coats were students, as anyone could tell. The short
white coats and white pants marked interns and residents. And
then, at the pinnacle, there were those long, heavily starched
white coats—a washday dream, they were, so white they made
even the bed sheets look gray. Need I say who wore those
coats?

Somebody had mentioned the name of the patient's disease,
and we were off and running on an intricate discussion of pH,
sodium ions, and glucose pumps, with articles from Houston,
California, and Sweden. Names flew back and forth in a kind
of academic Ping-Pong game. Who would get in the last name,
the latest change? We were nearly breathless with anticipation
when someone noticed that we were standing by the wrong
bed. The patient in front of us did not have the disease under
debate. That had ended the game without a winner, and we
had quietly moved on to the next bed. What the hell difference
it made I couldn't fathom, since we hadn't had time even to
look at the patient. Maybe everybody felt shy about discussing
one disease in the presence of another.

"Try to get some sleep, Mrs. Takura. Everything will be all
right." I glanced over my shoulder to see if the coast was
clear. The nurses hadn't paid much attention to me, mostly because they were busy with a man in the opposite corner. He

was wired up to an EKG monitor that showed a very irregular heartbeat. The woman was still sobbing quietly by the bed of her heavily bandaged teen-age boy. He had a head injury, the result of an auto accident; the poor fellow never regained consciousness. I headed for the door, pulled it open, and went out. Day changed to night. The bright lights, the sound of the machines, the bustle of the nurses were suddenly cut off as the door shut behind me.

I was back in the hushed dark air of the hospital corridor. To my left, a nurse sat at her station, her face silhouetted by the light directly in front of her. Everything else melted off into darkness. I turned into the completely black corridor. All I had to do was turn to the right, go down the stairs, and cross the courtyard to my quarters. There was still time to get some sleep.

Suddenly a light flashed behind me, and a voice shouted, "An arrest, Doctor. There's an arrest. Come quickly!" As I turned around, the light evaporated, leaving scintillating blotches in the center of my visual field. Berlin blockade, Cuban missile crisis, Tonkin Gulf: crises, all right, but not so close together or close to home. To me, this was a red alert, the type of catastrophe I dreaded most. My first thought was that I would be not only the first doctor to arrive, but also, since it was the middle of the night, perhaps the only one. Given a choice, I would have fled in the opposite direction, not worrying whether I was a coward or a realist. But there I was, running toward the patient, almost a cliché of the young intern dashing down a dark corridor with his stethoscope thrashing wildly in his tightly gripped fingers.

You've seen it all on television and movie screens, and it's thrilling—isn't it?—rather like the bugle call and the cavalry charge in the nick of time. But what is he thinking, this intern? It depends on where he's running. If it's pitch-black, he's trying to get there in one piece. Beyond that, it depends on how long he has been an intern. If not long, just a couple of weeks, then he's running scared—terrified, to be more exact. He doesn't want to be the first person to arrive.

Now he's there, a little out of breath but physically intact. His mind is another thing; what little information he owned appropriate to the situation has suddenly been drained out of his cerebrum by the shock of responsibility. Don't bother to learn drug names or dosages, the pharmacology professors insisted, just learn concepts. How do you tell a nurse to draw up 10 cc. of concept for a dying patient?

As I pushed open the ICU door, the weird world enveloped me again, and of course I found myself the only doctor there, quite alone with two nurses beside the bed of the man with the irregular EKG. While my mouth formed an inaudible obscenity, my fingers involuntarily clutched the side railing of the bed as if using it for support. I was no longer the television intern, but a real one, complete with inexperience and terror. Who would support me if this man died? The nurses? The medical-school professors? The attendings? The hospital? Most important, I had not yet learned to forgive my own mistakes.

Looking back at the door, I hoped against the odds that a resident would suddenly appear; it came home to me why many brilliant and dedicated students go all the way through medical school and then, facing internship, change course and switch to research or some paramedical field. Anything must be better than internship. Something's wrong here. Why can't the intern know something useful when he runs into the ICU during the first couple of weeks? And why don't the attendings back him up? Even the helpful ones are mostly no better than quietly aggressive. They seem to be saying, "We waded through all this shit. Now, goddamn it, you do it, too."

Well, I was doing it, here and now in the ICU, with no chance of any help, but this time I got lucky. The EKG monitor displayed on the oscilloscope showed a wildly erratic electrical impulse, like the scribbles of an irritated child. As its beeping sound rose higher and higher, to an extremely rapid staccato, I realized that the patient had slipped into ventricular fibrillation; his heart muscle was just a quivering, unco-ordinated mass. Now I knew what to do; I would "shock" him.

Actually, the decision was not so much mine as the nurses'. Always a step ahead, they had the defibrillator charged up and one of them was holding the greased paddles out to me.

"What's it charged to?" I asked, not really caring, but needing the control the question gave me.

"Full charge," answered the nurse with the paddles.

I put one of them on his chest, right over the sternum, and the other along the left side of the thorax. Oddly, he hadn't stopped breathing completely. Nor was he unconscious. The only sign of distress besides his gasping respiration was a sort of dazed look, as if the breath had been knocked out of him.

I pressed the button on top of the paddle handle. His whole body stiffened violently, and his hands shot into the air and down. The EKG blip was driven off the oscilloscope screen by the sudden tremendous electrical discharge, but it came right back, looking normal. I was reassured when the beep reappeared, too, suggesting a normal pulse rate, and the man took a deep breath. Everything seemed fine for about ten seconds. Then he stopped breathing, and right away the pulses went to zero, while the EKG continued along with the blip at a normal rate. That was crazy. EKG blips and no pulses was a combination not in the textbooks. My mind played a huge indoor tennis match, with concepts flying back and forth—electrical activity, electrical activity, but no beat, no pulse. "Get a laryngoscope and an endotracheal tube." One of the nurses already had them in her hands. He had to have oxygen. Oxygen and carbon dioxide had to move, and for that we had to insert an endotracheal tube and breathe for him.

The tube is put down by means of a long, thin flashlight affair called a laryngoscope. This instrument has a blade on the end of it, six inches or so long, that is used to raise the base of the tongue and bring into view the entrance to the trachea, where the tube must go. As the blade slides into the throat, you try to locate the lid that covers the trachea during swallowing—the epiglottis. All this time you are standing behind the patient, pulling his head far back, fighting through extraneous material like blood, mucus, or vomitus. Once you see the epiglottis, you slide the instrument past it, down a little farther, and pull up. With luck, you'll then be looking past the trachea at the vocal cords, which are creamy white, in contrast to the red mucosa of the pharynx.

That's the ideal situation. In practice, you must often push this way and that on the throat with your free hand, looking for the trachea, and sometimes you never do find it. And even when you do, your troubles are still not over, because sliding the tube down can be devilishly hard. The precious hole between the vocal cords will be obscured at the last second by the rubber tube. Nothing to do but push it in blind. Too often your dead reckoning leads the tube into the esophagus, so that when you try to ventilate the patient—force air into him —his stomach blows up instead of his lungs. And all the while there is usually someone else pounding on the man's chest, and the laryngoscope is clanking against his teeth or jumping out of his mouth, and the whole area may be filling rapidly with fluid of one sort or another. Putting down an endotracheal tube was, to me, a subject fit for nightmares.

But there was no one else around to do it, so I pulled the man's bed out and got behind his head with the laryngoscope.

"What's his basic problem?" I asked hastily, pulling his head back.

"He doesn't follow his pacemaker all the time," one of the nurses said.

Suddenly it made more sense. "What's he been on? What's in that bottle?" I said, motioning to the IV bottle. "Isuprel," came the answer, and I told them to speed it up. I knew that isuprel helped the heart with its contraction and was especially useful in cases where the heart wouldn't contract on its own.

"How fast?"

How fast? I hadn't the slightest idea. "Let it run." I couldn't think of anything better to say. His head was back now, and the laryngoscope far down into his throat, but I couldn't see the vocal cords. "Get me an amp. of bicarbonate." As one of the nurses vanished from the periphery of my vision, I realized that at last I had thought of something on my own. Then the vocal cords appeared. Their white contours stood out against the surrounding red like the gates to a subterranean chamber. For once I managed to get the tube into the trachea without too much of a struggle.

But no sooner had I slipped the tube in than the patient reached up and pulled it out. I was indignant, just for a second, until I realized he was breathing again. A strong, full pulse showed in his wrist. The nurse appeared with the bicarbonate. Stupidly, I wanted to give that stuff now, because I had thought about it and the nurses hadn't, and especially because I knew a lot about electrolytes and pH and ions. But I wondered what the effect would be on the calcium level. Both calcium and potassium combined with the pH in a tricky fashion. I was in danger of overthinking and getting all balled up, so I decided to save the bicarbonate; no sense rocking the boat.

Suddenly an anesthetist burst panting through the door, and another intern, followed by a resident, and another resident. All of them looked sleepy. One had no socks on, and there were pillow creases on the side of his head. The crowd continued to swell as another resident rushed in. This was about the time I liked to arrive, when everything was under control and decisions could be by committee. Actually, I was beginning to calm down, although my own pulse was still racing. The newly arrived house staff settled down on the counter and chairs. One of them leafed through the chart, while another called the private attending. I stayed beside the patient, who had started to talk. His name was Smith.

"Thank you, Doctor. I'm all right now, I think."

"Yes, all your signs are good. We're glad we could help you." Our eyes locked, his showing more trust than I thought I deserved, and mine trying not to give away my inner uncertainty. The isuprel was still running into him like crazy, and I didn't know whether to slow it down or not. Let the others carry the ball for a while. Mr. Smith wanted to talk.

"This is the third time for me, I mean the third time my heart has decided not to follow my pacemaker. When it happens, I don't have time to think, but afterward, like now, it all falls into a pattern. First, my throat tightens up, and then suddenly I can't breathe, nothing at all, and then everything goes gray and shadowy." I was listening hard, but only half comprehending. It was incredible to be talking with him when a few minutes ago he hadn't been there.

"A shadow, that's the best word I can think of, but the shadow doesn't pass. It goes deeper into blackness, until no light is left in the world." He stopped abruptly. "But do you know the worst part, Doctor?" I shook my head, not wanting to interrupt him. "The worst part is coming out of it, because it happens so slowly; not like going down, which is quick. First, I have these wild, chaotic dreams. No sense to them that I can find, until finally—it seems forever—the room and the bed and the people come into the dream and eventually take over. I can't explain why, but the last thing to come back is an awareness of myself, who and where I am, and the hurt. My chest feels caved in, as if I'm smothering from lack of air, especially if there's a tube in my throat."

"That must be why you pulled the tube out. Have you had many operations?" I asked.

"Enough to fill a book. Appendix, gall bladder . . ."

I interrupted him. "Do you remember what it was like to be put under anesthesia? Have you ever had ether?" That was one experience I remembered vividly, although it was a long time ago, when I was four or five. Back then, everybody had his tonsils out, and I remembered my terror as the ether mask was put over my face, the room began to fade, and an unbearable buzzing sounded in my ears. Then concentric circles moving faster and faster until they collapsed into a bright red center; then nothing, until I awoke vomiting.

"My appendectomy was in 1944," said Mr. Smith, thinking back, "while I was in the Navy, and I believe it was ether."

"Was that anything like the feeling you get when your heart stops? What about waking up?"

"No, not at all. The anesthesia is somehow pleasant, nothing like struggling with my heart—it seems literally like a struggle to keep it from jumping out of my chest, keep it under control. I can't remember waking up from those operations, but when my heart starts up again it is like a thousand unending nightmares."

He reached up and touched my hand, which rested on the bed railing. "God, I hope it doesn't happen again. You see, I can't be sure anybody will be there to help. You know, Doctor, there's another strange thing—this time I felt I was watching my own body from someplace outside of myself, as if I was standing at the foot of my own bed."

"Have you had that feeling before?" I asked, curious now; feeling outside oneself is a symptom of schizophrenia.

"Never. It was a unique sensation."

A unique sensation. A unique sensation. This man was telling me about dying, but the way he told it made death into a living process, something you could study in a textbook. Without that defibrillator, of course, he *would* have been dead, and with him all those thoughts. Tonight the line between life and death had hardly existed for three people—for him, for Marsha Potts, and for the old man with cancer. I was having trouble thinking about life and death at the same time, but I was happy this man wasn't dead, because he was so nice. What a stupid thought. Anyway, I couldn't imagine him dead. No matter what had happened he wouldn't have died, because he was alive right at that moment.

Does that make sense? It did to me. Who was I to think that I could have changed fate? Being alive and talking and thinking is so different from being dead and immobile that the transition seemed impossible now. It had been so simple, just a zap with the defibrillator, like slapping someone on the back to stop a cough, or running for a glass of water. Maybe he hadn't been fibrillating; maybe he would have come out of it on his own. He had before. I would never know.

The medical resident and another intern were still there, talking and adjusting the plastic tubes, scratching their heads and holding the EKG strips. They seemed happy and involved. As I went out I looked over at Mrs. Takura, who smiled broadly and waved with her free hand.

The strange nether world of the ICU vanished again as I turned down the corridor and descended the stairs. All of life seemed asleep. I thought of those nights in medical school back east when I had struggled to my apartment from the hospital through all that winter had to offer. Ironically, calm, star-filled nights like this one were even harder, so lonely you wanted to swear. In Hawaii almost every night was clear, blazing with thousands of stars and cooled by a gentle wind.

The thought of Jan back in my room kept me going. At times like this, when the medical tensions were beginning to evaporate, all I could think about was escaping the loneliness, being near someone alive and healthy, talking to her and loving her. A few times in medical school a girl had waited in my room while I went off to do something. That had always made it nice to come back. But too often she would just grunt a little in her sleep as I slid in beside her.

That "something" my medical-school peers and I found ourselves doing at odd hours of the morning was almost always a lab routine. The need for blood counts and Bence-Jones protein analyses seemed to occur to the residents primarily after midnight. So hundreds of times we had ended up spending the wee hours in what you might call the bowels of the medical ship, counting tiny blood cells, which grew ever tinier with the passage of time. Meanwhile, the resident on the bridge was steering the patient through, frequently complaining about the slowness of his blood counters in the hold. The truth about blood counts is that if you've done one you've pretty much done them all. The point of diminishing returns on the learning curve is reached quickly, particularly at 3:00 A.M., when your mind tends to dwell on getting back to your room and, perhaps, to the young lady.

In one twenty-four-hour period I had done twenty-seven blood counts, a personal record, though by no means a hospital record. My last few, in the small hours, were, of course, no better than half-educated guesses. Thus it went in the big leagues, where you were trained for a cost of $4,000 a year, to be a lab technician. All of us had worked up fantastic scenarios wherein we threw the urine in the resident's face and told him to jam the bottle up his ass, or we went on a sit-down strike in the cafeteria. None of these scenes existed outside our imaginations, because, to tell the truth, we were quite intimidated. As the professors never tired of pointing out, others were standing in line to wear our little white coats. What, in fact, happened was that late at night, when you felt pissed off and exploited, you cut a corner here and there and invented a plausible result. But this happened infrequently, and only late a night.

But worst of all was later, not having anyone to listen. The whole world seemed asleep and quite indifferent to your conviction that medical education was shitty and irrelevant. So you hurried back to your room, to the sleepy girl, grateful, finally, for her warm body.

Quite a few students got married at the beginning of medical school. I suppose they were not so lonely, having the omnipresent warm body. And the first two years *were* fine—courses during the day and hitting the books at night. They probably had a ball. But it was different when the blood counts came those last two years, and all the other Mickey Mouse in the middle of the night. Gradually, I think, some just gave up trying to communicate the frustration. The warm body wasn't enough. In any case, a lot of them weren't married any more when we finally got that piece of paper saying we were Doctors of Medicine. Actually, we had been champion blood counters, Doctors of Concept and Laboratory Trivia. Not one of us had known what dose of isuprel would save a life.

When I opened my door, I couldn't decide whether to make a lot of noise or be quiet. The kinder instincts won, and as the light from the hall flooded in I quickly rolled around the door and shut it. I took off my shoes. The room was perfectly silent, and so dark after the fluorescent lighting in the hall that I couldn't have moved around without knowing the position of the furniture. Some furniture! Of course, the hospital bed I slept on did have interesting characteristics. It could be cranked up into such a comfortable position for reading textbooks that I never managed to get through more than one or two paragraphs before falling asleep.

The rest of the furniture included an easy chair as hard as stone, a bookcase, and a desk designed for a small child. If I put both elbows on it, there was no room for the book, especially one of those five-pound, thirty-five-dollar jobs so popular with today's medical publishers. As I moved about in the dark, the only potentially serious obstacle was the surfboard I had hung from the ceiling. Gradually, as my sight adjusted, I could see the outline of the window and the bed, and I put my hand down on the covers, running it back and forth, faster each time, until I was sure she had left. Sitting on the edge of the bed, I rationalized that I was exhausted anyway, and she probably wouldn't have wanted to talk. It was past two, and I *was* exhausted; I really was.

The phone rang three more times before morning. The first two weren't important enough for me to go, just nurses with questions about some order and about a patient who wanted a laxative. On the matter of laxatives, I have made a small independent study. The study proves conclusively that five out of six nurses are ten times more likely to ask for a laxative order between midnight and 6:00 A.M. than at any other time of the day. As for the reasons, they are difficult to figure out, hinging perhaps on a Freudian interpretation of the nursing profession's anal hang-ups. In any case, I felt it was a near-criminal act to wake me up for a laxative order.

Each time the phone rang, I'd sit bolt upright as a shot of adrenaline whizzed through my veins. By the time I got the phone to my ear, my heart was pounding. Even if I didn't have to leave my room, it would take me about thirty minutes after each call before I calmed down enough to fall back to sleep. On an earlier evening, answering from a dead sleep, all I could hear was distant mumbling. "Speak louder," I had shouted, closing my eyes tightly and concentrating, barely able to make out the remote words. They had been telling me that I was speaking into the wrong end of the telephone.

The third call was at the opposite end of the spectrum from my fear of not knowing what to do. I could handle it for sure; so could a four-year-old child. Mrs. So-and-So had "fallen" out of bed. Patients don't usually hurt themselves falling out of bed—they're too loose, and, besides, the nurses know what to do. None of that mattered to the hospital administration. As long as they "fell" out of bed, the intern had to go say hello, no matter what time it was.

So I got up feeling—how to explain it?—well, it's not nausea, although you feel sick to your stomach, and it's not a high fever, though your forehead would fry an egg. The best nomenclature is a description. You feel just as you might expect to feel at being startled awake at 4:00 A.M. after about two hours' sleep during which you were awakened each time you sank off—having finally lain down after working for almost twenty hours, emotionally exhausted, physically, too—to hold the hand of someone who "fell" out of bed unhurt. Actually, most of them just sank to the floor on the way to the bathroom. But regardless of how they got there, even if they were twenty feet from the bed, the nurses always called it a fall, and up you went, in the observance of an absurd legality.

This formalism is even more absurd when one realizes that a hospital is otherwise dependent upon these same nurses to determine a patient's physical state and to call the doctor if need be. But for some inexplicable reason they cannot be depended upon to see if a patient has hurt himself sinking to the floor. Yet it's more, more than something useless and arbitrary you must do. About half your time since third-year medical school has been spent in pursuit of the useless and the arbitrary, which are justified by the diaphanous explanation that they are a necessary part of being a medical student or intern and becoming a doctor. Bullshit. This sort of thing is simply hazing and harassment, a kind of initiation rite into the American Medical Association. The system works, too; God, how it works! Behold the medical profession, molded to perfection, brainwashed, narrowly programmed, right wing in its politics, and fully dedicated to the pursuit of money.

These thoughts rumbled chaotically through my head as I went to the elevator and hit the button hard, half hoping to break the whole contraption. Returning to the hospital, down those sleepy corridors toward distant points of light, I tried not to wake up completely.

I once told a friend who was not in medicine the various reasons I got called out of my bed at 4:30 A.M. He didn't believe them. It was too disquieting for him; it shattered his colorful image of the intern awakened suddenly, all eager in white, flashing down the corridors, up the stairs by threes and fours, to save a life. Here was the real me, feeling shitty and stumbling down a hall swearing under my breath, on my way to say, How are you, patient? . . . Fine, Doctor. . . . That's wonderful. . . . Have a good rest, and please don't fall out of bed again.

When the phone rang again it was daylight, five-forty-five. Feet over onto the floor, sit up sideways, use my hands to push up. That slightly sick feeling again, and a momentary dizziness until the cold floor knocks it out of me. Over to the sink, hands on its sides, lean on it for a second. In the mirror my eyes are like aerial views of hot lava running into a muddy lake. The only reason the bags under them don't meet the corners of my mouth is that I can't smile. Ah, a trickle of water meanders out of the faucet. Holding on with one hand, I raise a few drops to my face.

Nothing about this morning was particularly noteworthy or different. It was just a morning, like other mornings. In two weeks I had worked up such a deficit of sleep that even when I did get six hours straight I felt the same way. The razor blade, much sharper than I was, left several points of blood on my throat. Mixing with the water on my face, it seemed like a lot of blood and, combined with my eyes and the dark under them, made me look like a Mafia heavy.

After thirty seconds or so I felt together enough to dress. Stethoscope, little flashlight, several different-colored pens, notebook, comb, watch, wallet, belt, shoes—on through the mental check list. Make sure socks are the same color. Mustn't spoil the tone of the place. One last visual sweep around the room to make sure there wasn't something else, some piece of paper, a book. Satisfied, I left, descended in the elevator, and stepped out into the morning air.

It had always been a point with me to walk around in front of the hospital on my way to the cafeteria. Somehow it lifted my spirits. This morning the sky was a pale faraway blue dotted with small clouds, half bathed in the east in golden tones of red; toward the west the colors faded off into pink and violet. The grass sparkled, still damp from the night air, even the trees sparkled, and birds were everywhere, producing an incredible din. Two types of birds predominated, the mynas, who strutted about gesturing awkwardly and making unharmonious, scolding squawks, and the less noticeable doves, moving more slowly, almost politely, some of them seeming to bob up and down as they fanned out their tail feathers and cooed in melodious voices. I liked that short morning walk. It was only a few hundred feet, but it made me feel happy.

Six o'clock in the morning is not my idea of the perfect time for a big breakfast, particularly after a sleepless night. But I forced myself to eat, stuffing the food into my mouth and relying heavily on water to take it down. By experience, I knew that if I didn't eat I'd be hungry in an hour or so, when it would be impossible to get food. Besides, I missed lunch about half the time because of the operating schedule. Another meal might not come my way for eight or ten hours.

After breakfast, I had about thirty minutes to see my patients before rounds started at six-forty-five. It was important to have everything in order before then, to know all the latest changes. The ICU was first. I never minded going there in the morning, or any time during daylight, for that matter. Having other doctors around diminished that feeling of being alone on a high wire. Mrs. Takura was sleeping peacefully after her preoperative medication; the tube hung still in her nostril, wrinkling her nose from the tension. Pulse, urine output, blood pressure, breathing rate, temperature, electrolytes, BUN, protime, proteins, bilirubin . . . all the recent tests were back and recorded. Pausing to write a note about her status in the continuation sheet, I hoped she was ready.

Back in one corner Mr. Smith's machines were still beeping

away, showing an EKG that looked pretty normal, although I was no ace at reading them, especially from the oscilloscope. He was sleeping, too. I went down to the wards.

On the ward, the name of the game was numbers and variety rather than crisis. I had several dozen patients, representing as many different types of people and problems. Most of them had had their surgery and were progressing well at various stages from postoperative, through having stitches out, to discharge. The length of their drains was usually a good indication of how many days had elapsed since they'd left the operating table. Drains are a somewhat awkward but quite necessary part of surgical practice. Planted deep with the wound at the end of the operation, they serve as an outlet for any unwanted fluid and help to keep down infection. The idea is to pull the drain out, inch by inch, beginning on the second postoperative day, thereby letting the wound heal slowly from the inside out.

Patients never understand these drains. To them, the dangling pieces of pale rubber are a source of endless conversation and discomfort, mostly mental. Mr. Sperry was two days postoperative for gastric ulcer, and it was time to begin pulling his drain. Grabbing it with a clamp, I gave the tube a good tug. But it held fast, just stretching a bit, so that it looked somewhat like a Chinese noodle. From his sitting position, propped up on two pillows, Mr. Sperry watched in dismayed fascination, his eyes as big as almond cookies and his hands gripping the sheets. Pulling at it again, I began to wonder if the drain had accidentally been stitched into the wound when gradually it let go and moved out a couple of inches. A bit of serosanguineous fluid escaped with the drain and was quickly soaked up with gauze.

"Doctor, did you have to do that?"

"Well, you don't want to go home with this drain hanging out, do you?"

"No."

I put a safety pin through the drain just above the skin to keep the tube from dropping back into the wound and then, with sterile scissors, I cut off the excess tubing. It was important to follow the right order in this simple procedure. Once, before I knew better, I had cut the drain off prior to placing the safety pin. The patient had been holding his breath all the while, and when he finally inhaled, the drain disappeared into his abdomen. Visions of a new operation crashed in my head, but fortunately a resident had retrieved the drain after taking out three skin sutures and fishing around with some forceps.

"Why don't you put me to sleep when you pull it?" Mr. Sperry looked at me, questioning.

"Mr. Sperry, putting you to sleep is not as easy as you think it is. Besides, anesthesia always carries a risk, but there's no risk in pulling out your drain."

"Yes, but then I wouldn't know about it."

"Did it really hurt when I pulled your drain?"

"A little, and it felt funny inside, like I was coming apart."

"You're not coming apart, Mr. Sperry. "You're doing great."

"Did you have to pull so hard?" he pressed.

"Look, Mr. Sperry, tomorrow I'll put these gloves on you, give you the clamp, and you can pull it out. How's that?" I knew that would get a response.

"No, no, I didn't mean that I wanted to do it."

Actually, I knew what he meant. After an operation I had once had on my legs, I felt the doctor was too rough when he took the stitches out. But I hadn't wanted to take them out myself. It's good for a doctor to be a patient now and then— makes him more responsive to all the patient's irrational fears. The solution is to tell the patient everything you are doing, even the simple things, because often it is what you take for granted that scares the patient the most.

"Mr. Sperry, you can move around as much as you like. In fact, movement is good for you. You are not going to pop open. This drain is the normal procedure. It lets out any bad juices while you heal. The safety pin is just to keep it from going back inside your abdomen."

All was well with Mr. Sperry, although I had surely given him something to talk about for the rest of the day: how the cruel doctor had yanked his drain and caused the wound to open and bleed.

That was the ward routine: checking drains, changing dressings, answering questions, looking at temperature graphs. Although Marsha Potts was not my patient, I paused in front of her door almost instinctively. She looked worse now, with the daylight exposing her jaundiced color and the skin on her face so tight and drawn that her teeth were bared in a perpetual grin. She was in terrible shape; we were doing all we could, but it would not be enough. Outside her room, where the grass came right up to the building, the birds paid no attention as they squawked and chattered over bits of toast tossed to them by the mobile patients.

Now, at seven o'clock, the ward had come alive, suddenly filled with breakfast trays and clanging IV poles as people made their way to the bathroom. Nurses scurried here and there, carrying pans, needles, ointments, and pills. Swept into this world, I no longer felt tired, at least as long as I stayed on my feet. There was an exhilaration to the routine; it seemed to say, "No one can die here, everything is under control." In the midst of all this bright efficiency, Roso was out cold from his Sparine. I had to shake him several times to get any response at all. But once half-awake he agreed he was more strong, Doktoor, before sinking back into sleep.

A lab technician asked me to help her draw some blood from a patient with bad veins. She had tried three times without success. Certainly I'd try, and willingly, because it was a source of great comfort to me having these technicians to draw blood in the morning. To nondoctors it might seem a small point, but medical students resented spending most of their time before morning rounds trying to milk blood out of patients; by the time rounds started they hadn't been able to see any of their patients and were therefore ignorant of their latest condition. When the questions started coming—"What's this patient's hematocrit, Peters?"—you had to guess, because you hadn't had a chance to look at the chart, either. But it must not sound like a guess. Snap back, without hesitation, "Thirty-seven!" as though you'd stake your life on it. It was not a matter of honesty. Better to play the game than to tempt disaster by saying you didn't know, whatever the reason. No one cared whether you had done those twenty-seven blood counts except if you didn't do them. So you shot back thirty-seven so quickly that half the time the professor would pass on without thinking. But if he paused, you were in trouble, unless you could distract him by referring to a recent article bearing on the disease. Of course, if he checked the chart, you lost totally, unless by wild chance the hematocrit was, indeed, thirty-seven; otherwise, you said somewhat lamely that you had another patient in mind. This would bring about the last, fatal pause as the professor leafed through the chart, looking for another question.

"What about the bilirubin, Peters?"

Now you were really up against the wall, faced with an all-or-nothing gamble. If your bilirubin guess was wrong, too, the professor's suspicion that you were lax on patient care would spread like ripples through the hospital. But in the happy event that you were right, you were returned to a state of grace and moved on to the next patient to watch another student get his interrogation. Bilirubin is different from hematocrit in that everyone's hematocrit varies a good deal, whereas the bilirubin value is usually pretty much the same in everybody, except in liver and blood cases. So you decided to gamble, saying, "It was about one, sir." In medical school most of us learned to play the game; if you played it well, you won more than you lost.

In Hawaii, the technicians had lifted this blood burden, and I didn't mind helping them occasionally. Besides, I was pretty good at it. I should have been, after having drawn several thousand blood samples in medical school. We students had started by drawing each other's blood, which was generally a snap, although some of us made it look pretty difficult. Even this exercise had not been without its dramatic moments. One time, after vigorously palpating the arm vein of another second-year student, I had it standing out like a cheap cigar. The tourniquet had been on for about four minutes while I built up my courage, and when I finally pushed the needle in, my friend just disappeared. It all happened so fast. I went directly from concentrating on the needle breaking the skin to staring at a needle and no arm. My "patient" was spread out on the floor in a dead faint. We had all dreaded those practice sessions, but they were easier than having each student draw blood from himself.

I'll never forget the first time I drew blood from an actual patient. It happened early in third year, when we students were beginning ward medicine. As bad luck would have it, our first day on the ward had coincided with a shift change among the interns and residents. To the new residents, the opportunity was irresistible. They decided to check the diagnoses of all the patients, and for this they needed proof—cold facts, incontrovertible laboratory evidence. As a result, we students had to draw about a pint of blood from every patient assigned to us. My first patient, poor fellow, was a chronic alcoholic with advanced liver cirrhosis. His surface veins had disappeared years ago, and I had to stick him twelve times, groping around inside his arm with the needle, feeling each needle point break through unknown inner structures with a sudden, almost audible popping release. Finally, I had had the good sense to give up and be instructed by the intern on how to get the needle into the large femoral vein in the groin, a procedure known as a femoral stick.

Now the laboratory technician was having much the same problem with a Mr. Schmidt, whom I palpated for the usual arm veins as she handed me a syringe. It was obvious why she hadn't been able to get any blood: I couldn't feel a single decent vein in his arm. So I did a femoral stick, and it was over in a flash.

Farther along the ward I came to Mr. Polski, who was a problem for me mainly because I had failed to achieve any real rapport with him. He had diabetes, very poor peripheral circulation, and a deep infection of the right foot. About a week previously we had done a lumbar sympathectomy, cutting the nerves that were responsible for contracting the walls of the blood vessels of his lower legs. But he was showing very little improvement. Because of the pain, he insisted on hanging his leg over the side of the bed, and that merely inhibited what meager circulation he had. At first I had tried the friendly approach, explaining carefully what happened when he let the leg hang over the side. Regardless, every morning when I appeared, there it was hanging down. Switching tactics, I had pretended to be angry, yelling in feigned rage—which didn't change the situation except to make him like me even less. The foot, now black and gangrenous, was scheduled for amputation.

I nodded my head to Mrs. Tang, an elderly Chinese lady with a cancer growing inside her mouth. She couldn't talk, so we just nodded. The cancer was so big that it had dissolved some teeth and the bone of the jaw on the left side, becoming finally an uncontrollable, fungating mass that occasionally broke through the side of her throat. She was like many older Chinese people who thought of a hospital only as a place of death and would not come to us until the very end. There was little we could do for Mrs. Tang but try some X-ray therapy. The cancer got bigger every day, and somehow Mrs. Tang every day seemed less real—perhaps because she couldn't talk, or maybe because she was so resigned.

There were others: a lymph-node biopsy, a breast biopsy, two hernia repairs. I greeted each of them, passing from bed to bed, using their names—I knew them all by now. I even knew the families of many of the patients who had been with us quite a while. The other intern and a handful of residents arrived, including the chief resident, and morning rounds began. This was a rapid affair; we probably looked like a bunch of myna birds, moving awkwardly and quickly, almost stepping on one another in our haste, as we went from bed to bed. The haste was necessary since we now had only half an hour until the first scheduled operation. No articles were discussed; we didn't do much more than just count heads to make sure everybody was still there. Gastrectomy, five days postop, going smoothly. Hernia, three days postop, probable discharge. Varicose veins, three days postop, also probable discharge. Gastric ulcer, X rays complete, scheduled for surgery. Did the X ray show the ulcer? Yes. Good.

In the next ward, we stood in the middle and twirled slowly on our heels. Mass lesion, mediastinum, aortogram pending. I ran through a staccato capsule description on each of my patients. The other intern did the same. There were four such wards, and we finished the last case in the fourth ward exactly seventeen minutes after starting.

"Peters, you do another cutdown on Potts while we go to the ICU and pediatrics." The little troop disappeared around the corner, and I turned toward Marsha Potts's room, confused and irritated, silently protesting. She wasn't even my patient. I knew I had been chosen because I didn't have any surgery until eight, instead of the usual seven-thirty, but even so I didn't want to get involved with her again, after fooling around with that venous pressure setup the night before. Moreover, a cutdown could be tricky. I hadn't done many of them. But mainly it was just so damn unpleasant in there. Still, Marsha Potts needed a cutdown because she needed intravenous fluid and food; with no more superficial veins that we could use for her IV, we had to cut down on a deeper vein.

As I entered that room, the cheerful morning bustle faded away. Even the bird sounds became inaudible to me, although of course they were still there. The smell was almost overpowering, so pungent and revolting it made the air seem heavy. It was the hot smell of rotting tissue mixed with the sweet, syrupy smell of scented talcum powder being used in a vain attempt to counteract the stench. The talcum powder only made it worse for me. Trying not to look at the poor women's face, I put on three surgical masks to fend off the smell, but the layers made it hard to breathe and my diaphragm struggled to draw in the thick air. I didn't want to touch too many things in there. Death seemed spread on everything, almost contagious.

I pulled up the sheet from the bottom and bared her right foot. There were open ulcerations on the underside of her leg and the back of her heel. In fact there were sores all over her body, wherever it touched anything. After focusing a bright light on the medial aspect of her ankle, I pulled on the rubber gloves and opened the sterile cutdown tray.

The knife slipped through her skin with zero resistance. She was a little edematous on the foot, so that clear fluid rather than blood began to run from the wound. I was lucky to find the vein right away, and lucky I hadn't accidentally cut it. After making a little nick in the wall of the vein, I slid the catheter easily inside it, first try, as drops of sweat appeared on my forehead from the heat of the bright light. Using silk, I tied the catheter in place and closed the little wound, watching the IV run freely. With my foot I pushed the tray away, snapped off the gloves, and walked rapidly out toward the sunlight and the birds.

Washing my hands, I felt a deep disgust with myself, and I didn't know exactly why. She was a human being; I was supposed to help her. But the situation and her condition revolted me so much I had trouble accepting the responsibility. Where was my compassion; where was it going?

My first scrub was at eight, a cholecystectomy, or gall-bladder removal, with a private surgeon. My patient, Mrs. Takura, was scheduled for another operating room, to follow a ganglion removal; her operation should begin about nine, barring complications with the ganglion. Obviously I was going to be late for Mrs. Takura, but that was typical. The intern is a kind of pawn in the medical game; he is the first line of defense, sacrificed without remorse, disposable in the end, but needed, it seems, in the middle.

I pushed into the surgeons' locker room and began to put on a pale green scrub suit. It was so cramped in there that everybody always got shoved around a little, in a good-natured way. In fact, the sense of equality and the recognition of everybody as a person made scrubbing there a pleasure. Back in med school, the students and house staff had dressed in a completely different area set off by doors and a separate stairway from the sanctum sanctorum of the attendings' dressing quarters. It was almost as though a surgeon's image would crumble if you saw him in nature's state.

One med-school attending was so nasty that students actually shook while presenting their cases. A friend of mine—an excellent doctor, though inclined to stage fright—once had a complete lapse of memory at a bedside as he started to run through the facts in front of this attending. I knew he had the case down cold, but he could not get it out. "This woman presents an . . . uh . . . uh . . ." His face flushed and his pulses hammered at the sides of his neck. The attending could have eased the situation by suggesting that we come back to the case later, or even by giving a key word from the chart to bump the student's memory chain. Not a chance. He had flown into a rage, shouting in wonderment that a person so stupid could have gotten into medical school and ordering the student out of his sight until he knew his patients well enough to present them. Not all the attendings were like that, but a significant number were, even, sometimes, the chief of the service. Naturally, after one of those episodes, rapport between student and patient was in bad repair when it came time to draw blood the following morning. As time goes on, many details of medical school will blend and merge into generality, but not, I think, the scenes of rant and frenzy staged by overbearing surgeons. Some of them behaved so violently that it almost seemed as if they hated medical students; and yet these men were our mentors, our teachers and models.

After the green gown, I put on canvas boots and plodded down the long surgical corridor. Some of the OR doors were closed, and as I passed their small windows I could glimpse Ku Klux Klan-like groups clustered in the center of the room. Other doors were open, some with cases going on, others empty with anticipation. Dozens of nurses moved about, highly organized and busy, many of them looking quite pretty—a high achievement for anyone in one of those shapeless suits, with her hair tucked under a scrub hat. Others, however, might have done well at defensive tackle for the New York Giants, playing without equipment and just scaring the opponent into submission. Everybody said good morning; it was a friendly place.

When I moved up to the sink to scrub for the gall-bladder operation, the surgeon and a resident were already there. The resident was Oriental, small, silent, and respectful. I smiled to myself, thinking of my friend Carno's description of the resident as being so small he had to run around in the shower to get wet. The smile started an itch under my mask. Uncanny how that always happened. Always after scrubbing came the itch, usually along the side of my nose or at the corner of my forehead. Of course, I couldn't scratch it until the operation was over and we broke scrub. Twisting my face and wrinkling my forehead occasionally brought minor relief. But the itch remained, fluctuating with my degree of concentration on what I was doing. For me, it was the most annoying part of the OR —aside from the retractors.

"Your name's Peters, huh? Where you from? Where'd you go to school? Oh, one of the big boys from back east, huh?"

There it was, reverse prejudice. It seemed crazy now that one of my strongest motivations for applying to medical school had been the idea of becoming a member of a highly educated fraternity, a group whose dedication and training put it beyond the trivialities and pettiness of everyday society. Needless to say, I no longer labored under that delusion; it had been riddled early in medical school. Nevertheless, the competition to get in was so keen that if you made it to one of the top few medical schools, it almost invariably meant that you had really whizzed through college, usually with straight A's. Therefore, the guys who had to settle for their fifth or sixth choice of medical school usually felt like victims of a system in which performance was gauged by the harsh and immutable reality of the transcript. They thought the ivory-tower types looked upon them as second-class citizens. It was all nonsense. Everybody came out on the other side of that huge medical machine looking and thinking exactly the same, and with the same license to practice medicine. In fact, it was the sameness of these men that frightened me, not their differences, which were superficial. I had begun to suspect of late that the machine was producing a lopsided product.

Scrubbing is an invariable, monotonous, ten-minute routine. First under the nails, then a general wash, then the brush. Each surface in turn up to the elbow, then each finger. Start again. Back and forth.

The scrubbing done, I backed through the door, ass first— the perfect symbol of the intern's position—my hands raised in surrender and submission. That's too theatrical. Actually, I was resigned by now. After all, it had been my own decision to go into medicine; no Romeo had ever panted harder after his Juliet. Too bad she had turned out to be such a bitch. These pseudophilosophic ramblings bore no fruit, changed nothing, but they did help to pass those interminable hours in the OR.

Towel, gown, then gloves, from a rather perfunctory nurse whose eyes I couldn't catch, and the routine was complete. We draped the patient while the surgeon, who was part Hawaiian, and the anesthesiologist, an Oriental, maintained a half-intelligible conversation in pidgin English.

"I go Vegas next week. You want go?" It was the anesthesiologist, looking blankly over the other screen.

"What, you think I that kind gambler?"

"You surgeon, you dat kind gambler."

"Fuck you, *pake*. At least I ain't no fly-by-night gas passer."

"Ha! No gas, no work for you, *kanaka*."

I was on the right side of the patient, between the surgeon and the anesthesiologist, so that such priceless wisdom and Hawaiian linguistic exotica had to go right by me. The resident stood on the other side, inscrutable.

With everything ready, the surgeon picked up a knife and made the skin incision under the right rib cage. About halfway through the cut, everybody realized that the patient wasn't anesthetized deeply enough. In fact, he was twitching and moving about as if he had a generalized, unbearable itch. The surgeon and the anesthesiologist simultaneously gave nervous little laughs, the surgeon's a bit cynical, because he actually wanted to tell the anesthesiologist he didn't know what the hell he was doing. I don't know why the anesthesiologist laughed, except maybe to fend off the surgeon's broken-record sarcasm. Surgeons are not known for their tact or their love of anesthesiologists.

"Hey, brudda, whatcha madder wich ya? You saving da kind gas for the next patient? Geevum, man, geevum."

The anesthesiologist didn't say anything, and the surgeon continued, "Looks like we going to do this case with no help from the gas passer."

I was unavoidably a kind of referee in this verbal pugilism, literally squashed against the draped anesthesia screen by the surgeon. Not until they were finally inside the belly was I handed the all-too-familir handle of a retractor, the intern's joy and *raison d'être*. There are thousands of different kinds of retractors, but they all do the same thing: hold back the edges of the wound and the other organs so the surgeon can get at his target.

The surgeon positioned one of the retractors to his liking, motioned for me to take it, and told me to lift up rather than pull back. Well, I'd lift up for about two or three minutes, and then I'd pull back. From where I was standing, my leverage on the retractor handle was negative. Two or three minutes was my limit. "Lift up, goddamnit. Here, let me show you." The surgeon took the retractor out of my hands. "Like this." Amid further comments on my ineptitude, he lifted on the retractor for about two seconds before giving the handle back to me, whereupon I lifted up for two or three minutes and then pulled back. It was unavoidable. Show me the man who can lift up rather than pull back through a five-hour cholecystectomy, and I'll follow him to the ends of the earth.

Cholecystectomy is simply the medical name for the removal of a gall bladder. The gall bladder is tucked far up under the liver, and the intern is needed to pull back the liver and the upper portion of the incision so that the surgeon, with the help of the resident, can take it out. The gall bladder is a pretty unreliable organ, and, therefore, removing it is one of the most frequent surgical procedures. Of all the memory aids I'd learned in medical school, I best remembered the one about the average gall-bladder patient: the four *f*'s—fat, female, forty, and flatulent.

Throughout the operation, my arms were more or less under the surgeon's left arm. He was pivoted away from me, presenting his back, which totally obscured the incision, somewhere over his shoulder. When the anesthesiologist switched on his portable radio and began glancing through a newspaper, and the surgeon began alternately humming and singing, both out of tune, the scene came less and less to resemble the tense silence of medical school—except for those outbursts of displeasure by the surgeon. They were the same.

"Okay, Peters, take a look." I peered over into the incision, a red oozing hole with surgical tapes holding back the abdominal organs. There was the gall bladder, the cystic duct, the common duct, the . . . "Okay, that's enough. Don't want to spoil you." The surgeon moved back, muscling me out, chuckling with the anesthesiologist. The operating room is a feudal world, with an absolute hierarchy and value system, in which the surgeon is the divine and almighty king, the anesthesiologist his sycophantic prince, and the intern his serf, supposedly grateful for any small scrap of recognition—a look inside or perhaps even the chance to tie a knot or two. That glimpse into the wound had been my reward for being there holding the retractors and watching either the surgeon's back or the hands of the wall clock as they crept slowly around.

The atmosphere was congenial enough, however, until the surgeon asked for the operative cholangiogram, an X-ray study, to make sure he had the common duct well cleaned of gallbladder stones. This could be determined by injecting an opaque dye into the ducts and then X-raying the area. Any remaining stones would stand out.

When no X-ray technician appeared magically at the snap

of his finger—all were busy on other cases—the surgeon cursed and waved his scalpel about, threatening dire reprisals. The nurses were immune to this display, as was the anesthesiologist, whose radio continued to drum out its patter of music and news. This familiar scene was played just about every time the need arose for a mid-operation X ray.

A technician finally came and took the shot, returning in a few minutes with a foggy blur, which the surgeon pronounced the most inept attempt since Roentgen himself. Did he want another taken? No! There is much to learn about the surgeon. I was sure, on reflection, that he wanted that X ray because he had read about it in some journal and thought it would look good on the operative record. The practical effect of the X ray was at best neutral—the way he utilized it, at any rate.

The next day a radiologist would struggle with the X ray, trying to figure out which end should be up and why the hemostat showed in the middle of the ductal system. His report would be sheer guesswork. The unhappy ending of this episode would come later, when the surgeon said something sarcastic to the radiologist, who would smile wryly and reply that if the surgeons could organize themselves a little, radiology might be able to do something. In truth, the surgeons are often at war with everyone—with radiology, pathology, anesthesiology, the operating schedule, residents, nurses, interns—constantly surrounded, they feel, by an ungrateful and inept staff. In a word, many of them are quite paranoid.

Once the retracting had been completed, I prefaced a request to leave with a brief explanation about Mrs. Takura and was excused from the rest of the cholecystectomy. As I stepped out of the operating room into the corridor, the surgeon was still deep in his complaint about X-ray and the anesthesiologist still absorbed in his newspaper.

The work had already started on Mrs. Takura when I began scrubbing the second time. I could see the chief surgical resident and the first-year resident, Carno, busily inserting subcutaneous clamps. Carno and I had come to Hawaii at the same time, for the same reason—to get away from the pressure and have a little fun. In the first few days we had hit it off pretty well, and had even considered getting an apartment together. But now our schedules made it hard to get together.

Friendship among medical people is difficult and elusive, much harder than in college. There is so little time for it. Everyone tends to draw more and more inward, become almost autistic, even when free. In the later years of medical school, the on-call schedules are so different that you can't count on anybody showing up for dinner or a party. Sometimes I couldn't even count on myself. I'd often make plans and then feel too washed out to carry them through.

Also, there was the unavoidable competition. It had settled on us from our very first day, like the spores of a fungus, beginning with the premise that medicine was at its zenith in the research-oriented university center. That was where the "good guys" ended up. To get there, you first had to have a residency at a university center, and for that you needed an internship in one of a handful of princely hospitals. We had been told right off that the top four or five in the class would be asked to stay on as interns, the golden ticket to advance one more giant step. Pressure! There were about 130 of us, all good students in college, and all stumbling around in a haze, sopping up facts as fast as we could and accepting the value system that told us we had to stay on the top. The alternative, too horrible to contemplate, was that we would FAIL and end up in a small-town general practice. That was made to sound bad, really bad, like going from the executive suite to the mail room.

It didn't make any difference if you did well; everyone in the group could do that. After all, we were horses trained to run, and we ran like hell. The real point was to do better than the next guy. That didn't create a congenial environment for friendship, especially when you were short of time, and the time you did have you invariably wanted to spend with a girl.

The system affected that, too, especially during the last couple of years. At first, being a medical student gave you a certain mystique at cocktail parties—everybody thought you were sure to make it into the big money someday. But gradually, since your schedule was so screwed up, you couldn't count on being anywhere at the right time, and you came to be considered a bad risk. All those lovelies from Smith and Wellesley, the ones you were used to, drifted away to more fertile ground. So we had turned to the girls who were there, the ones with the crazy schedules just like ours. And they turned to us. The hospital was full of girls—technicians, instructors, nurses, nursing students—many of them damn nice, and most of them conveniently available.

As our training forced us into the mold, we withdrew into ourselves and into the artificial world of the medical school and the hospital. The change was imperceptible, almost unconscious, but steady; once on the escalator leading to the ivory tower, we stayed on it, intellectually. Even though I'd come to Hawaii, I hadn't split totally. Never would. I still had a foot in the door back east; at least, I hoped so. I wasn't a rebel or a revolutionary, just a little worried about where I was going.

Right now I was going into the OR with Mrs. Takura, backing in again with my hands up, ready to be gowned and gloved. They were just getting into the abdomen, and the chief resident motioned me to his left side. After I had squeezed into my position between him and the anesthesia screen, he handed over the legendary retractors and we settled, in, this time for eight hours.

It was hard to recognize nice old Mrs. Takura. Instead of being her usual agreeable and considerate self, she was bleeding all over the place. She had had a cholecystectomy several years back, and it was difficult operating through all the adhesions and fibrous tissue. About two hours into the operation, we took time out to plug a little puncture in the bowel, and then a strong "bleeder" that was squirting on Carno's chest. As her blood pressure sagged, full bottles of blood replaced the empty ones. It was a tough, long procedure, but the chief resident seemed to be doing a good job. Any levity that might have existed earlier disappeared as fatigue crept over us.

Although you would never know it from watching television, humor plays a big part in the operating room. To be sure, it is often grisly, and often at the expense of an unwitting and innocent patient. Most surgeons can regale an operating team for hours with bizarre and off-color tales from the past. With my limited experience, and therefore a limited repertoire, I was mostly silent during these performances, but just before getting serious about Mrs. Takura, when everybody was still feeling good, I ventured a story that was a favorite in my medical school.

It seems that an enormously obese lady had once appeared at the hospital during a time when the OR was covered only by two interns and a resident. She complained of an agonizing abdominal pain. Elbow deep in fatty tissue, the three examined her, conferred, re-examined, and conferred again, unable to agree on a diagnosis. Finally those who thought she had a hot appendix won out, and up the lady went to the OR, where she was literally draped all over the table. Hearing of the action, a small band of six or seven others had gathered by the time the resident began cutting down through the layers of fat toward the peritoneal cavity. After repositioning the retractors several times, as he moved in deeper and deeper, he suddenly stopped and had the overhead light readjusted. Then he asked for a pair of tongs, and while everyone watched in anticipation, he brought up through the lady a piece of white cloth. A stunned silence fell over the assemblage until, simultaneously, everyone realized that the resident had cut all the way through to the operating table. The patient's abdomen, being so large, had skewed off to the left, causing the resident to miss the abdominal cavity entirely.

But the laughter from that story had long since drifted away. We labored now inside Mrs. Takura, and the muscles in my hands and arms were numb from maintaining tension on the retractors in that awkward position hour after hour. As lunchtime approached and receded, my stomach growled in protest, a counterpoint to the itch on my nose. My bladder was so full I didn't dare lean against the operating table. Time crept on. I seldom saw into the wound, although I could tell what was happening from the surgeon's comments. Fastidiously the vessels were sewn together—a side-to-side anastomosis—and the final suture was placed and run down with tired fingers. When I was at last relieved of the retractors, I couldn't even open my fists; they stayed clenched until I bent the fingers back one by one and soaked them in warm water.

Although it was almost four o'clock, we were not through. We still had to close. Like all the others, I was tired, hungry, and uncomfortable in every way. Suture after suture, wire, silk, wire, slowly working up the long incision, starting from the bottom and working with rapid ties, the gaping portion very slowly but progressively drawing closed until the last fascial suture. Placed. Then the skin. By the time we snapped off our gloves at the finish it was past five—the beginning of my glorious night off.

I urinated, wrote all the postoperative orders, changed my clothes, and had some dinner, in that order. As I walked across to the dining room, I felt as if I'd been run over by a herd of wild elephants in heat. I was exhausted and, much worse, deeply frustrated. I had been assisting in surgery for nine straight hours. Eight of them had been the most important hours of Mrs. Takura's life; yet I felt no sense of accomplishment. I had simply endured, and I was probably the one person they could have done without. Sure, they needed the retraction, but a catatonic schizophrenic would have sufficed. Interns are eager to work hard, even to sacrifice—above all, to be useful and to display their special talents—in order to learn. I felt none of these satisfactions, only an empty bitterness and exhaustion.

After supper, even though I was not on call, the usual ward work was still to be done, and I moved perfunctorily through a series of dressings, drains, and sutures. I rewrote IV orders, looked over laboratory reports, and did a history, physical, and preoperative preparation on one new patient, a hernia. Roso's hiccups had started again as he came out of his hibernation with the Sparine. Anything I wanted to ignore I did so by leaning on my tiredness, rationalizing. I avoided even looking into Marsha Potts's room.

Sleep was impossible, though I had been without it for most of twenty-four hours. Besides, I wanted to go somewhere away from the hospital, to talk with somebody. My confused and angry thoughts were rocketing around in my head too much for me to deal with alone. Carno couldn't be located anyplace; probably he was with his Japanese girl friend. But Jan, thank God, was there and available. She wanted to go for a drive, perhaps a swim. She wanted to do anything I wanted to do.

We drove eastward, moving toward the silvery violet of the evening. The road took us up over the Pali to the windward side of the island, gradually climbing and opening out the view of the colors from the setting sun on the expanding panorama of ocean behind us. The scene had a poetry that kept us silent until we were through the tunnel and out in the shadow again, in Kailua. There we found a beach where we were alone. My head gradually cleared of hostile thoughts, and the prison of the day, with its creeping clock and stiff fingers, seemed far away as I floated in the shallow water, letting the small exhausted waves rock me with their surge. Later we lay on a blanket and watched the stars come out.

Wanting to hear Jan talk, I asked her questions about herself, her family, her likes and dislikes, her favorite books. All at once I wanted to know all about her, and to hear her tell it in her small, soft voice. She grew weary of this after a time and asked me about my day.

"I spent all day in surgery."

"You did?"

"Nine hours."

"Wow, that's wonderful! What did you do?"

"Nothing."

"Nothing?"

"Well, practically nothing. I mean I was the retractor, holding back the wound edge and the liver so that the real doctors could operate."

"You're silly," she said. "That was important and you know it."

"Yes, it was important. But the problem is that anybody could have done it, anybody at all."

"I don't believe it."

"Yeah, I know you don't believe it. Neither does anybody else. No one thinks that anybody but an intern can take an intern's place. But let me tell you, in that operating room, no one could have done the nurse's job except another nurse, ditto the anesthesiologist and the surgeon. But me? Anybody! The guy off the street. Anybody at all."

"But you have to learn."

"You hit the problem on the head. The intern is frozen in one spot, eternally retracting. They call it learning—that's the rationalization—but it's a hoax. You learn enough about retracting after one day. You don't need a year. There's so much to learn, but why at this snail's pace? You feel so damn exploited! They ought to hire people to retract, and put the intern over there tying knots and watching the surgeon work."

"Can you tie good knots already?" she asked.

That stopped me. I could remember telling her that I wasn't very good with knots, but still, her comment seemed discouragingly off the mark. It indicated that I wasn't getting through to her and it was useless to try. Even so, I felt better, almost as if my own thoughts had focused. I told her no, I couldn't tie very good knots, but I'd probably learn if they gave me the job.

She was getting to me again, turning me on. We ended up running through the shallow water. She was so beautiful, so full of life, I wanted to yell with joy. We kissed and held each other close, rolled up in the blanket. I was wild for her, and knew that we were going to make love, and that she wanted to as much as I did. But she felt obliged to talk some more first, and tell me some personal things about herself. For instance, that she had made love to only one other boy, but that he had tricked her because it turned out that he hadn't really loved her. This went on for five minutes or so, slowly turning me off again, and I decided that making love was probably a bad idea, after all. She couldn't believe this, and wanted to know why. The real reason, my inner frustration, would not have satisfied her. Instead, I told her that I loved the sheen in her hair and her sense of life but I didn't know if I loved *her* yet.

That pleased her so much she almost made me change my mind again. Driving back to the hospital, I got her to sing "Where Have All the Flowers Gone?" over and over again, and I felt at peace.

"You think you didn't do anything today, but you did," she said, suddenly turning toward me.

"What was that?" I asked.

"Well, you saved Mrs. Takura's life. I mean, you helped, even if you thought that you should have been doing something else."

I had to admit her point, a very nice point, which I had almost forgotten. For Mrs. Takura I would stand holding a retractor for weeks.

Back at the hospital I jumped into my whites and dashed over to the ICU to see how she was doing. Her bed was empty. I looked at the nurse, questioning, holding back the thought.

"She's dead. She died about an hour ago."

"She's what? Mrs. Takura?"

"She's dead. She died about an hour ago."

As I stumbled back to my room, my thoughts piled up, tumbling over into tears, draining me of every thought except that the day had been a horrid abortion, unredeemed even by the act of love. In bed, I fell into a troubled sleep.

Emergency Room

My ears were trained to separate its sound. Somewhere off in the distance I could hear the unmistakable high-pitched undulations building and cycling, growing progressively louder as it drew near. The clock said 9:15—A.M. I was seated behind the counter of the emergency room—waiting.

For some people, even those closer to the ambulance than I, the siren would be inaudible, mixed with the general background noise. Others, aware of their good health, or unaware of their bad, would be content to let the siren diminish, melting away into the subconscious, intermingling with the noise of cars, radios, voices. For them it was a distant thing. It belonged to somebody else.

For me it invariably got louder and louder, because I was the intern assigned to the emergency room— the ER to those who knew and loved it. My duties in the ER could be subsumed under the title of official hospital welcomer to all who came. And come they did—the young and the old, the sleepless, the depressed, the nervous, occasionally even the injured and the sick. There I worked, often feverishly; I frequently ate; I occasionally sat. But, always waiting for the dreaded ambulance, I almost never slept.

Its sound meant trouble, and I was not ready for trouble, nor did I believe I ever would be. Although I had been assigned to the ER for more than a month, and had been an intern for almost half a year now, my most prevalent emotional state was still one of fear. Fear that I would be presented with a problem I couldn't handle and would screw it up. Ironically, I had been plunged into this new environment, one that demanded radically different medical choices, just when I was beginning to develop a certain degree of confidence on the wards and in the OR. Except for a group of highly capable nurses, I was on my own in the ER, solely responsible for what happened. It was not so bad during the day, when other doctors were around—the house staff was only a few seconds away—but at night five minutes, maybe even ten, might pass before anyone else from the house staff arrived. So things could be crucial. Sometimes my hand was forced.

Even the schedule in the ER was different. On duty twenty-four hours, off twenty-four. That doesn't sound so bad until you do it for a solid week. If your work weeks starts at eight on Sunday morning, by eight Wednesday morning you have already worked forty-eight hours, with another forty-eight to go. The result is that after two weeks your system is in total rebellion; you have headaches, loose bowels, and a slight tremor. The human body is geared to work only so long and then sleep, not go for twenty-four hours straight. Most organs of the body, particularly the glands, must rest; their function actually changes in a time-honored way over a twenty-four-hour period, whether the whole body sleeps or not. So after sixteen hours on duty your glands have more or less gone to sleep, but the same decisions are there to be made, with the same consequences. Life is no sturdier at 4:00 A.M. than it is at 12:00 noon. In fact, some studies suggest that it is frailer. Your patience hardly exists, everything is a struggle, the slightest hindrance becomes a major irritation. . . .

The siren approached, very near now. I listened hopefully for the end of the build-up and the receding Doppler effect that we occasionally got as an ambulance sped off to one of the smaller hospitals nearby. Not this time. I couldn't see it, but I could tell from the way the siren suddenly trailed off that it had entered the hospital grounds. Within seconds it was backing up toward the landing, and I was there to greet it.

Through the small rear windows I could make out the chaotic resuscitation efforts of the ambulance crew. One of the attendants was giving closed-chest cardiac massage by compressing the patient's breastbone; another was trying vainly to keep an oxygen mask on the face. As the ambulance stopped I reached out and twisted open the door. A few passers-by paused and looked over their shoulders. To them the event was closed. The ambulance had arrived, the doctor was waiting with an assortment of strange and miraculous instruments at hand, all was saved. For me it was just the beginning. I was glad that no one could see into my mind as I tried to prepare for what was to come.

"Bring him inside to Room A," I yelled to the crew as they slowed their resuscitative efforts. I helped lift the stretcher out and roll it fast through the short hallway, asking how long it had been since the patient had made any respiratory attempts, any sign of movement or life.

"He hasn't, and we got to him about ten minutes ago."

He was a bearded man of about fifty, and so large it took all of us to lift him onto the examining table. Seconds stretched into what felt like hours as the necessity for making a decision drilled into me—the kind of decision that isn't much discussed outside hospitals. I must either call a cardiac arrest or declare this simply a case of DOA—dead on arrival. Surely it was unfair to demand such a decision based on what I could remember from a textbook! Still, it had to be made, and made fast.

What would happen if I called a cardiac arrest? Six weeks earlier, we had restored a man to life after only eight minutes of clinical death. He lay now in the ICU, a vegetable, alive in a legal sense but dead in every other way. Seeing that man day after day, I had come to feel that in giving him the half life technology made possible we had somehow deprived him of dignity. For six weeks the body had functioned—the heart beating, the lungs mechanically pumping, the eyes dilated and empty; and his relatives were being drawn out to the limit of their emotional and financial reserves. Whose hand will dare to pull the plug of the machine that breathes, whose will cut off the IV, whose mind relax the attention necessary to maintain a proper ionic concentration in the blood stream so that the heart can beat on forever without the brain? No one wants to kill the grain of hope that lingers in even the most objective mind.

But there is the problem of the bed. It is needed for others —people who perhaps are more alive, and yet will be just as dead if deprived of the resources of the ICU. It comes down to a decision based on subtle, undefined gradations of life versus death. It isn't a matter of black or white, but of varying shades of gray. What does it really mean to be alive? A perplexing question, the answer to which evades a mind numbed with fatigue.

Where does the exhausted intern look for guidance in these moments? To college, where sterile concepts of truth, religion, and philosophy invariably lead to an automatic acceptance of life as the opposite of death? No help there. To medical school? Perhaps, but in the ivory tower the complexities of the Schwartzman reaction and the sequence of amino-acid cycles have pushed aside the fundamental questions. Nor will there be any help from an attending physician. He always remains silent, perhaps perplexed, but hardened by repetition. And the relative or friend standing by? What would he say if you meekly put forward the proposition that there may be halfway points between life and death? Alas, he cannot think beyond the poor soul that is, or was, Uncle Charlie. Unassisted, then, the intern gropes inside himself and makes arbitrary decisions, depending on how tired he is, whether it's morning or night, whether he is in love or lonely. And then he tries to forget them, which is easy if he is tired; and, because he's always tired, he always forgets—except that later the memory may surface from his unconscious. Angry and uncertain, he has once more been tested and found unprepared. . . .

Paradoxically, even with six people around me I was alone, standing there next to the nonbreathing hulk of the bearded man. His extremities were cold, but his chest was quite warm; he had no pulse, no respiration, dilated fixed pupils. One of the ambulance attendants kept talking, telling me what he had heard from the neighbor who had been with the man. The man had called his doctor after an asthma attack that morning, but it had gotten worse—so bad, in fact, that he started toward the ER, driving with a neighbor. In mid trip he had experienced an attack of acute dyspnea, an inability to breathe. He had stopped the car, jumped out, staggered a few steps, and collapsed. The neighbor had run for help and the ambulance was called.

"DOA," I said firmly, trying not to show doubt. In fact, my mind was a jumble of loosely connected thoughts racing around in search of a pattern. Strangely, in the ER mornings are an intern's most vulnerable time. Despite the surface refreshment of a night's sleep, his decision-making abilities are undercut by the deep exhaustion of the twenty-four-hour cycle. His experience is insufficient for him to make critical decisions with the certainty not of rational thought, but of pure reflex. One takes for granted the old aphorism that familiarity breeds blind acceptance. And so it is. Very often, in the beginning of his career, the intern is faced with a situation in which his mind is clear enough to think, yet he can find no answers. As with the schizophrenic who cannot handle an overabundance of sensory input, information remains unassociated in his mind. So the intern absorbs these experiences that rush in upon him; they hang around his mind in a loose conglomerate until he is tired enough to relegate them to his unconscious, and eventually he does reach a point at which experience brings familiarity, and familiarity brings acceptance without thought. By then a large part of his humanity has dropped away. . . .

All this mental activity happened in milliseconds. I didn't stand pondering and uncertain while the bearded man lay there. From the time I opened the back of the ambulance to the time he was pronounced DOA, less than thirty seconds elapsed. But it seemed much longer, and it affected me for hours. I did have one thing to be thankful about. My training had advanced far enough so that I would not be popping back in to feel for a pulse.

The central, cutting question remained: why should I be allowed to make such a decision? I felt somehow an accomplice of evil, an agent in this man's death. It's true that if I hadn't done so, someone else would have pronounced him dead; I was not necessary to the drama. That's easy enough to say if you're not involved, but I couldn't dismiss the matter so quickly. I had made the decision without which the bearded man would not have been technically dead at this moment. We'd have had him all wired up by now, and we would have been pushing on his chest, breathing for him, keeping him legally alive. So I felt that, because I had cut off this possibility, I was the one responsible for his being dead.

Had I been too hasty in calling him DOA, in taking the easy way out? As soon as I said it, all the medical doors clanged shut. Had the decision gone the other way, in favor of an attempted resuscitation, my first move would have been to insert an endotracheal tube so that we could breathe for him. I had always found this a very difficult task. Maybe I had pronounced him DOA partly to save myself the trouble. Or maybe it was because I knew all the beds up in ICU were full, and figured that even if we did manage to resuscitate him, he'd only be another vegetable anyway. I now think these are questions without answers, but at the time they were driving me crazy. In that state, I walked out into the hallway to face the wife and child. The wife was tall and thin, almost gaunt, with dark, deep-set eyes. She wore sandals and some sort of floor-length granny dress. Up against its ample folds, really wrapped in it, was a little girl of about seven.

The situation was right out of a prime-time television program—"The Interns" or "The Young Doctors"—ingredients for either a dramatic or a terribly sentimental confrontation. The reality, again, was nothing Ben Casey would have recognized. Facing the dreadfully concerned and frightened wife and child was neither dramatic nor sentimental, only one more hurdle for me to jump. Perhaps an omniscient third party would have read more into it. I was hardly that. I knew what had happened in the room behind the curtains, but I had no idea what these people were thinking, what they needed to hear. Worst of all, I was hopelessly swamped in my own crazy thoughts about death and responsibility, about what might have been. I wanted to beg them to hear my lectures on the Krebs cycle or some other medical elegancy. How poorly medical school had prepared me for this. "Just get the concepts, Peters. The rest will come." The rest—death—you learned about by trial and error, and finally, gratefully, you did fall back on the comfortable stock phrases of television.

"I'm very sorry. We did all we could, but your husband has passed away," I said softly. The banal words rolled out, seeming good enough, really quite satisfactory under the circumstances. Perhaps I had a future in television. The only bothersome part was that business about doing all we could; we hadn't done anything. What I said, however, was only a stupid self-serving hypocrisy. It would pass. Wife and child simply stood there, frozen, as I turned and walked away.

Thank God no other patient were waiting to be seen. I signed the sheet of paper making it official that I was the reason the bearded fellow was dead, and then I went quickly into the doctors' room, slamming the door behind me. In the process I jarred off the wall a picture a drug firm had given us of a bunch of Incas opening up some poor devil's skull; but the *Playboy* calendar opposite only rustled a little in protest, and Miss December hardly seemed disturbed. I sank into an enormous old leather chair. It was a large room, with blank walls except for the Inca picture and Miss December. A low, crowded bookcase stood at one end, and a small bed and a lamp at the other. The chair I sat in faced the pale green wall that was supporting Miss December. I longed for my mind to become as empty as that room, and as placid.

Miss December helped; in fact, she had me mesmerized. What did *Playboy* have against body hair? Aside from the required abundance on top of her head, Miss December was as smooth as a piece of marble—no hair around her breasts, under her arms, or on her legs, and apparently none between her legs, either, although that was difficult to tell for sure because of the artfully draped Christmas stocking. Maybe *Playboy* was misjudging a good part of its market. I didn't think pubic hair was so bad. In fact, remembering the night before, I decided that Joyce Kanishiro's pubic hair was one of her most appealing features. No offense meant—it's just that she had very pretty pubic hair, and a lot of it. When she was naked, you saw it no matter what position she was in. I thought it would be hard to put Joyce on a *Playboy* calendar.

Miss December, Joyce, and the esthetics of body hair couldn't drive the bearded man entirely out of my mind. It certainly wasn't the first time death had confronted me in the ER. In fact, on my very first day on ER service, when I trembled to see even a patient with mild asthma, an ambulance had pulled in, its siren trailing off, and disgorged a twenty-year-old boy on whom the ambulance crew had been performing artificial respiration and cardiac compression. I had stood on the landing virtually wringing my hands and hoping that someone would call a doctor. This was ludicrous. I was the person they had been racing to, running red lights, risking life and limb.

I had looked down at the boy and seen that his left eye was evulsed. Its distorted pupil looked off into nowhere. What on earth could I do with that eye? Actually, I didn't have long to think about it, because the boy wasn't breathing and his heart had stopped. The crew rapidly informed me that he had not made the slightest movement since they picked him up, in response to a call from a neighbor. As they rolled him onto the examining table, I glimpsed a wound in the back of his head. I tried to get a better look at it, but my view was blocked by little pieces of brain oozing out of a hole about an inch in diameter, and I suddenly realized that he had been shot, that a bullet had gone through the left eye and out the back of the head. The nurses and ambulance crew stood by, panting from their efforts, while I went through my routine. It was sheer nonsense to fuss with my stethoscope—nothing would make any difference—but for lack of another strategy I put it on his chest. All I heard were my own thoughts, wondering what to do next. The intern is always expected to do several things, yet this boy was so dead he was practically cold.

"He's dead," I had said finally, after feeling for pulses.

"You mean DOA, Doctor? No arrest, is that right?" That was right, dead on arrival. The medical jargon was reassuring; it made me feel secure. That boy with the hole in his head had been very different from the bearded man. Sure, the hole had scared me half to death, and I had been greatly relieved to be rid of the responsibility of figuring out what to do with that eye. The main point, however, was that he had had a big hole right through his head that pre-empted any action by me; hence, I had felt little responsibility. On the other hand, even now, without the sheet that covered him, the bearded man would look quite normal, as if in a deep sleep. That's the thing about death from asthma. You don't find much even at an autopsy, unless the victim has had a massive heart attack.

Sitting in the doctors' room, I tried to picture Joyce Kanishiro in the center fold of *Playboy*. That would be something. She even had a few black hairs around her nipples. They'd have to touch up the photo a bit.

Joyce was a laboratory technician with a strange schedule like mine. That was no problem, but she did have one gigantic drawback: her roommate was always at home. Every time I took Joyce back to her apartment, the first few times we went out, her roommate was there eating apples and watching television. There was a bedroom, but it was never opportune for us to go into it. Anyhow, the roommate, a confirmed night person, would probably have still been there staring at the test pattern when we came out at 5:00 A.M. After a few nights of situation comedies followed by the late news and the late movie, I knew Joyce and I would have to change the locale.

My reverie about Joyce was interrupted by another memory, an episode that had taken place in the late afternoon some two weeks after I started ER duty. The same routine—siren, red flashing lights—and this fellow had looked normal, too. As the attendants unloaded him and rushed him inside, they told me he had fallen fifteen stories onto a parked car. Had he moved? No. Tried to breathe? No. But he looked normal, quite peaceful, somewhat like the bearded man only a lot younger. How long did it take to get him here? About fifteen minutes. They always exaggerated on the low side, to forestall criticism. With an ophthalmoscope, I looked into the fellow's eyes, focusing until I saw the blood vessels. Concentrating on the veins, I made out clumps that could only represent blood clots. "DOA," I said. "No arrest." I had been pretty upset about that case, too, although falling fifteen stories onto a parked car was generally conclusive.

Then the family had started arriving, in spurts—not the immediate family, at first, but cousins and uncles, even neighbors. It seemed that the man—his name was Romero—had lost his footing while painting the outside of a building. After the nurses called his wife to tell her that Romero was in critical condition, word of the accident had spread quickly, and by the time Mrs. Romero arrived the place was jammed with people demanding to know how he was and waiting to see him. As I informed Mrs. Romero of the death in my best quiet and confidential tones, she raised her hands to heaven and began to wail. Taking their cue from her, the rest of the crowd began wailing, too. For an hour or so from that moment I witnessed the most incredible and frightening performance by the Romeros and their friends as they continued to drift in and engulf the ER. They beat the walls, tore their hair, screamed, cried, fought with each other, and finally began to break up the waiting-room furniture. I had no time to brood over the metaphysical implications of the case, being much too busy protecting myself and the rest of the staff. Interns have been killed in the ER. That's no joke.

Later I had seen in the pathologist's autopsy report that Romero's aorta was severed. That made me feel a little better. But I knew that the pathologist would probably find nothing so plainly wrong with the bearded man.

Dozing and musing in the old leather chair, I played with such thoughts and memories while Miss December's gigantic, almost hilarious breasts seemed to grow even larger. Joyce didn't have breasts like that. We had moved to my room to avoid the TV addict, and I vaguely remembered waking up at four-thirty that very morning as she left via the back door before anybody else was up in the quarters. It was her idea; I couldn't have cared less. But that was how we got away from Miss Apples and TV. It was a great schedule. During my twenty-four hours off, I surfed in the afternoon, read in the evenings, and then about eleven, after her work, Joyce would arrive and we'd go to bed. She was an athletic girl, who liked to bounce all over the place. She had great endurance, really insatiable. When she was around I didn't think about anything else.

But the hospital bed in my room made a hell of a lot of noise, and it was pretty small. When Joyce got up to leave at four-thirty or so, it always felt delicious to expand all over it, luxuriating in the spaciousness. For a while I had gotten up with her—it seemed the courteous thing—and waved as she went down the stairs and drove away. But lately I had just propped up on one elbow, watching her dress. She didn't seem to mind. This morning she had come back over to the bed, all starchy white, and kissed me lightly. I said we'd get together soon. She was an okay playmate.

When the phone rang to wake me up three hours later, such a short time had elapsed that I half expected to see Joyce still standing there. I must have fallen asleep before she got out the door.

Saturday, busiest day of the week in the ER, 7:30 A.M. Even though I had been in bed for eight hours, I felt physically bankrupt and out of phase. It was that twenty-four-hour baloney. I had followed my usual routine, which started when I balanced against the sink and studied my bloodshot eyes and ended with my arrival at the ER at one minute after eight, as always. Strangely, despite a general tendency toward tardiness, I always managed to arrive promptly at the ER to relieve my colleague, who would slink off gratefully with blood-spattered clothing and drooping eyelids.

Until the arrival of the bearded man this had been a relatively quiet Saturday morning, with no big problems, only the usual procession of people who had dropped a steam iron on their toes or fallen through a plate-glass window. Everything had been handled quickly.

A half hour had come between me and the bearded man, and obviously nothing untoward had happened outside the doctors' room, else I would not have been allowed to sit there musing. My watch showed 10:00 A.M. I knew it was only a matter of time.

After a perfunctory knock, a nurse entered to say that a few patients were waiting. Feeling almost relieved at being tugged from my reverie, I went back into the daylight and took the "boards" the nurse had prepared. My hat is off to these nurses. They routinely escorted each patient into the examining room, took all the administrative detail, the blood pressure, and even the temperature if they thought it was necessary. In other words, they screened the patients very well. Not that they decided whom I should see, because I had to see everyone, but they did try to establish priorities if the place was busy, or to give me a little peace occasionally if it wasn't. Whenever a new intern arrived, I guess the nurses were tempted to handle everything alone, because most of the stuff that came in really didn't rate as an emergency.

But I was the intern and in charge, dressed in white coat, white pants, and white shoes, stethoscope tucked and folded into my left pocket in a very particular way, equipped with several colored pens, a penlight, a reflex hammer, a combined ophthalmo-otoscope, and four years of medical school—apparently ready for anything. In fact, really, only for the ailments I had already seen and dealt with. Considering that the variety of bodily ills approaches infinity, I wasn't ready at all. My inadequacy was like a shadow that fell away only when the place was jammed with crying babies and suturing to be done.

After about ten hours, I usually got so tired that even if there were no patients I couldn't think. So the morning was toughest, just getting through to the afternoon; the rest seemed to take care of itself.

The first of the two new patients was a surfer who had been hit in the head with a board, leaving a two-inch cut over his left eye. He was oriented and alert, with normal vision. In fact, he was fine except for the laceration. I called his private doctor, who, predictably, told me to go ahead and sew it up. That was the way it worked. The patients came in, and I saw them and then called the private physician. If they had no doctor, we picked one for them, provided, of course, they had the means to pay. Otherwise they were considered staff patients, and I or one of the residents would take responsibility for treating them. "Suture it up" was the invariable reply from private doctors on these laceration cases. During the first few days I often speculated as to whether the private doctors then billed their patients for the suture, although we weren't encouraged to investigate that.

Actually, I was now rather good at knot tying and suturing, by virtue of having forced my way into several operations, including three hernias, a couple of hemorrhoids, an appendectomy, and a vein stripping. Mostly, though, I had gone on holding those damn retractors and, occasionally, cutting off warts.

Cutting off warts is an intern's reward for behaving himself; it's about on a par with hemorrhoid removal, although hemorrhoids are rather higher on the ladder. We had taken off dozens of warts in medical school, during dermatology, since the procedure was essentially without risk and well beneath a surgeon's dignity. My first Hawaiian wart had come with the Supercharger, a surgeon nicknamed for his matchless slow-motion incompetence. We scrubbed together on a simple breast biopsy, which is normally a thirty-minute job, unless you find a malignancy. Not so with the Supercharger. He rooted around for an hour or so before sending off a little wedge of mangled tissue to pathology. I stood by hoping that the tissue was benign—luckily it was—and then the Supercharger closed the wound. Being an assistant on a breast biopsy is not a thrilling procedure under any circumstances; this one was made worse for me because I hadn't done anything, not even retract. When the Supercharger finished tying the last knot, he had stepped back, snapped off his gloves, and magnanimously informed me that I could now remove the wart from the wrist, which I dutifully did—to the accompaniment of a lot of bad advice from the Supercharger, who couldn't understand why I wasn't more grateful.

My next operation, however, had been more involved; in fact, it had almost wiped me out. It was a vein stripping, and the surgeon was a private M.D. I had never scrubbed with before. As we washed our hands he told me that he expected me to do a careful job on my side. I blinked a little, knowing he had mistaken me for a resident, but I let the misconception stand. When I answered that I would try to do a good job, he told me trying wasn't enough, and that I'd either do it right or not at all. I didn't have the guts to tell him that I had never done a vein stripping before. I had *seen* several of them, but only from behind retractor handles; besides, I wanted to try it.

Needing to follow the surgeon's lead, I delayed beginning until he was well under way. The patient was a woman of about forty-five, with bad varicose veins. Having been assigned to the case only a few minutes before it started, I hadn't seen the patient beforehand, so I had to guess what her veins looked like when she was standing. Although I knew the theory, I wasn't quite up to the practice. It was like having read all about swimming, knowing the names of the strokes and the movements, having watched other people swim, and then getting thrown into deep water. My job was to make an incision in the groin, find the superficial vein called the saphenous vein, and tie off all the little tributaries. Then I was to move down to the ankle, make another incision, isolate the same saphenous vein there, and prepare it for the stripper. The stripper was simply a piece of wire, which I would thread up through the vein to the groin; after tying the end of the stripper to the vein, I would pull both stripper and vein out through the incision in the groin. That was what I was supposed to do, and I knew it by heart; I'd read about it, watched it, and thought about it.

Almost without pressure, the supersharp scalpel cut smoothly through the skin in the groin region. I began to dissect with the scissors, but I couldn't control them very well. I changed and used a hemostat clamp, not to clamp a vessel, but to bluntly separate the tissues by opening the clamp after I pushed it into the fat. That method caused less bleeding, and I began to make some headway, going deeper into the thick layers of fat. Down there, deep in the groin, I saw nothing I recognized, nothing; it was like feeling around in the dark—until I stumbled on to a vein. I had no idea which vein it was, but, by slowly cleaning around it, I was able to follow along it to a larger one, which I hoped was the femoral vein. If I was right about that, then the first vein I had encountered was the coveted saphenous vein, but I wasn't sure. I was all thumbs, dropping the instruments once or twice, altogether nervous about my role. After all, what would the surgeon say if I told him I hadn't operated before except to put in cutdowns for IV's and remove warts? I thought about asking him if I had the right vein, but such a confession of ignorance would only have gotten me removed from further participation.

At any rate, I plunged on, hoping I'd found the saphenous vein and not a nerve. The job grew progressively more difficult. In fact, it was a mess. I pushed and pulled on the vein, trying to strip it out, bluntly spreading the hemostat, dabbing blood with a gauze sponge to keep the field clear. Several times the vein broke and blood spread, but I somehow managed to stop it with a hemostat after a few wild stabs in the dark. There was some consolation in this bleeding, because it proved that the structure I had isolated was indeed a blood vessel.

Perhaps the hardest part was trying to get a tie around the hemostats that I had placed deep in the wound to stop the bleeding. Putting the silk around the tip of the hemostat was easy enough, but trying to maintain tension on the first throw seemed all but impossible. Then, when I released the hemostat, the tie I had just made would pop off and the bleeding would start again. All in all, from a technical standpoint I might as well have been butchering a hog. I glanced self-consciously over at the surgeon from time to time, but he seemed oblivious to my trials and intent on his side, where all was under control.

What a way to learn, I had thought. But it seemed the only way. If he had known I was a novice at vein stripping, he wouldn't have let me do it. It was as simple as that. So I pushed on, finally freeing up all the tributaries to the saphenous vein. Even with the tributaries isolated, I was nervous about cutting the vein in two, an irrevocable act. So I went to the ankle and made a cut, locating the saphenous vein easily there because it was the same one I had used doing IV cutdowns. I threaded a stripper up inside the vein and pushed it out through the inguinal incision. After tying the vein to the stripper at the ankle, and with a bit of force, I pulled the whole thing up through the leg, ripping out the vein. A spurt of blood, a sharp crunchy sound, and the vein came out, all shriveled up at the end of the stripper. The surgeon had long since finished the other side and disappeared for coffee, leaving me to sew up the whole job. I never heard anything dire about the day's results, so I assume that the lady was none the worse for my debut.

Despite my having sewed hundreds of incisions in the OR, the first few emergency-room lacerations had been major affairs for me. For one thing, in the ER almost every patient is awake and sharply observant. On my first ER day, when the nurse asked me what kind of suture I wanted, she might as well have asked me for the population of Madagascar. In the OR, the surgeon stipulates what kind of suture material he wants for the skin before the case starts; you merely take what the nurse gives you, even if the surgeon has already departed the room. But in the ER I was faced with a variety of choices —nylon, silk, Mersilene, catgut—which came in all sorts of thicknesses. The nurse wasn't trying to put me down; she just wanted to be told.

"What sutures will you be using, Doctor?"

I had no idea. "I'll take the usual, Nurse."

"The usual, Doctor?" Obviously, there was no usual.

"Uh, nylon," I tried.

"What size?"

"Four-0," I told her, wondering what I was ordering.

Needless to say, I quickly learned about sutures, and also about suturing, but always by trial and error. On the first case, I put in too many stitches, and on the second case, I came to the end of the laceration with too much skin on the top. Slowly but surely I learned the little tricks, like excising beveled edges, and even fancy stuff, like small Z-plasties to change the axis of a laceration in order to reduce scarring. I came to enjoy suturing quite a bit, because it was a clear problem with a neat, clean solution that I quickly enough learned to provide. It made me feel useful, a rare and cherished sensation.

All that learning was behind me now. The surfer was waiting, a sheet over his head. Through the little window at the site of the laceration, I began to clean and anesthetize the area with xylocaine. After trimming the edges slightly, I poised the needle with the attached nylon suture about midway from either end of the laceration and back a few millimeters from one edge. Guided by a rolling motion of my wrist, the needle pierced the skin, traversed the laceration, and emerged on the opposite side. I withdrew it with the needle holder. Then, barely catching the edges of the wound with the needle, I brought the suture back to the original side and tied it, not tight, but just a little loose so that the swelling of the wound would bring the edges together. Four more sutures finished the job.

The other patient was a somewhat mysterious twenty-year-old girl who appeared chronically ill. She admitted to having been diagnosed and treated for systemic lupus erythematosus. The name alone sounds forbidding, and, indeed, lupus is a serious disease. It was one of the diseases we had discussed *ad nauseam* in medical school because, being so rare and ill-understood, it was good for a lot of academic speculation. So I didn't feel entirely unprepared—except that she was complaining of abdominal pain, which wasn't a common symptom for someone with lupus. Trying to connect the two in my mind, I palpated her abdomen and asked questions about her condition, which either she or her mother answered. Then, needing to think, I went back to the desk-counter in the center of the ER and racked my brains for some association between her pain and her basic disease. While I was trying to come up with a suitably exotic lab test, mother and daughter walked by, said that the pain was gone, thanked me, and went out the door. So much for my challenging diagnostic mystery, and one of the few ER cases that four years in medical school had prepared me for.

At that point, Almost came rushing in and practically collapsed in front of me, putting his forehead on the counter, panting and wheezing. His real name was Fogarty, but we called him Almost because he invariably held off until the very last moment before coming into the ER to be treated for his asthma. It was like waiting until you ran out of gas so that you could coast into a filling station. The nurses led him, blue and heaving, into one of the rooms while I prepared some aminophylline. I had seen Almost several times, beginning with my second day on ER duty. From medical school I knew quite a lot about asthma in terms of pulmonic pressure gradients, pH changes, smooth muscle function, and allergic phenomena, and I even knew about the drugs that were useful—epinephrine, aminophylline, bicarbonate, THAM, and steroids. But I hadn't known a thing about dosages. So, that first time, while Almost was in another room puffing on the positive-pressure breathing machine, I ran into the staff room and looked it up in a paperback. Anything to avoid asking the nurses. Actually, from ward cases I had an idea of what and how much to give a reclining patient. But this guy was walking around, not lying in bed, and that makes a big difference. You cannot use the same amounts. To ask the nurses something else would have demoralized me. Anyway, old Almost and I had gotten used to each other, and an aminophylline IV did the trick, as usual.

While the ER sometimes got so crowded that patients sat on the floor or stood against the walls, it was more usual to have a steady stream over the twenty-four-hour period, amounting, perhaps, to 120 or so on weekdays and twice that on Saturdays. It was now about 10:30 A.M. The stream had started to run, and I was on my feet, moving quickly from one room to the next, calling the private M.D.'s, not really thinking too much, almost unaware of the omnipresent fear of the next big case.

One chart read "Chief complaint, depressed." Thirty-seven-year-old lady. As I walked into the room she lit a cigarette, cupping her hands around the match as if in a great wind. Throwing her head back with the cigarette precariously perched in the corner of her mouth, she looked at me blankly.

"I'm sorry, ma'am, you can't smoke in here. Those green metal bottles are filled with oxygen."

"All right, all right." Obviously irritated, she ground the cigarette relentlessly in a small stainless-steel dish accidentally left on the examining table. She was silent now. When the cigarette was totally destroyed, she looked up and stared aggressively into my eyes, about ready to explode, I thought.

"Your name is Carol Narkin, is that correct?"

"That's right. Are you the only doctor here?" She wanted to get at me.

"Yes, the only one here now. But we'll call your doctor, too. His name is Laine, it says here on the chart."

"That's right, and a damn good doctor, too," she said defensively.

"Have you seen him recently?" I was trying to calm her down with routine questions, working around to why she had come to the ER.

"Don't get smart with me."

"I'm sorry, Miss Narkin, I must ask a few questions."

"Well, I'm not answering any more. Just call my doctor." Angrily, she looked away.

"Miss Narkin, what am I to say to your doctor?" She didn't budge. "Miss Narkin?"

Clearly, I couldn't help her, and so I walked out, thinking I'd go back after the next patient. Why had she come here? There was no point in calling her doctor without being able to give him some sort of report. When I returned to see her after a few minutes, she was gone. That was typical of ER work—brief, inconclusive encounters and a lot of wasted time.

Next the nurse pressed five charts into my hand and pointed a bit sheepishly into the next room, where I was confronted by an entire family—mother, father, and three kids—standing there waiting to be treated.

The mother spoke. "Doctor, we came because Johnny here has a temperature and a cough."

I looked at the chart. "Temperature 99."

"And as long as we were here, I thought you wouldn't mind looking at these spots on Nancy's tongue. Show the doctor your tongue, Nancy. And Billy fell at school last week. See his knee, see that scrape? Well, it's been keeping him at home, and he needs a note. And George, he's my husband, he has to have a doctor sign his welfare statement because of his back condition, since he doesn't work and since we just came from California. And I've been having trouble with my bowels for the last three or four weeks."

I stared at the faces. The husband didn't meet my eyes, and the kids were busy climbing on the examining table, but the mother was loving it, looking at me excitedly. My first impulse was to throw them out. They should have been at the clinic, anyway, not the ER. We weren't set up for routine outpatient care. But if I indulged my temper, I was sure the mother would complain to the hospital administrator that I had failed to see them in their hour of need. The administrator would report to the attendings in charge of the teaching service, and I would end up getting shit on. That was how much you could count on support.

Besides, it was still morning; bright sun flashed through the windows, and I felt pretty good. Why spoil it? So, instead of getting angry, I looked perfunctorily at the spots and the scrape, and gave them a few pills. But I drew the line at the welfare paper. I couldn't tell anything about a bad back with the resources of the ER; and lots of times I'd treat these guys and see them running around on motor scooters the following day.

The next patient, a drunk called Morris, was also a frequent visitor to the ER. His chart read "Intoxicated, multiple bruises"; the description fit. Apparently the man had fallen down a flight of stairs, as was his habit. When I entered the room, he propped himself up on his elbows with great difficulty, his eyelids half covering his pupils, and bellowed, "I don't want an intern, I want a doctor!" Incredible how such remarks could sink into the tenderest recesses of my brain and cause such havoc. That stupid drunk really hurt my feelings. He made me aware again that I often had to run to the review book for a dosage, that I was scared most of the time, that I had spent four years memorizing a million facts and didn't seem to know anything. With him, I couldn't hold myself back. "Shut up, you drunk old fart!" I shouted.

"I'm not drunk!"

"Any more comments like that and I'll throw you out of here on your head."

"I'm not drunk. I haven't had a drink in years."

"You're so drunk you can't even keep your eyes open."

"I am not." He practically rolled off the examining table trying to point his finger at me.

"You are so." Our level of communication was not high. We continued the childish exchange while I examined him roughly, actually bending my reflex hammer as I pressed it against his Achilles tendons but proving he had tactile sense in his lower extremities. I ended up sending him to X-ray, more to get rid of him for a while than to get films of the bones under his bruises.

About that time of the late morning, the number of patients coming in began to exceed the number going out. A bunch of screaming babies arrived together, as if by conspiracy, and were distributed to various rooms. I really didn't enjoy treating babies. It was rather like my conception of veterinary medicine—zero communication with the patient. Half the time I was forced to ignore the child and try to make some sense out of the mother. Moreover, I found it nearly impossible to hear anything through a stethoscope on the chest of a screaming two-year-old. The usual problems were colds, diarrhea, and vomiting—nothing serious. These kids seemed to anticipate my arrival, saving up so that they could either urinate or defecate while I was examining them.

That Saturday morning was no exception. Children were all over everything, up to their usual tricks. The first baby had had a discharge coming out of its right ear for several days, which the mother thought was Pablum, but she became suspicious when the discharge continued even after she changed the baby's diet. From the general hygiene of the two of them, I thought possibly it was Pablum, but it turned out to be pus. The baby had a roaring infection in both middle ears, behind the eardrums. The right drum had ruptured, causing the discharge; the left drum was still intact, bulging outward from the pressure behind it. It would have been proper to make a little hole in the left drum to release the pus, but I didn't know how to do that, and when I talked to the private doctor, he only wanted me to treat with drugs—penicillin, as usual, and gantrisin, a sulfa drug. When I emphasized the seriousness of the unruptured left eardrum, he cut me off, saying he would see the child Monday morning. Dutifully, I wrote the prescription for the penicillin and the gantrisin.

The next baby had not been eating well for a week. Some emergency. The next one had diarrhea, but only once. It seemed incredible to me that a mother would rush her child to the hospital after a loose bowel movement, but one soon learns that nothing is incredible in the ER. A few other children had colds and stuffy noses and mild temperature elevations.

In order to be thorough, I had to look in every ear, down every throat. This work was often more like wrestling than medicine. Children, even young ones, are surprisingly strong, and although I always entreated the mother to hold the child's arms against its head during the examination, she'd invariably let go and the kid would grab for the otoscope, pulling it away and bringing with it a little drop of blood from the ear canal. That made everyone joyous and confident, naturally, but I'd try again, peering into the little hole in the contorting, screaming infant. If any of them had really high temperatures, 104 or over, I'd ask the mothers to give them tepid sponge baths. That morning we had two such cases going. All in all, the ER was sometimes like a pediatric clinic. Of course, there were occasional emergencies, but not as often as the public thinks. Mostly the problems were trivial, stuff that should have been treated in the clinic.

When the odd and horrible thing did happen, the whole staff would become somber and withdrawn for several hours. One morning, a small, dark lady had come in quietly, carrying a small baby in a pink blanket. At the time I hadn't paid any attention to her, being busy with someone else. A nurse took a clean chart and disappeared with the mother. A few seconds later, she reappeared on the run, saying that I should see the child immediately. When I entered the room, the child was still swathed in the pink blanket. Opening it and pulling it back, I saw a blue-black baby, its abdomen swollen to twice normal size and hard as a stone. I couldn't be sure how long it had been dead, but I guessed for about a day. The mother sat in the corner, not moving. We didn't talk; there was nothing to say. I had just looked at the baby, marked the chart, and walked out.

About once a week a pair of hysterical parents charged into the ER with a convulsing child. The child was usually pretty young, and the first time I saw one of those I almost passed out from anxiety. This little girl was about two years old. She lay doubled up, with her arms pressed against her chest; saliva and blood drooled from her mouth, and her whole body shook with rhythmic, synchronous, convulsive jerks. As usual in such cases, the child was out of control of both her urine and her feces. Still terrified, but relieved because the doctor was there, the parents put the girl down on the table. Since they were too hysterical to be of any help, I asked them to wait outside. I also wanted to avoid their judgment of my action—or inaction—for, in truth, I didn't know what to do. Then one of those great nurses bailed me out by handing me a syringe and offering to hold the child while I tried to find a vein. Suddenly I remembered: amobarbital IV. The next problem was getting the needle into a vein. Even on a quiet, resting child, finding a vein can be difficult. On one who's convulsing, it can approach the impossible. How much drug to inject was another dilemma, but I thought I'd just give a little and test the reaction. Finally getting into a vein, after several abortive probes, I gave a squirt, and the child's convulsions suddenly slowed down and then stopped; her breathing stayed strong, thank goodness. My terror of convulsing children decreased somewhat after that experience, especially after I learned to use Valium, or paraldehyde and phenobarbital intramuscularly. But that first time it could have gone either way.

An even bigger scare concerning children had occurred with a seemingly routine case. It served to reinforce my fear that an ordinary situation would deteriorate before my eyes, leaving me helpless. The boy was about six years old, a cute little guy, brought to the scary ER by his overly solicitous parents. He wasn't feeling too well—that was apparent, because he had vomited three times and had other telltale symptoms adding up to the flu syndrome. For the parents' sake as much as the child's, I treated him with an antiemetic drug called Compazine, something I'd used successfully hundreds of times after operations. However, this time I got one of those adverse side reactions you read about at the bottom of the manufacturer's product information sheet—the type of episode the drug detail men don't like to talk about and doctors seldom see. Two minutes or so after the injection the child went into a convulsion, his eyes rolled back, he couldn't sit up unaided, and he developed an obvious rhythmical tremor. The parents were aghast, especially since I had been explaining to them that the boy was not very sick. I frantically sedated the child with a little phenobarbital. While I was at it, I probably should have given some to the parents, too, and taken a little myself. I ended up having to admit the child to the hospital. Needless to say, the parents had not been very pleased by this performance, nor had I.

So the early hours of Saturday passed, a combination of glorified pediatric clinic, suturing factory, and occasional true crisis. The few suturing jobs had been routine and rapid. My only disturbing problem had been that bearded fellow, but the hours and the tedium dulled it sufficiently so that the day became a typical one of generalized monotony punctuated by infrequent but memorable moments of terror and uncertainty.

I was actually beginning to like the quick, uninvolved routine of the ER. No patient required such deep attention as to make a real claim on my emotions. I could remember when it had been different, six months ago, back at the beginning of my internship. Mrs. Takura, for instance, had gotten to me. We had become friends; her long operation, throughout which I held the retractors, unable even to see her wound, had been a physical and emotional trauma. When I finally got away from her operation, out to the beach with Jan, I had been secure in my intuition that Mrs. Takura would pull through. Returning to find her dead had been the final, backbreaking straw in my disenchantment with what was happening to me as an intern. I had blown up at the system—at petty day-to-day harassment, the retractors, the lack of teaching, and the constant, nagging fear of failure. It had taken me a long time to get over Mrs. Takura, and, finally, I hadn't so much accepted her fate as merely put it aside, vowing not to get emotionally involved again. It became easier, then, not to let patients get inside me. I began to think of them in hard, clinical terms, as so many hemorrhoids, appendixes, or gastric ulcers.

Roso had also been a trial. Unlike the short time with Mrs. Takura, my rapport with him had developed over several months. I even gave him a haircut, after he had been with us so long that his hair was a shabby mane flowing halfway down his back. He didn't have any money, so I offered to cut it if he wanted me to. He was delighted; perched high on a stool in the sunlight of the alcove by the ward, he seemed proud to be alive. Everybody thought it was the worst haircut they had ever seen.

Roso had always smiled, even when he felt terrible, which was most of the time. In fact, he had nearly every complication I had ever read about, and a few that were not even in the medical literature. His vomiting and hiccups had persisted until another operation became imperative. I was in my familiar position, both hands clenched around pieces of metal and looking at the back of the chief resident for six and a half hours while Roso's Billroth I was converted to a Billroth II; his stomach pouch was now attached to the small intestine at a point about ten inches farther down than usual. It was hoped that this procedure would end Roso's troubles, because the obstruction in his digestive system that was causing them was at the very connection between the stomach and the intestine that had been made in the first operation. But even after this second operation everything on his chart hovered near critical; his course was like a sine wave. Hiccups, vomiting, weight loss, and several horrendous episodes of upper gastrointestinal bleeding kept me busy—especially those bleeding episodes. A week after the Billroth II, Roso vomited up pure blood and rapidly sank into shock. I stayed with him several nights in a row, continuously irrigating his stomach with iced saline, and pulling out the nasogastric tube when it got clogged and pushing it back in. He hung on, somehow, through our mistakes and my miscalculations, and through his own relentless, troubled course.

After the bleeding, nothing would go through his stomach until I was lucky enough to pass a nasogastric tube down through the anastomosis and into his small intestine. Using that as a start, I fed him directly into the intestine with special stuff. Some stayed down—but he got diarrhea. Then one day he sneezed out the nasogastric tube. I had him on intravenous feedings off and on for four months, balancing sodium and potassium and magnesium ions. He developed a wound infection, inflammation of his leg veins, a touch of pneumonia, and a urine infection. Then we became aware of an abscess under his diaphragm, which was causing the hiccups; back to surgery again. Somehow he managed not only to live through all this, but actually to recover. It took me four hours to do his discharge summary; his chart weighed five pounds—five pounds of my own writing, frequently stained with blood, mucus, and vomitus. When he left the hospital, I was happy to see him alive and vastly relieved to have him gone. His case and my attachment to it had been almost too much to bear on top of everything else. At times during his bleeds, administering the iced saline and seeing to his tube, I had begun to wonder if I had set him up as a challenge just because everybody said he wouldn't make it. Maybe I didn't give a damn about him, was just using him to prove to myself that I could handle a tough case. Eventually, though, I stopped examining my motivations and began to treat my patients as hernias, or whatever they had; it was infinitely less wearing. The ER was easy on a brooder. You were always too busy or too tired or too scared to think. . . .

Eleven-forty-five in the morning. I was about to go to lunch when a rather pale young woman in her early twenties walked in with two girl friends. After a hushed consultation with the nurse, the pale one followed her into one of the examining rooms. The other two sat down and nervously lit cigarettes. The sound of a New York accent drifted out of the examining room as I wrote the last sentence on a baby's chart and put it in the "Finished" basket. Eager to get away for lunch, I pushed into the room where the nurse had taken the girl. The chart indicated vaginal bleeding for two days, clots that morning. The girl took out a cigarette.

"Please, no smoking here, Miss."

"I'm sorry." She carefully put the cigarette back and looked at me, then away. She was of average build, and dressed in a short-sleeved blouse and a miniskirt. With some color in her face, she would have been pretty. Her conversation suggested no more than a high-school education.

"How many days have you been bleeding?"

"Three," she said. "Ever since I had the D and C." We were both nervous. Wondering if my uncertainty showed, I tried to stand motionless and appear knowledgeable.

"Why did you have a D and C?"

"I don't know. The doctor said I had to have it, so I had it, okay?" She feigned irritation.

"Where was it, here or in New York?"

"New York."

"Then you came here right away?"

"Yeah," she said. She really had an accent. The fact that she had come to Hawaii so soon was off center. A six-thousand-mile trip directly after a D and C was not standard medical procedure.

"Was it done by a professional person?" I asked.

"Of course. Whaddaya mean, by a professional person? Who else?"

What to do? If she had had an abortion—and I was pretty

sure of it—I knew I would have some difficulty getting a private M.D. Also, I remembered all too well from medical school a string of girls in endotoxin shock from infections caused by bad D and C's. It can happen so fast; the kidneys give up and blood pressure disappears. However, this girl's blood pressure was obviously all right for the moment. In fact, she was functioning well in all respects, except that she was quite jumpy and a little pale. I wondered if she were trying to follow my thoughts. She need not have worried. I didn't care how she had gotten into her condition, only how to get her out of it. My chances of discovering the exact cause of her bleeding were pretty small. She'd probably have to have another D and C. In that case, I would try to locate a private gynecologist, but few of them cared to get mixed up in such an affair —picking up someone else's pieces, so to speak. One way or another, a pelvic examination was in my future, and that was the last thing I wanted right before lunch.

The memory of my first pelvic floated across my consciousness. It had been during a second-year medical-school course in physical diagnosis. I had had no preconceptions, which was fortunate, because my patient was quite a hefty lady. She was a clinic patient in for a regular checkup. At first I didn't think my arm was long enough to reach the uterus, and the guy after me claimed he lost his watch—although he found it later in the bag where we threw the gloves. At the time, we had not yet been through obstetrics or gynecology, and reaching into the lady was strangely unsettling. But after a hundred or so, a pelvic examination is a routine like any other. The only problem is finding the cervix—which might seem absurd, because it's always there. But when there's a lot of blood and clots, the job can be hard, particularly if the patient is unco-operative. Moreover, you don't want to hurt the patient by fumbling around. So it pays to take a few minutes extra and do a good job. But not before lunch.

"How long had you been pregnant?" I suddenly asked the girl from New York.

"What?" She was sputtering again, in obvious surprise. Since it was important for me to know, I let the question hang in silence. "Six weeks," she said finally.

"And was it a doctor or someone else?"

"A doctor in New York," came the resigned answer.

"Well, we'll do what we can for you," I said, and she nodded in relief.

Leaving the room, I told the nurse to get her ready for a

pelvic. In a matter of minutes the nurse reappeared to say that everything was ready, and when I walked back in the patient was draped and waiting nervously in the stirrups, with her skirt rumpled around her waist. As I prepared to insert the speculum, I couldn't help recalling a night six weeks before when I had been waked up by a nurse saying that she couldn't catheterize an elderly patient with a full bladder because she couldn't find the right hole. I had gotten up and been halfway over to the hospital before the ridiculousness of the situation hit me. If the nurse couldn't find it, how could I? But I did, after a while; it was just a matter of persistence.

It was the same with finding this cervix. Persistence. Surrounded by blood and clots, which I cleared away as best I could, the cervix suddenly popped into view. The orifice was closed, and no new blood appeared when I dabbed it with a sponge stick. I pushed down on the abdomen, to the girl's great discomfort, and got nothing. Then I noticed a small tear, bleeding very slowly, on the posterior aspect of the cervix. Almost surely that was the problem. I cauterized it with silver nitrate, called a gynecologist, explained things, and walked over to lunch with a unique feeling of accomplishment. Miraculously, I was still hungry.

Lunch was a rapid affair; fifteen minutes of stuffing down two sandwiches and a pint of milk amid careless banter of surfing, surgery, and sex. Nothing serious—there wasn't time for it. I made some tentative plans with Hastings to go surfing late the following afternoon, about four-thirty. Carno was eating at a distant table; except for seeing each other at the hospital, we rarely got together any more. I also talked with Jan Stevens for a few minutes. I hadn't seen much of her lately, although during July and August, early in my internship, we had had quite a spree, culminating in an unusual weekend trip to Kauai.

The first day, Saturday, had been great. We stocked the car with beer, cold cuts, and cheese, and drove to the big Kauai canyon. On the way, the road rose and fell among the clouds, moving us in and out of quick rain squalls as the sugar-cane fields rolled by on either side. The canyon was even more expansive and spectacular than we had expected. I found a lookout for us, and Jan turned the groceries into sandwiches. I asked her not to talk—a necessary precaution, because as our relationship had developed so had her desire to communicate. The view was wonderful, what with rainfall, waterfalls, and rainbows sparkling in the corners of the steep valleys that branched off from the main canyon. I was totally at peace.

By late afternoon we had driven to the end of the road on the northern shore, right at the beginning of the Napali coast. In a secluded grove of evergreen trees, I put up our borrowed pup tent, and as the sun prepared to set among the puffy little clouds along the horizon, we swam naked in the still waters within the protective reef. It didn't matter that there were campers in full view at the other end of the beach—although I wondered why they were so near the water, rather than where we were, on higher ground among the pines.

Somewhat self-consciously we ran up to the car. I pulled on a pair of white jeans and Jan wriggled into a nylon windbreaker. Even another meal of cold cuts and beer couldn't destroy the atmosphere. Night descended rapidly, with the sound of breaking surf on the reef mingling with the soft whisper of the breeze through the evergreen trees above us. The night creatures began their eerie symphony, increasing in intensity until they dominated even the sound of the surf. The western sky was just a smudge of red. Jan looked beautiful in the half-light, and the idea of her in nothing but that nylon windbreaker seemed fantastically sexy. In fact, I was delirious with the sensuality of the moment.

Naked once again, we returned to the beach. As we slid into the water the full Hawaiian moon floated over a ridge of trees; the scene was so perfect it seemed unreal. I couldn't stand it a second more. Holding hands, we ran back to the tent and fell together on the blankets. I wanted to devour her, to capture the moment in my mind.

Slowly and reluctantly, from the depths of this wet embrace, I became aware of the whine of mosquitoes. In our desire to make love, we tried to ignore them at first, but they began to bite as well as whine. No passion could have resisted that onslaught. In dreadful seconds the whole sensual atmosphere disintegrated, ending with Jan's departure to the shelter of our Volkswagen. Still shaking with desire, I resolved to stick it out in the tent rather than sleep crammed into a car built for midgets. I rolled up in one of the blankets so that just my nose and mouth were vulnerable. Even so, the mosquitoes bit me so relentlessly that my face began to swell, and finally I surrendered, trudging back to the car accompanied by a swarm of mosquitoes who seemed as unfulfilled as I was.

I knocked on the window and Jan sat up, wide-eyed, opening the door with relief when she recognized me. I stumbled in wearily and told her to go back to sleep. After smashing the mosquitoes that had come in with me, I somehow fell asleep myself, under the steering wheel, in a contorted ball. In about two hours I awoke sweating. The temperature and humidity had risen to Turkish-bath levels; the moisture was so thick it had condensed on all the windows. Opening a side window, I felt a cool rush of air and about fifty mosquitoes come into the car. That was that. I started the engine, told Jan to relax, and drove out to the main road and back toward Lihue, until I found an elevated spot with a good wind, where I managed to doze until the sun came up. My breakfast was bread and cheese mixed with ants and sand and washed down with warm beer, all eaten off the hood of the car. Then I woke Jan up and we drove back to town.

Somehow Jan and I had drifted apart after that. Not that I blamed her for the weekend. It was more because she began heckling me a lot, especially after we started sleeping together, wanting to know if I loved her, and why not, and what was I thinking about. I loved her sometimes, in a way that was hard to explain; as for what I was thinking, most of the time we were together my mind just drifted. Anyway, I couldn't cope with her questions. It had simply become convenient to let the whole thing slide back into casual friendship. But it was nice seeing her in the cafeteria. She was still a great-looking girl.

The ER had completely changed in the fifteen or twenty minutes I took for lunch. A new group of people stood waiting, and eight fresh charts were waiting in the basket. Obviously no real emergencies were at hand, or the nurses would have called me immediately. Just more routine stuff. One of the new people was a chronic visitor to the ER, in for his usual shot of xylocaine to ease an alleged back disorder. His arrivals were so frequent and predictable that the nurses always had a needle full of xylocaine ready and waiting for me on the tray next to the patient. Kid Xylocaine, as we called him, had developed a certain expertise about his conditin, and this was his time to shine, as he directed me where to insert the needle, how to insert it, and how much to give. Feeling somewhat victimized by this ritual, I nevertheless did what he wanted; he sighed with apparent relief and left.

Walking next into Room B, I was greeted once again by my drunk friend Morris, who had returned at last from the X-ray department. Flopped on an examining table and secured by a wide restraining belt, Morris held a large manila envelope filled with fresh X rays. He greeted me. "All I ever get is a goddamn intern. I don't know why I come here any more."

Lunch had made me mellow and somehow able to ignore this prattle as I took the X rays out of the envelope and began to hold them up, one at a time, against the light of the window. I didn't expect to find anything of consequence, except perhaps in the upper left arm, which was badly discolored. Earlier, when I lifted and rotated the arm, Morris had rewarded me with a stream of obscenity. Something might be amiss there. I went through the whole stack of X rays—left knee, right knee, pelvis, right wrist, left elbow, left foot—on and on, without finding anything for the left arm and shoulder. Not there. Nothing to do but have the nurse return Morris to radiology. "They're going to love you up there, Doctor Peters," said the nurse. "He terrorized the X-ray department all morning and used up two boxes of film."

"That doesn't surprise me," I said, picking up a handful of new charts and heading for Room C.

The afternoon babies were much like the morning babies, suffering mostly from colds and diarrhea. One had to be sponged for a temperature of 104.2, and another, about four years old, needed suturing for a laceration on his chin. Suturing children is very, very difficult. Their terror at being brought to a hospital, often bleeding and in pain, is only made worse by the papooselike contraption they are strapped into to keep them still. Not even the papoose could immobilize this boy's chin; it was like hitting a moving target. The worst part for him was being under the sheet with the hole in it. After the sting of the xylocaine, he didn't feel much of anything but pressure and slight pulling. Yet he screamed just the same, and hated it all the way. So did I.

A thirty-two-year-old man in another room had a catalogue of complaints, beginning with a dry throat and proceeding down the body. His real aim was to be admitted as a hospital patient, and when he realized that the dry throat hadn't impressed me very much, his trouble shifted to a right-side chest pain. To test his reaction, I finally told him the hospital was already overcrowded, whereupon he stormed out in a rage, complaining that when you really needed a hospital it was always full.

The afternoon drifted by in a carelessly busy way. By now I had seen about sixty patients, par for the course, with no more than the usual sweat. But Saturday night was approaching, and that always meant trouble. Two older men with asthma walked in together, and the nurses put them into separate rooms with the positive-pressure breathing machines. The gentleman in Room C was wheezing away, his bony chest held at almost full inspiration, his back straight, hands on his knees. I asked him if he smoked. No, he answered, he hadn't smoked in years. Reaching down, I slowly pulled the pack of Camels out of his shirt pocket, his eyes following my hand until he saw the cigarettes. When he looked up at me, the expression on his face, even in his suffering, was so comical yet warmly human that I couldn't help smiling. It was like catching a small boy in a piece of silly mischief. Much of the emergency room's appeal lay in its lavish display of the variety and folly of humankind.

Old friends kept turning up. Another drunk, well known to us, stumbled in, complaining of a fall over a rocking chair that had left him with a chronic leg ulcer! I had seen the same ulcer a few weeks before when the drunk was a ward patient— an eventful time for all of us. Despite rigorous security measures, he had stayed drunk for days on end, and his discharge was probably hastened when the chief resident found him behind the blood bank with two bottles of Old Crow and a female patient. This time I bandaged his ulcer and told him to come back to the clinic on Monday.

Between the drunks and the crying babies with colds, an ambulance pulled up unannounced, without siren or flashing red light. That meant it wasn't much of an emergency. When the stretcher was unloaded, it revealed a thin lady of about fifty dressed in dirty, ragged clothes. I followed one of the nurses, who was saying they couldn't get any response from this patient. And neither could I. The lady just stared at the ceiling, breathing heavily. She had a small laceration in the hairline of her forehead, but it wasn't even suturable. She seemed fully conscious, and yet she was totally immobile. I began a neurological exam, testing first her pupils and then her reflexes. No bad signs. But when I tried to do the Babinski test, by lightly scraping the bottom of her foot with a key, she practically hit the ceiling, screaming that there wasn't anything wrong with her feet, it was her head that hurt, and why was I fooling with her feet? She jumped off the examining table and disappeared down the hall, with a nurse in hot pursuit. Finally, we called the hospital administration and the police, who ended up dragging her away still screaming that she was all right.

Down in Room F was an elderly gentleman who had run out of his diuretic, or water-eliminating, pills and whose legs were swollen with excessive fluid. He turned out to be one of those people with a remarkable talent for talking continuously and apparently sensibly without saying anything at all. A torrent of words rolled out as I tried to examine him. He spoke of his extrasensory perception and of the many times he had been able to use it, especially in communicating with his wife, who had died several years previously. Against my will I paused to listen while he described how he could take a bottle of water and distill it into his own model of the universe. In fact, he thought the earth was one small portion of one molecule of some gigantic object from another universe in another dimension. A little dazed, I gave him a supply of pills, told him to stay off his feet for a while, and took up the next chart.

It was important to listen to these patients, despite the craziness and trivia. Every so often their ramblings were significant. Once in the medical-school hospital a man had checked in to the ER complaining that he had eaten several shot glasses, without the usual complement of bread. The resident and intern began to escort him out the door, with the suggestion that he return in the morning, when the psychiatry department was staffed. Seeing their disbelief, the man grabbed at the intern's pocket, coming away with a test tube and a wooden throat swab, both of which he quickly chewed up and swallowed while the house staff watched in paralyzed disbelief. They turned him around, then, and led him back to the examining room, softly suggesting that he stay overnight. In the X ray, his abdomen had looked like a bag of crushed marbles.

"Goddamn hospital. I'm never coming here again. Next time I'll go to St. Mary's." This was from the ubiquitous Morris, as he was rolled by on an examining table. Evidently he was to haunt me all day long, although I took some hope from the fact that now he appeared to be holding the X ray of his upper left arm. Perhaps I could get rid of him, after all.

"Doctor, a call for you on 84," said one of the nurses.

I already had the receiver to my ear, listening to a busy signal from my third effort to reach a Dr. Wilson, one of whose patients had come in suffering from a urinary-tract infection. Feeling frustrated, I pushed the button for 84.

"Dr. Peters."

"Doctor, my boy has a terrible headache, and I can't find my doctor. I don't know what to do." Her story hung in my head, blending with the din of crying babies in the background. We didn't need another aspirin case, but there was no way for me to tell her not to come. Reluctantly I answered, "If you are convinced that the boy is ill, then by all means bring him to the emergency room."

"Doctor, a call on 83." I told the nurse to put it on hold while I redialed Dr. Wilson, steeling myself for another busy signal. Instead, there was a ring and Dr. Wilson answered. "Dr. Wilson, I have a patient of yours here, a Mrs. Kimora."

"Mrs. Kimora? I don't think I know her. Are you sure she's one of my patients?"

"Well, she says so, Dr. Wilson." It frequently happened that doctors couldn't remember their patients' names. Perhaps a description of her problem would jog his memory, and it seemed to as I went on. "She has a urinary-tract infection, with heavy burning on urination, and her temperature—"

"Give her some gantrisin and send her to my office on Monday," he said, interrupting me.

I paused, fighting an urge to hang up. Why didn't he want to hear about the case—her temperature, urinalysis, blood count? "How about a culture?" I asked.

"Sure, get a culture."

"Okay," I pushed 83 to take the call on hold.

"Doctor," a voice wailed on the other end, "I just had a bowel movement and there's blood in it?"

"Was it bright red on the toilet paper?"

"Yes." We established that her hemorrhoids were the probable cause of the bleeding and that she wouldn't have to come in to the emergency room, just see her physician on Monday. With a sigh of relief and profuse thanks, she hung up. The nurse was holding another call, on 84, but this sort of thing could go on indefinitely, and I ignored it. Instead, I went back to Mrs. Kimora and explained very carefully about the gantrisin, that she would have to take two of the pills four times a day. A nurse took the urine for culture.

Now for Morris. Immobile on the table and apparently somewhat less drunk than before, he greeted me with his usual cheer. "I wanna get outa here." At least we agreed on that. Taking up the new X rays I held them against the light and saw immediately, with great disappointment, that he had a sharp fracture halfway between his elbow and his shoulder, as if he had taken a good karate chop. He would be with us a while longer.

"Mr. Morris, you have a broken arm." I looked at him sternly.

"I do not," he countered. "You don't know what you're doing."

Wanting to avoid another yes-you-do-no-I-don't series, I retreated and rapidly wrote an order commending Morris into the hands of the orthopedic resident. The nurse called the switchboard operator and put the resident on page.

By midafternoon I was barely keeping abreast of the crowds. About 4:00 P.M. we were briefly overwhelmed by a bunch of surfers with lacerated scalps, cut fingers, and deep coral cuts. The surf was up! The babies seemed unending, crying in every corner, with their temperatures, diarrhea, and vomiting. I was suturing madly, sending people to X-ray, and desperately trying to look into the ears of totally unco-operative children. One mother came in quite frantic, saying her baby had fallen down a third-floor rubbish chute with the garbage. I was tempted to inquire exactly how that had happened. But instead of asking any questions, I examined the child, and removed onion rings from his ear lobes and coffee grounds from his hair. Amazingly, he was quite intact. But I sent him to X-ray because his right arm appeared to be a little tender, and it did turn out that he had a greenstick fracture of the right humerus—about the least you could expect after falling three stories into a pile of garbage.

Meanwhile, the X rays were piling up, all different kinds, from skulls to feet. I was the first to admit I wasn't much good at reading those things. But that was the system—the intern read the X rays at night and on weekends. It didn't make any difference that we were badly trained for the job; we had to do it as best we could. Knowing my lack of qualifications, I was always fearful of missing something important—especially after the humbling experience with the toe. That incident had occurred one other Saturday night, when a girl came hobbling in on the arm of her boyfriend. She had stubbed her toe. When I sent her up for an X ray, her friend went along. About an hour later, in the middle of pandemonium, I looked at the X rays, mostly at the metatarsals, and told them that they were apparently negative and— The friend interrupted quietly to say that when he saw the film he thought there was a fracture. I paused and gulped, "You did?" Back at the X-ray view box, he pointed out a line in the middle phalanx of the third toe that was definitely suspicious and could have been—indeed, was—a fracture. So it goes in on-the-job training!

Morris was now conveniently stashed away in the orthopedic room, out of earshot. The orthopedic resident had responded to his page, examined Morris and his reams of X rays, and disappeared, after trying unsuccessfully to reach the on-call staff orthopedic attending. Morris would stay in the orthopedic room until the attending was contacted. So Morris was an albatross still to be carried, but he wasn't around my neck any more. I forgot about him.

Around five-thirty the whiplash injuries started trickling in. That was standard whenever traffic got heavy and cars began piling into one another out on the freeways. Anyone claiming a whiplash injury needed a careful palpation of the neck, a thorough neurological exam, and a cervical spine X ray before his doctor could be called. All these X rays looked frightfully the same, and when I slipped one of them on the gigantic view box in the middle of the ER I felt as transparently vulnerable as the negative itself. Moreover, the patients were always there, peering anxiously over my shoulder while I read their films. I only hoped they were impressed with my wizardry at making so much out of those smudgy black, white, and gray pictures of bones and tissue. It was mostly for their sake that I generally faked a thorough analysis, lingering a little longer than necessary over some part of the negative. Actually, anything I could diagnose had to be pretty far out of line or clearly broken in two, which took about ten seconds to determine. Anything else was a lucky hit. But you couldn't let the home team down, so I would gaze knowingly at the negatives, mumbling to myself and making notes, while the patient fidgeted, expecting the worst.

As the clock slid around to six, our traffic unaccountably fell off, giving me a short respite. I even began to get a little ahead, and after I dug a large fishhook out of a middle-aged man, no one else was waiting. The ER was suddenly peaceful; outside, the golden afternoon sun cast a long shadow of violet across the parking lot. This was the calm before the storm, a temporary armistice between battles. Feeling tired and lonely—surprisingly lonely, with so many people around—I ambled over to dinner. On the way I passed a few people waiting for rides home. Those who had come from the ER nodded pleasantly and smiled; I smiled back, glad to have the unusual second contact and hoping I had done right by them. Interacting with the patients outside the hospital made all of us seem more real and took away some of the fear that dogged us as we came to expect disaster in every movement of the clock.

Sitting down was a luxurious experience. I stretched my feet out under the table onto a chair opposite. Joyce came along and sat by me, which was pleasant, although we didn't have much to say to each other. She was full of laboratory gossip and blood counts, which threatened to give me indigestion; nor did I want to discuss the ER. I ate rapidly, knowing that each bite might be my last for the night. At least that part of television's view of medicine is dead right. We ended up talking about surfing with another intern, named Joe Burnett, from Idaho.

Every intern needs an outlet, a safety valve; surfing was mine. It provided the perfect detachment and escape. Not only was the environment different in sound, sight, and feeling; on top of a decent wave, struggling and concentrating to make the shore, no other thought was possible. As the months passed and my addiction to surfing grew, I began to understand why people follow the sun in search of the perfect wave. I suppose it's healthier than drugs and alcohol, but its grip is just as strong, and a bad move can kill you. Hawaii does not publicize that last fact very widely.

But never mind that. Even if the waves weren't good, beauty was all around. And who could tell?—any minute a big one might rise up to challenge you. Surfing is its own thing, basically unlike any other sport, although it superficially resembles snow skiing. The difference is that in skiing the mountain stays still; on a wave everything moves—you, the mountain, the board, the air around you—and when you fall off your board in a big wave you have no say about where you go. All you know is you weren't meant to be there. So Joe and I talked about surfing, excitedly describing little episodes, our hands and feet motioning and moving, telling how the waves curled, how we got locked in or wiped out, everything. And I forgot about the ER.

Curiously, surfing is not a sociable sport except when you are away from the water talking about it. Out there on your board you hardly speak. You're part of a group of detached people held together by a bond of water, but you are unmindful of the others except to curse if someone drops in on your wave. Every wave you catch is somehow *your* wave, even though you don't go surfing alone. You always go with someone, but you don't talk.

The phone rang for me, and I had to break off with Joe; the ER was getting some business. It wasn't peaceful any more when I arrived. During my thirty minutes away, more babies had come in, crying with the usual complaints. A teen-aged girl complained of cramps. I asked her how much relief she had obtained with aspirin. She hadn't tried any aspirin yet. I gave her two. Another miracle cure worthy of four years of medical school. And the colds. There were several people with plain old garden-variety colds—runny nose, irritated throat, cough, the usual. Why they had to come to the ER was beyond my comprehension. Even though I had reached my third wind after dinner, any humor in the situation was going right by me unnoticed. People were waiting to be sutured, and I had to see those with runny noses.

One of the suturing jobs was a little out of the ordinary. A lady had cleanly sliced off the tip of her index finger with a carving knife. She had been swift enough to rescue the little piece, and after I soaked it for a while, I sewed it back in place with very thin silk. All this was done while the private M.D. gave explicit instructions over the telephone. Had I seriously expected him to come down and do it himself?

One of the back rooms held an elderly man who was troubled by back pain and inability to hold his urine. The latter symptom was clear enough from the smell in the room, which nearly overpowered me as I examined the man by degrees, ducking into the hall from time to time for fresh air. Bad smells were still my bête noire. I thought maybe he should be admitted to the hospital, since he had a urinary-tract infection and obviously couldn't take care of himself. However, the first attending I called knew him and didn't want him as a patient. He told me to find another doctor. Seems that the old man was a notoriously bad patient, famous for disappearing from the hospital without being discharged, and always turning up again on weekends or in the middle of the night. The next doctor refused, too, and suggested yet another. Finally, after calling five M.D.'s, I got one to agree to take him as a patient, but as the nurses were preparing the man for admission they discovered he was a veteran. All my efforts on the phone flew out the window; now we had to ship him off to a military hospital.

Passing by the entrance on my way to see another patient, I nearly bumped into a young woman of about twenty, clutching a poodle as she was propelled by a man not much older than she. She was screaming that she didn't want to talk to any goddamn doctor. That was fine with me; I proceeded into the room where I was going. But I had to see her anyway, eventually, and when I did she wouldn't say a word; it would have been easier to communicate with the poodle, still tightly clutched. I decided to let her sit a while, but that was a mistake, because a few minutes later she dashed down the hall and disappeared. I was too busy to take much notice—until the family psychiatrist arrived shortly thereafter with the girl's parents. It seems that the hospital had called the police when the girl was found outside pulling up flowers. I was a little surprised to see the psychiatrist—I always had so much trouble getting any of them to come in on weekends or after 4:00 P.M. I could count on having two or three psych patients on Saturday night, a bad time for them. Since I never got a psychiatrist to come around, I just did what I could to make the patients quiet and comfortable; but a light sedative and kind words don't do much for them.

"Doctor, 84," a nurse called to me from the main counter. I picked up the phone outside Room B and poked the 84 button.

"Peters, this is Sterling." Sterling was the orthopedic resident. "I finally got hold of Dr. Andrews, who's covering staff orthopedics this month, and he thinks that a hanging cast would do for Morris."

There was a pause. I began drawing interconnected circles on the scratch-pad by the phone. This bastard Sterling didn't intend to come down and put on a hanging cast, whatever the hell that was.

"Why don't you have a go, Peters? And if you have any trouble let me know, okay?"

"I've got about eight patients here I haven't even seen yet."

"Well, if he has to wait too long, call me back."

"For Christ's sake, Sterling, he's been here since ten o'clock this morning. Don't you call that long? I mean nine hours?"

"Aw, that's all right. Give him a chance to sober up."

Arguing with Sterling involved more effort and thought than I wanted to put into it, and, furthermore, it went against my new determination to keep my distance, not to get pissed off. "Okay, okay, I'll get to it as soon as I can." I hung up the phone, mentally mapping out the next half hour.

"Nurse, have the attendant draw up some warm water and get a supply of plaster ready down in the ortho room."

"What size plaster, Doctor?"

"Two- and three-inch, four rolls of each."

Putting on my most nonchalant air, I wandered into the doctors' room and quickly scanned the shelves for a book on orthopedics. Mercifully, I found one and turned rapidly to the index. There it was—cast, hanging, see page 138, which turned out to be a discussion of breaks and fractures of the proximal humerus, just what I was looking for. Despite my apprehension at being shoved into still another strange task, I was impressed by the ingenuity of the hanging cast, which did, in fact, work by a kind of traction. Rather than encasing the patient's whole arm and shoulder, the cast was placed only around the area just above and below the elbow, where its weight would pull downward on the fractured bone and ease it back into alignment. The whole arm was then pulled into the body by swathing the cast to the chest; this held the arm immobile but allowed movement in the shoulder. Amazing.

A nurse stuck her head in. "Doctor, there are nine patients waiting."

I knew that I would hear from the nurses if a real emergency arose; now was the time to get rid of Morris once and for all. After replacing the book, I headed toward the ortho room, somewhat better prepared to make a hanging cast than I had been five minutes before. As I entered the room, it became obvious why Morris had been easy to forget for the past hour or so. He lay on the examining table fast asleep, snoring lightly, cinched in place by a broad leather strap. Nor did he awake when I cranked him into a sitting position, holding his head to keep it from flopping over. Damn that Sterling; this was his job. I had heard the television blaring in the background while he was talking on the phone with me. After cutting Morris's left shirt sleeve off at the shoulder, I fashioned a piece of stockinet for the underside of the cast and slipped it on his arm, trying not to disturb the fracture.

"Doctor, there's a call on 83."

I didn't even answer the nurse, hoping that whatever it was would solve itself.

"Ohhhhh." Morris came to when I positioned his arm for the cast. "What are you doing to me?"

"Mr. Morris, you broke your arm falling down the stairs, and I'm putting a cast on it."

"But I don't—"

"Yes, you do! Now don't say another word." I hoped Sterling would ask me for a favor some day. After soaking the plaster rolls in water long enough for the bubbles to stop, I wrapped them around and around Morris's arm, building the cast up layer on layer. I made it big, almost an inch thick. Since it functioned by its weight, mine was going to work very well.

"Now just stay where you are, Mr. Morris. Don't move. Let it dry."

Reaching the main portion of the ER, I picked up 83, but no one was there. Good strategy. It was only seven-thirty; I was already eleven patients behind, and I knew it would get

worse. Grabbing a handful of charts, I started off, glancing at
the top one: "Skin rash."

Skin problems drew a blank in my mind no matter how
many times I read and reread the descriptions of papulosqua-
mous erythematous pruritic vesicular eruptions. The words lost
all sense, twisting and turning in my memory so that if I saw a
patient with anything other than acne or poison ivy I was lost.
And there in front of me stood a man with a violent pruritic
eczematous erythematous rash. I knew what it was, because a
dermatologist had used those words to describe my sunburn
after an Easter week in Miami during medical school. It meant
itchy, wet, and red, but dermatologists preferred complicated
scientific jargon. In fact, dermatology is the only branch of
medicine still using Latin to any great extent—appropriate, in
a way, since I couldn't see that the science had advanced very
far since the days of alchemy. Although the terminology and
the diagnosis of skin disorders were difficult, the treatment was
simplicity itself. If the lesion was wet, you used a drying agent;
if the lesion was dry, you kept it wet. If the patient got better,
you continued what you were doing; otherwise you tried something else, ad infinitum.

The patient standing before me was a skinny, sallow-faced
fellow with dark hair, bushy and unkempt. Looking at his
hands and his arms, I couldn't think of a thing except how little I knew about dermatology. He didn't have a private doctor,
which meant I would have to call one, and I wondered what I
could say without sounding like an idiot.

I noticed that the rash was on the palms of his hands, too,
and some distant bells began ringing in my mind. Only a few
dermatological disorders occur on the palms of the hands.
Syphilis is one. Hmmm. I was so involved with my own
thoughts, I hardly heard the patient when he said that he had
neurodermatitis and needed more tranquilizers. I was still
trying to remember the exact list of those diseases that occur
on the palms when his words suddenly scored in my consciousness. Neurodermatitis. With practice, I had developed an
ability not to show surprise or gratitude when such sudden
gifts of diagnosis were presented, and I continued to look at
his arms knowingly until sufficient time had elapsed. It made
me feel that my knowledge of dermatology at least equaled his
when I guessed correctly, that he was on Librium. He was
thankful to get some more.

As evening spread into night, my steps became labored and
slow, and my fears mounted, giving rise in my imagination to

a series of hopeless cases waiting to descend upon me. There was no pause in a continual stream of patients that kept me always five or six people behind. My suturing became more rapid, out of a combination of necessity and diminishing interest. Whenever I sutured, the people waiting stacked up, so I had to be fast, dispensing with trimming the edges and other fancy stuff. I was not haphazard, just less careful, and perhaps more easily satisfied. As, for instance, with the man who had a flap laceration on his arm. During the daytime I probably would have excised the flap and closed it as a linear cut. Now I just sewed it up, flap and all, hoping for the best.

In the eye-and-ear room a four-year-old boy sat forlornly on the examining table. His grandfather stood nearby. As I entered, the boy started to whimper, putting his arms to his grandfather, who held him while I read the chart. It said, "Foreign body, right ear." After talking quietly with the little guy for a few minutes, I convinced him to let me look in his ear. Far up in the canal I could see something black; it looked like a raisin or a small pebble.

Since the grandfather didn't know an ear, nose, and throat man, I picked one out of the M.D. roster, a Dr. Cushing, and gave him a call.

"Dr. Cushing, this is Dr. Peters at the ER. I have a four-year-old boy here with a foreign body in his ear."

"What's the family name, Peters?"

"Williams. The father's name is Harold Williams."

"Do they have health insurance?"

"What?"

"Do they have health insurance?"

"I haven't the slightest idea."

"Well, find out, my boy."

What a scene, I thought, retracing my steps into the eye-and-ear room. With a dozen people waiting, I've got to find out about the health insurance. No, the grandfather said, they were not insured.

"No, no insurance, Dr. Cushing."

"Then see if any of the adults are employed."

Once again I returned to the eye-and-ear room to quiz the concerned grandfather. Actually, I knew that this information gathering was easier than calling a dozen or so physicians until I found one who wasn't so concerned about getting paid; but it seemed gross and inhumane, just the same.

"Both the parents are employed, Dr. Cushing."

"Fine. Now, what is the problem?"

"Little David Williams has a foreign body in the ear, something black."

"Can you take it out, Peters?"

"I suppose so. I can try."

"Good. Send them to my office on Monday, and call me back if you have any trouble."

"Oh, Dr. Cushing."

"Yes?"

"I had a little girl in here this morning with infections in both middle ears." The Pablum child suddenly came back into my consciousness. "One drum was ruptured, and the other was bulging out. Should I have drained it?"

"Yes, probably."

"How do you do that?"

"Use a special instrument called a myringotomy knife. You merely make a tiny incision in the lower, posterior part of the eardrum. It's very simple, and the patient gets immediate relief."

"Thanks, Dr. Cushing."

"Not at all, Peters."

Thanks for nothing, Dr. Cushing. After all that nonsense, I had to go fumble for the foreign body myself. As for incising the eardrum, I decided that I should consider myself instructed on the procedure.

Back in the eye-and-ear room, I immobilized the boy and reached into his ear, trying to grab the black object. It came apart as I pulled the forceps back, and when I looked at what came out I didn't want to believe my eyes. It was the back leg of a cockroach. The little fellow was sobbing now as I dug out the cockroach piece by piece, feeling sorry for the boy and wanting to have it over and done with, nearly vomiting with revulsion. The last few pieces came out with a great gush of irrigation. The boy's crying gradually subsided, and I swabbed out the ear with disinfectant. He seemed all right, but I felt pretty faint.

Throughout the last of this procedure, a nurse had been fidgeting behind me. She now informed me, somewhat icily, that Morris was still waiting down in the ortho room. Sometimes these nurses bugged me nearly to death, especially at night. I did feel a bit guilty about Morris, though, because he had been with us for almost twelve hours now, and I suppose my guilt added to my animosity toward the nurse. Being deep in sleep, Morris couldn't have cared less. His cast was quite dry. Unfortunately, I had to wake him up in order to bind the cast to his body with an Ace bandage, and in so doing I came in for a little more verbal abuse, which seemed to me not quite up to Morris's usual standard. What bothered me a bit was whether Morris would be able to move his shoulder, with his left arm bound so closely to his chest. But I was doing it by the book, and the clinic would bail me out on Monday if anything was amiss. Returning to the main part of the ER, I told the fidgety nurse that Morris could go home, if she could find time between coffee breaks to give him a tetanus shot.

By ten o'clock the place was really hopping, jammed full of all manner of bodily ills. With the rise in clientele, I had fallen slightly further behind, perhaps by a dozen charts. Standing quietly in the middle of the main waiting room was a woman who wanted me to examine a small puncture wound on the bridge of her nose inflicted some eight hours earlier by a pair of pruning shears. Her name was Josephs. I didn't know why Mrs. Josephs had waited so long, but, in any case, her doctor had sent her to the ER for a tetanus injection. That was sound enough. However, the tetanus toxoid only helps the body to build immunity; furthermore, it is a slow worker. It seemed wise to supplement the tetanus shot with some premade antibodies for temporary protection, especially on a wound over eight hours old. We had just received a new shipment of a very good human-antibody serum called Hypertet, but I couldn't give it to Mrs. Josephs without first calling her physician, a Dr. Sung, who was well known for his sharp tongue and antiquated medicine. I dialed his number with trepidation.

"Dr. Sung, this is Dr. Peters at the ER. Mrs. Josephs is here, and I am about to give her the tetanus shot, but I feel she should have something to hold her until the shot takes effect."

"Yes, you're right, Peters. Make it a dose of horse antitoxin, and do it quickly, please. I don't want her to wait."

"We have a very good human tetanus-immune globulin called Hypertet, Dr. Sung. Wouldn't that be better than the horse serum? It's much faster, and besides—"

"Don't argue with me, Peters. You don't know everything. If I wanted Hypertet, I'd order it."

"But, Dr. Sung, if I use horse serum, there's a chance of allergy, and I'll have to skin-test her. All that takes time."

"Well, what the hell are you getting paid for? Now, get on it."

The sharp crack of the disconnection shot into my ear. Well, screw it. Old Dr. Sung was practicing very bad medicine,

and someday it would catch up with him. Why should I get
steamed up? Too bad about the Hypertet, though, all nicely
packed and ready for injection. Ten to one the old bastard
hadn't ever heard of it. So this is what we get paid for, I
thought, grimly working through a long set of directions for
sensitivity testing on the side of the horse-serum bottle while
fifteen people waited outside.

But I didn't get very far with the horse serum. A siren, off
in the distance, brought back the old fear. To my horror and
disbelief, three ambulances pulled up simultaneously, and the
crews jumped out and started unloading pieces of people, all
victims of the same automobile wreck, putting them in rooms
where others were already waiting. One smashed body would
have been terrifying; five were simply overwhelming. While
the nurses called upstairs for help from the house staff, I tried
to do something, anything, before the situation immobilized
me. One of the patients was a young boy with the side of his
head crushed in. His breathing was extremely stertorous; at
times it stopped altogether, only to resume seconds later. I
started an IV, which the kid probably didn't need right off.
But he would need one eventually, and I kept busy putting it
in and getting some blood for type and cross match. Inserting
an endotraceal tube came next, an automatic choice. Normally
a very difficult procedure for me, this one was easy because
the boy's lower jaw was so broken up that I could pull it away
from his face. After sucking out his mouth and throat, bringing up bits of bone and a lot of blood, I put in the tube for
him to breathe through. Surprisingly, his blood pressure was
all right. I wanted to stay by the boy, even though there was
nothing more for me to do for him just then, but the other patients were lying everywhere, crying for help—and, anyway, a
neurosurgeon was on his way down. Later I heard that the boy
had died a few minutes after leaving surgery. It bothered me
for a while, until I rationalized that he had been virtually dead
when I got to him.

Now, after all these months, it was easier for me not to get
emotionally caught up in any one case. Other problems were
waiting, demanding attention. The lady in the next room, for
instance—she was critical, too. A huge area of skin and hair,
running from her left ear to the top of her head, could be
flapped back, revealing a network of multiple skull fractures,
like a cracked hard-boiled egg ready to be peeled. The pupil
on the left side was widely dilated. Where to begin? While
I was looking at the skull, she suddenly vomited a pint or

so of blood, which splattered off the table onto my pants and shoes. Thank goodness for the IV, providing some direction for my chaotic thoughts. I hurriedly got that going, at the same time sending up a blood sample for type and cross match to get some blood available for transfusion. Since she had vomited blood, I thought we might need eight units rather than the usual four, although her blood pressure was surprisingly strong. This matter of acceptable, even normal, blood pressure in the face of clear body failure had begun to bother me. All the books cited blood pressure as a prime and reliable indicator of general systemic function, but most of my experience seemed to be going against that rule. At any rate, I poked around at the woman's abdomen, trying to think where that blood might have come from.

Just then a nurse urgently called me into another room, where a man was barely breathing and, she thought, convulsing. Apparently hit in the stomach, he had been one of the drivers, I guessed. The nurse handed me some amobarbital to stop the convulsing, but before I could give it I realized that, instead of convulsions, he had what some call the dry heaves, a kind of retching. He vomited a little, too, not blood but a stale-smelling alcohol that also managed to splash on my shoes. When Dr. Sung called back in the midst of all this wanting to know if I had given the horse serum yet, I was tempted to unload on him, but I just said no, we were busy.

A motorcycle hd been involved in the same accident. The rider was virtually skinned alive. He had abrasions all over him except on his head. He was one of the few who actually wore a helmet. Every weekend had its quota of wiped-out easy riders. For sheer gore they were unmatched—so bad, in fact, that a standard hospital joke went around about the motorcycle patient who arrived at the hospital in several ambulances. Total body bruise, fracture, and abrasion was a better description for this one. If they could talk at all, these fellows would staunchly insist that a motorcycle wasn't so dangerous, because you got thrown free when you had an accident. But being thrown free at sixty miles an hour, onto concrete, on your head, and then getting run over didn't leave us much to work with. This one was not only totally abraded; his left lower leg was crushed as well. The two bones were hanging out at a forty-five-degree angle, with the foot attached only by some threads of sinew. Pants, socks, bits of sneaker, and asphalt were squashed into the wound.

Surprisingly, he was conscious, although dazed.

"Do you have any pain?"

"No, no pain. But I have something in my right eye."

God, with all that injury he was worried about a cinder in his eye. I took it out. His blood pressure was all right, the pulse a little high at 120. I started an IV and sent up a sample for type and cross match, arbitrarily picking five units of blood to be available. He apparently didn't need blood right away, but he obviously was facing some bone surgery. With a hemostat I tried to stop a little of the blood oozing out of the leg muscles, which were in plain view. It amazed me how little he bled.

I went back to the lady who had vomited up the blood and was relieved to find her blood pressure holding up well. Perhaps she had just swallowed the blood, I reasoned; after all, she was bleeding from both nostrils. Twenty minutes had passed since the ambulances pulled in, and some others from the house staff were there now, helping to stabilize the patients. I got X-ray to come down and shoot a group of heads and chests and other bones. No description could capture the uproar of that time. It was total chaos, as colds and diarrhea and babies and asthmatics mingled with broken bones and crushed heads. Nor did matters improve much when the attendings arrived and began ordering everyone about. The OR, alerted earlier, finally began to absorb the automobile-accident patients.

Dr. Sung called again, threatening to file a complaint with the hospital if I didn't get right on that horse serum. At that point I didn't give a damn about his horse serum, so I hung up on him. This brought him storming in about twenty minutes later, ready to give me hell, just as we were moving the last of the critically injured up to surgery. I stood there, covered with a mixture of blood and vomitus, vaguely hearing him rant. This lunatic could get me into real trouble, so I didn't say anything except to mention the Hypertet again, and how much quicker it would have been. That made him even madder, and he stomped out taking his patient with him. Sure enough, a written reprimand showed up in my box a few days later. So much for priorities.

By eleven the cyclone had passed, leaving the usual jumble of patients with lesser complaints, a much larger number than usual because of what had gone before. They were everywhere —inside, outside, sitting on the ambulance platform, on the floor, in chairs. I began to go from one room to another, half listening, performing like a tired machine. One man had fallen by his pool during a party, breaking his nose on the diving board as he went down and cutting his thumb on a gin-and-tonic glass. The nose was straight, so I left it alone. The laceration I sutured rapidly, after telling his private M. D. the sad story. Even *he* sounded drunk.

It was, in fact, a big night for drunks; most of them were suffering from minor cuts and bruises or premature hangovers, with nausea and vomiting. And the kids were still coming in, long after bedtime, with their diarrhea and runny noses and fevers. Occasionally I had one with a temperature of around 104, yet I wouldn't be able to find anything wrong. This made me very uncomfortable. As a human being you have an almost irresistible desire to treat; you are expected to treat. The parents almost invariably clamored for penicillin, but I had enough sense not to give in most of the time. To treat a symptom like fever without a firm diagnosis is bad medicine; and yet I often got only a fleeting and rather limited look at the eardrums or the throats of those miniature screamers. Sometimes I treated, sometimes not; always I went on half-educated guesses.

It went on being a typical Saturday night in the ER. The crowd thinned out about 1:00 A.M. From now on we would see less of the various things that drove people away from their TV sets during the evening to seek the sanctity of the ER —things like colds, diarrhea, and minor puncture wounds. In about an hour, the problems that were keeping them from falling asleep would begin to appear. The same ailments they had ignored all day and through the early evening would, of course, keep them awake, forcing them to the ER in the middle of the night to see the astute and understanding intern. Like itchy thighs. On another tour of duty, I had fallen asleep around 5:00 A.M. only to be awakened because some patient had itchy thighs.

Slightly after one an ambulance pulled up without its siren, and the crew unloaded a peaceful-looking girl in her early twenties who was in a deep sleep approaching coma. Ingestion. The usual, as I found out: twelve aspirins, two Seconals, three Libriums, and a handful of vitamin tablets. All of these drugs, except maybe the vitamins, could be dangerous—especially Seconal, a sleeping pill—but you had to take quite a few of them if you were really serious. Otherwise it was only a gesture, a childish cry for attention within the social fabric of the individual's life; the usual ingestion case is a young woman lost in the unreal world of *True Romance* magazine. I could be interested and sympathetic, but not in my state; I was so tired that any sense of empathy had long since dissolved into irritation. How could this stupid girl pull such a stunt so late on a Saturday night? Why couldn't she throw her little show on Tuesday morning?

As they always did, several members of the family and some friends arrived shortly after the ambulance. They stayed in the waiting room, nervously talking and smoking. I looked down at the girl sleeping on the table. Then, put my hand on her chin, I forcibly shook her head and called her by her first name, Carol. The eyes opened slowly, so that only half the pupils were showing, and she whimpered, "Tommy."

"Tommy, shit." Irritation became anger as my exhaustion and hostility sought expression and won. I ordered some ipecac from the nurse and decided to pump her out. The pumping-out procedure was no bargain for either of us, but I wanted to make her remember the ER. Besides, I knew that when I called her private doctor he would ask what I had gotten out of her stomach.

An ingestion stomach tube is half an inch in diameter. After cranking her into a sitting position, I crammed one down her throat, through her left nostril. Her eyes suddenly shot open all the way as she retched and struggled to get free of the attendants holding her. She vomited a little around the tube as I pushed it farther down into her stomach, and then everything in her stomach came up, including an undissolved Seconal and a portion of one of the Librium capsules. When I pulled the tube out, what remained came with it. A few minutes later the ipecac took effect, causing her to vomit again and again, even though her stomach was empty. By now Tommy had joined the others in the waiting room. Perhaps he also wanted some ipecac, so as to play a full role in this melodramatic event.

After sending up a blood sample to see if the aspirin had changed the acidity of the blood, and finding out that it hadn't, I called Carol's doctor. I told him what she had taken and that, aside from being sleepy, she was all right now, nicely tranquilized.

"What did you get when you pumped her out?"

"One Seconal, bits of Librium, not much else."

"Fine, Peters, good work. Send her home, and tell her father to call me on Monday."

Soon after that Carol was taken home, in all her glory, covered with vomitus. I never questioned my harsh attitude toward her, not after eighteen hours in the ER, and, while I'm not proud of it now, that's the way it was.

Back around midnight a new shift of nurses had come on. It was now two, and I was really sagging, but the new nurses were a clean and spirited bunch, displaying remarkable agility and garrulousness for that time of night. The contrast made me feel even lousier, like a silhouette. And the next patient didn't help. Her chart read, "Depressed, difficulty breathing."

As I walked into the room, my dismay was instantly confirmed by the sight of a lady in her late forties who was wearing a light blue negligee. She lay on the table, one hand pressed dramatically against her ample upper chest. Two other ladies stood nearby hysterically telling me and the nurse that their friend was unable to breathe. I could see from a distance that the lady was breathing very easily.

"Oh, Doctor," the lady whined, drawing out the word in a deep southern accent. "I cain't hardly breathe. You have to help me."

She smelled like week-old martinis. One of the hysterical ladies produced a prescription bottle. I looked at it. Seconal.

"Oh, those little red pills. I did take two. Was that all right?" The southern lady looked at me with fluttery eyelids; she was having a hell of a good time at two o'clock in the morning. I had a strong impulse to throw her neurotic ass out of the ER. That was a sure administrative bomb, however—perhaps even career suicide. Despite my disenchantment with the system, I hadn't come to that.

"Do you hear anything strange, Doctor?" I was forcing myself to listen to her chest, which was totally clear. "Oh, you're going to take my temperature and blood pressure," she said gleefully. "I do feel rather faint. I just cain't understand what's happening to me." On her arm went the blood-pressure cuff and into her mouth the thermometer, silencing her at last. I was glad of the opportunity to get away from her for a few minutes by calling the doctor who covered the hotel where she was staying. He said to give her Librium.

Back in her presence, I coaxed myself to be civil. "Madam, the hotel physician has suggested Librium for you."

"Librium, Doctor? Are those the little green and black pills? Well, I'm afraid I'm allergic to those. They make me so gassy, and sometimes," she said, sitting up now, moving into high gear, "sometimes it's so bad my hemorrhoids pop out." With this, we were fully launched into her extensive pill history and the dreadful details of her lower gastrointestinal tract. In the

middle of her recital, a performance worthy of Blanche Du-
Bois, I interrupted to say that perhaps orange Thorazine would
do just as well.

"Orange Thorazine!" She virtually squealed with delight.
"I've never had that! I just cain't thank you enough, Doctor.
You've been so sweet." And out she went, chattering gaily
with her friends about the wonders of medicine.

One of the nurses from a private ward appeared, limping
slightly. She had fallen down a flight of stairs, with apparently
no serious damage, but she had thought it best to have it
checked. I agreed. Her name was Karen Christie, and nothing
seemed wrong with her hip, but I suggested she have a pelvic
X ray, anyway, to be perfectly sure. Hospitals are understand-
ably sensitive to any threat of personal-injury claims on the
part of the staff. When Miss Christie's X ray appeared fifteen
minutes later, I snapped it up on the view box amid an assortment of skulls and broken bones. My eyes were a little blurry
as I ran them over her femur, acetabulum, ilium, sacrum, and
so on. All was normal. I almost missed the white coil toward
the center, and when I did see it I couldn't figure out how the
X-ray technician had managed to get such a strange artifact in
his picture. Then it dawned on my sleepy mind that I was
looking at an intrauterine contraceptive device, which served
the double purpose of making Miss Christie a much more interesting case and lightening my mood for a moment.

Unfortunately, my sour humor returned with the next patient. He sat quietly sobbing because he had hurt his nose
when the car he was riding in hit a fire hydrant. With no encouragement from me, he loquaciously told the whole story.
He had been minding his own business when he got picked up
by a lesbian, who turned out to be so upset with her roommate
that she ran the two of them into the fire hydrant. I didn't ask
what had happened to the lesbian, being grateful not to have
her, too. I thought wryly, and unkindly, that this fellow was
the fag end of the night in more ways than one. Putting up
with him was almost more than I could tolerate in my state of
zero compassion. All I was prepared to handle were simple
medical problems—diagnosis and cure. This guy needs more.
He refused to do anything but sit and cry, and ask for Uncle
Henry. When Uncle Henry arrived, not even he could persuade the man that an X ray was not lethal. Finally, when
Uncle Henry agreed to stay constantly by his side, they disappeared to X-ray. The film showed a broken nose, and his private physician admitted him to the hospital by phone. Some-

what later, a policeman arrived with the real story. It had been a simple punch-out in one of the local "gay" bars; the lesbian was imaginary.

Off in the distance, again, I picked up the fateful sound of a siren, hoping it would pass us by. Instead, the ambulance screeched into the parking lot and backed quickly to the platform. I was in no shape for what I saw, the human wreckage of yet another automobile accident. The two girls on stretchers had obviously gone through the windshield. They were bloody from the waist up, with first-aid bandages covering their heads and faces. After the girls, two men stepped out of the ambulance under their own power, showing only minor bruises.

As I removed the bandages from one girl's face, a geyser of blood spurted straight up onto my face and chest. A textbook case of arterial bleeding, I thought, replacing the bandages. I put on a pair of sterile gloves and a mask and then jerked the bandages off suddenly, immediately pressing a piece of gauze into the wound, working my hand along a gaping laceration that ran from her forehead down between her eyes almost to her mouth. Bleeders were spurting little jets of blood in various directions. With great difficulty, I managed to get mosquito hemostats on the bleeders, but before I could tie them the girl ripped them off. She was drunk. For a minute or so we went through a cruel, gory routine, she taking the hemostats off as fast as I put them on. I won by dogged persistence, finally tying off the bleeding vessels, but of necessity leaving enough work to enrich a plastic surgeon. Meanwhile, a resident had arrived to work on the other girl. Then we discovered that the two girls were military dependents, and since they were stable—meaning they weren't going to die in the next hour—off they went to a military hospital. That left me with the two fellows, who were in relatively good shape. I cleaned their abrasions and mechanically sutured a couple of scalp lacerations without uttering a word.

By about three-thirty there was only one more patient to be seen, a baby sixteen months old. I was really dragging by then, and I don't remember much about the case except that the parents had brought the child in because he really hadn't been eating too well for the last week or so. Thinking I must have missed something, I had them repeat that several times. All the while the child was sitting there smiling and alert. With a touch of sarcasm, I asked if they didn't think their behavior was a little strange. Why strange, they wanted to know; they were worried. A slow burn came over me as I silently examined the perfectly normal baby, and then fled to the telephone to call their private doctor, who was equally irritated because I'd waked him up. That was absurd, too. The doctor was angry because his patient was bothering me at 3:30 A.M. I ended up turning everything over to the nurses, who sent them all home. I couldn't talk to them again.

After the child left I wandered out on the platform, peering blankly into the silent blackness. I felt nauseous and drained, but I knew from sore experience how much worse I would feel to be waked up for the inevitable next patient after sleeping for only fifteen or twenty minutes. All the nurses were busy with small jobs except one, who was having coffee. I felt strangely detached, as though my feet were not firmly on the ground, and thoroughly lonely. Even fear was gone, banished by exhaustion. If anything serious came in now, all I could do would be to try to keep it alive until a doctor arrived. Well, that was a useful function, of sorts. Of course, I would continue to do miracles with the drunks and the depressed and the kids who weren't eating too well—my true constituency.

Somewhere near and coming nearer, a Volkswagen's horn was beeping, disturbing the deceptive tranquillity of the ER. As the beeping got louder, it began to remind me of the cartoon character called the Road Runner—an absurd association, but somehow appropriate to my mental state. Beep-beep. Maybe it *was* the Road Runner. Thirty seconds later fantasy was replaced by a VW that pulled up, still beeping, next to the platform. A man jumped out yelling that his wife was having a baby in the back seat. After calling for a nurse to bring a delivery kit, I ran down to the VW and opened the door on the right side. There in the back, sure enough, was a woman lying on her side, obviously in the last stages of labor. The light was very poor, obscuring the birth area; everything would have to be done by feel. As she started into another contraction, I felt the baby's head right on the perineum. The woman's panties were in the way, so I cut them off with some bandage scissors, and while she grunted through the contraction, I kept my hand on the baby's head to prevent it from popping out. After convincing her to roll over on her back, I pushed the front seats forward, and got one of her legs braced on the rear window and the other one draped over the driver's seat. My hands were moving by reflex now, leaving my mind to do absurd things, such as remember an old joke—what's harder than getting a pregnant elephant into a Volkswagen? Getting the elephant pregnant in a Volkswagen. With the contraction over, I got the baby's head out slowly, rotated it, pulling it down to get one shoulder out and then up for the other shoulder, and suddenly I was holding a slippery mass. I almost dropped it trying to back out of the car. Thank God, just then the baby choked and started to cry. Not knowing what to do through all this, the father had been behaving oddly; he interrupted his audible anguish about the upholstery, which was pretty messy by now, to ask whether it was a boy or a girl. In the dark I couldn't tell. Must not be this guy's first child, I thought. I wanted to suck the newborn's mouth out with the bulb syringe, but the baby was too slippery to hold in one hand. Instead, I gave the infant to one of the nurses, with explicit instructions to keep it level with the mother, and, after putting on some clamps, I cut the cord. Then everyone—attendants, nurses, and father—helped lift the mother out of the car. The after-birth came away without effort in the ER. I was amazed that there were no lacerations. The whole crew disappeared up to the obstetrics area.

That baby redeemed the night. Maybe they would name it after me. More likely they'd call it V. W.

I almost didn't even mind seeing the dirty drunk who had come in during the excitement of the birth. He had a scalp laceration, which I sewed up without anesthetizing it while he swore at me. Actually, he started to swear and swing at me as soon as I appeared. He was so drunk he was beyond feeling. After the last stitch, I went into the doctors' room and plopped down on the bed, instantly asleep.

That was 4:45; at 5:10 a nurse knocked and came in to say a patient was waiting to be seen. At first I was disoriented, literally unable to recall where I was and aware only of the hammering of my heart. In the twenty-five minutes between then and now, sleep, the great healer, had incapacitated me, leaving me dizzy and weak, with scintillations in the periphery of my visual field. These passed as I began to move around. Even so, my left eye refused to focus, and when I opened the door the light in the hall was like a thousand flash bulbs. I felt just about as shitty as I could feel and still function.

The patient, where was the patient? The chart in my hand said, "Abdominal pain, twelve hours." Jesus! That meant I had to record a complete history and probably wait for lab reports. I walked into the room and looked at the patient. About fourteen, soft silky hair of shoulder length, skinny, large nose. Mother sat over in a corner. The check list of questions for possible appendicitis is a long one, and I started in on it. When did the pain start? When did you first feel it? Did it move? Was it like indigestion cramps? Did it come and go or remain steady? Meanwhile, I casually felt the abdomen for sensitivity, through Bermuda shorts, reasonable apparel in Hawaii's climate—but underneath them was something odd, the distinct outline of a girdle? Crazy. Did you eat today? Tonight? Did you feel like vomiting? The stomach seemed soft. It could not have been very tender, for moving my hand over it evoked no sign of discomfort. Did you move your bowels? Was it normal? I took out my stethoscope. Has your urine been normal? I put the stethoscope in my ears and rested the bell of it on the abdomen, the patient's words filtering through the earplugs. Have you had trouble with abdominal pain before? Have you ever had an ulcer? For some reason I always left the questions about the menstrual cycle until last. It was just a small propriety. When was your last period? The answer came rather apologetically: "I'm a boy."

I looked at her—him—for a minute, my dull mind reeling. Long silky hair, loose purple velvet shirt. No, it was a blouse. Girdle! Putting my hand under the girdle, I lifted the whole works up, practically raising him off the table. No doubt about it, that was a penis. The mother just looked away. I was unprepared for such sudden reverses. It all seemed a huge, cruel joke. Here I was struggling to make some sophisticated intraabdominal diagnosis, and I was wrong even on the sex. Anyway, he didn't have appendicitis or anything else terribly serious. Probably a simple case of abdominal cramps. I thought to myself, If I told him they were menstrual cramps he'd be pleased.

Being a slow learner, I immediately fell asleep again. Crash! The door came open and a delighted nurse informed me that I had a patient. The same process occurred, the same agonizing gauntlet of getting up and blinking and gradually clearing as I emerged into the light. This one was a dandy, a Samoan lady towing along her ailing mother, who couldn't speak a word of English. With so many languages in use around the islands, we were accustomed to working through translators, but in this case the daughter's English was not even a serviceable pidgin. Besides, the complaints were so numerous that every organ system seemed to be involved. She had pains here, pains there, headache, weakness, couldn't sleep, and generally felt crappy. Sounded like me.

Very carefully I asked the daughter if her mother had any burning sensation when she passed her urine, and was rewarded with a blank look. Rephrasing it, I asked if her mother had any pain when she made pee-pee, wee-wee, shishi, umm . . . my mind had run out of synonyms . . . when she makes water. I thought this brought a glimmer of understanding, so I put it together again. Does your mother have pain when she makes water? The answer was great, made me want to give up medicine entirely. She said she didn't know. The lexicon of English does not hold a word to describe my frustration. I said, for Christ's sake, ask her, then. So she asked her. Yes. That was how it went with every question. Slowly, and every answer was yes. She had burning on urination, frequency of urination, nausea, vomiting, vaginal discharge, diarrhea, constipation, chest pain, cough, headache. . . . Since the mother was quite emphatic about her chest pain, I tried to take an electrocardiogram, but the machine broke. When the birds started singing outside, it was as if they meant to attack me with their song; but of course they were only heralding the light. I was so tired I just didn't care about the old lady, about anything. In the firm conviction that she would not die within the next few hours, I gave her some Gelusil, which she liked enormously, and set up an appointment in the clinic. It was glorious morning by the time she left.

Before I could disappear into the doctors' room again, a baby and an old man came in simultaneously. The mother had dropped the baby on its arm, which was a little swollen, and the man had strained his back several days before. With the baby and the man up in X-ray, I fell asleep in a chair by the counter, smack in the center of the ER. When my relief came to take over, he let me sleep on. Forty-five minutes later I woke up feeling as bad as before, but knowing that this time I could go back to my own bed. Where are the television cameras now? I mused, trudging along home looking like a Jackson Pollock action painting made of dried mucus, vomit, and blood. It was a strange and wonderful feeling to take off my clothes and slide between the cool, slightly coarse sheets.

Thus my twenty-four hours off began. After more than a month of the ER routine, I was a mental and physical shamble. I became lucid around lunchtime, when I was waked by a combination of the birds, the sun, and hunger. A shave and shower made me feel somewhat human, and by the time I had walked over for lunch in the warm noonday sun, I was back in the real world again.

Following lunch, I succumbed to an imperative somewhere in me to get away from the hospital. More sleep would have been the prudent course, but I had discovered through experience that, no matter how tired I was, the general afternoon din around my quarters would keep me awake. So I put on my bathing trunks, loaded the surfboard on to my car, threw some medical books into the back seat, and took off for the beach.

It was a relief to drive out there and let the clutter of colors and movement capture my mind. People seemed to be everywhere, all of them strangely whole and healthy. In the hospital, one often feels that everybody in the world has diarrhea or a chest pain. But there they were, busily and happily walking around, laughter mixing with the physical activity, sun tans, and brightly flashing bikinis. These people looked so *normal*. With my morose thoughts, I was somehow an outsider, not belonging. Too tired to swim or play volleyball, I propped myself up against the surfboard, facing the sun, and let the scene roll by.

I didn't try to talk to anybody and no one approached me, which was just as well. I was so full of the ER that I would quickly have turned off anybody in his right mind with my yammer about blood and broken bones. But that wouldn't be my real subject; my real subject would be me—my anger, exhaustion, and fear. Come on, now, I thought, too many dire and dramatic nouns; stop wallowing in self-pity. That's about all you've been doing lately, feeling sorry for yourself. So what if it's a crappy deal being an intern? Change it if you can, but stop feeling sorry for yourself. That doesn't help anybody, least of all you. I still wished, however, that our culture would take some of the pressure off by realizing that a white coat and a stethoscope do not confer wisdom. Much less instant nobility.

Well, screw it. I'd take a nap instead.

I fell asleep there in the sun by myself, in the middle of all that gaiety and laughter. Actually, this happened every afternoon I was off during the period of ER duty. Sleep in the morning, eat, sleep in the afternoon, eat. Do nothing for a while, then sleep, only to wake and find the twenty-four-hours-on cycle beginning again, wondering where the time had gone. When I awoke it was late afternoon; the people had thinned out and the sun was much weaker. No one bothered me as I continued to sit and look at the sun on the water. It was like watching a bonfire. Its activity seemed an excuse for my stillness and undirected thought. Not that I was unconscious; everything around me came into my mind—all movement, sound, and color. I just wasn't connecting.

Hastings had to wave his hand in front of my face a few times before I got him into perspective. Surf? Sure, why not, if I could get myself and my board down to the water. I felt immobile, as if the sun had sapped all my remaining strength. This was another part of the afternoon-off routine. Hastings would meet me down at the beach, quite late, and we'd surf, not talking to each other except to say a few words like "outside" if a large wave was coming. I didn't understand why we made such elaborate plans to meet and then ignored each other. But both of us liked it that way.

Paddling out was the high point of the day, a kind of catharsis. I felt my body and mind join again. I used my arms and feet to paddle, feeling the strength that was there and the touch of water under me, cool and gently moving. The expanse of the ocean, spreading to apparent infinity around me, made me feel small yet real, the true center. People vanished; their voices changed, became muted and distant as they were swept off by the waves. The setting sun turned the whole western sky into warm, soft oranges and reds reflecting millions of times from the surface of the water, like a Claude Monet painting. To the east, silver blues and violets began to appear among the pinks and faraway greens. Sailboats were dotted around haphazardly, little dabs of color against water and sky. The island rose up sharply from the water's edge, and sunlight cast contrasting shadows among the canyons, creating a texture as soft as velvet, making the soaring ridges fly like buttresses off a Gothic cathedral. Deep violet clouds hovered over the island, concealing the peaks, forming the prismatic reflections of rainbows in the shadows of the valleys. Whatever effect it may have on others, this beauty cradled me, drained all other thoughts and made me whole again.

The waves added to the atmosphere with their impetuosity and rhythm; one minute an organized vibration of harmonic motion, the next a swirling mass of senseless confusion. I caught one of the waves. I felt its power, the wind and the sound. Twisting as the board responded, I made my body work against the force to fall; speed and crucial milliseconds. Down the wave and then a twist of my torso, running my hand along the sheer wall of water and the crash and swirl, yet still standing, my feet on the board lost beneath a swirl of white foam. Finally the sudden kickout, with a violent but controlled backward twist, made me want to shout with the joy of being alive.

Darkness erased the scene slowly and drove us back to

shore. Hastings went his way and I mine, to the hospital for a shower. Back in the geometric, sanitized world of clean floors, utilitarian showers, and fluorescent lights, I dressed and left the grounds again. Driving up Mount Tantalus, I pleasantly anticipated the night to come.

Her name was Nancy Shepard, and I had met her—how else?—through the hospital. Her father had been a gall-bladder patient whose progress I followed closely after assisting a private M.D. in the operation. Every time I changed his dressing, he had mentioned that he wanted me to meet his daughter, retelling how she had gone to Smith and spent a year at Boston University working on a master's degree in African history. In truth, I grew a little tired of hearing the stories, although I remained interested in meeting her. Finally, the day before her father left the hospital, she had appeared, and she *was* nice—very. In fact, she looked a little like another girl from Smith I had dated while I was in college. Anyway, we went to the beach a few times, which we both enjoyed. She could talk about almost anything; it was fun to be with someone educated and intelligent. A political-science major, she was fond of arguing heatedly over small points of government, especially about Africa. Despite a number of successful dates and my admiration for her, I stopped asking her out very often, mostly because of lethargy and lack of time. In fact, that night's invitation to dinner had come out of the blue. Not that I didn't want to see Nancy. I just never got around to it—and by then Joyce had become pretty convenient.

The dinner was fine. Nancy's parents and two brothers were also there, all of them lively talkers. After coffee, Nancy and I wandered out into the large, verdant yard and began an argument about Jomo Kenyatta and Tanzania. Why had Africa failed to produce more Kenyattas? She was emotional on the subject; it was good to see her color rise as she warmed to the argument, making her even prettier.

But then she started asking me questions about medicine. Because she was really interested, not just passing the time, like so many, I worked hard to make her understand, answering as well as I could. Inevitably, she asked why I had gone into medicine. To this question an intern develops many answers. Most of them are evasive half-truths. But with her I decided to try for the whole truth.

"Well, Nancy, I don't think I'll ever know exactly. In the beginning I suppose I had some vague notion about helping people by entering a noble profession. But now that I have a lot of medicine behind me, I think I was attracted just as much by the idea that being a doctor would give me a sort of power that other people don't have—a power over people as well as disease. Few things mean more to Americans than good health, and those who have that to give, or claim to have it, are automatically authority figures in our society."

"What do you mean by power and authority?"

"Just that, I suppose. It's something like the power a medicine man holds in a primitive tribal society. He holds a high position only so far as he's able to play on the fears of his fellow tribesmen and make them think he can control nature. It's a kind of legitimate hoax—legitimate because he performs a more or less useful function, and a hoax because he doesn't really control anything but the tribal psychology. I think modern medicine is the lucky heir to that kind of psychological misconception. My patients don't fall prostrate before lightning and thunder, but they're sure as hell terrified by cancer and lots of other diseases they don't understand. When they come to the hospital, they are looking for a medicine man in more ways than one. Before I went into medical training, I was like any guy in the street. I mean I believed in the power of medicine to do almost anything, and I wanted that power, wanted to be looked up to as the agent of that power."

"But surely you mean the power to help people?" She still didn't understand.

"Sure, I can help people. Not as much as I'd like, and nowhere near what they hope for, but some. But that kind of power is severely limited. Medicine is still fairly primitive. We just don't know enough. It's the other kind of power, the more abstract kind, that I'm talking about. That's nearly unlimited. For example—I played a little football in high school, and one time a fellow broke his leg in practice. I was right next to him in the pileup, and I found myself there looking straight at him, wanting to do something, but totally helpless. When I thought about it later, what I remembered was the envy I felt toward the doctor. I know now that he didn't do much except say a few soothing words, administer a painkiller, and haul the guy away. But to me, to all of us, he was a kind of god. The more I thought about it, the more I wanted a piece of that power."

"But what about the idea you started with, of medicine as a noble profession, of just helping the boy with the broken leg. What happened to that?"

"It got all mixed up with the god idea. Anyway, I went on to college planning to become a doctor. Although a lot of new avenues opened up after that, no pressing alternative appeared. So I finally just drifted into medical school, not really having anything else in mind, wanting both kinds of power, and realizing I could have them in the medical profession, plus the social status and a reasonable income. Now that I've more or less made it, all those abstract notions have fallen apart on me. I don't have much social status, no money at all, the god-power thing seems utterly empty, and as for the power over disease itself—I hope to heaven I never have to undergo any surgery. I know too much about the limitations of medicine."

I should have been sharp enough to notice the slight chill Nancy was giving off, but I didn't. She had been waiting for the "ever since I was a little boy" story so dear to television and other fictionalized accounts of medicine. But she had made me reach down into myself, searching for answers, and the little boy wasn't there.

"Then you don't feel you have any special quality that made you go into medicine? No vocation, so to speak?" She was still looking for Ben Casey.

"No, this is definitely not like the priesthood for me. The closest I can come to medicine being a vocation is that I did well in both science and the humanities in college, and medicine is a logical combination of the two."

"Well, you don't sound like you have the same motivations as the doctors I know." She was flaring up. And so was I.

"Just how many doctors do you know, Nancy? My whole world is made up of them. I live with them—interns, residents, attendings, the medical-school crowd—and I can tell you that, in general, what happened to me happened to them, and what I feel is pretty much what they feel, if you can get them to admit it."

"Well, I think it stinks."

"What stinks?"

"That our society has let you get this far. You're the wrong person to train as a doctor, because you don't care enough about helping other people."

"I just told you that I want to help people, and I do, but the whole thing is more complicated than that. Hell, I'm just like everybody else. I don't have one consuming goal that shuts everything else out. I want to live, too. Besides, a lot of the idealism I had was smothered in medical school. It's just not oriented that way."

"Don't you like being an intern?" she interjected.

"No, not really."

She was again surprised. "Why not?"

"Basically I feel so tired, really exhausted, all the time. And yet I lack any sense of real usefulness. I realize most of the things I do could be done by someone without the training I've had. Plus I'm constantly scared, thinking I'll screw something up and look like a fool. You see, medical school didn't seem to prepare me very well at all." By now, the resolution of that afternoon to keep my mouth shut had dissolved in the intensity of the moment.

"Well, I think that's understandable. Medical school can't do everything," she said.

"It might be understandable from a distance, but when you're right in the middle of it, you don't understand what's happening to you. And when I do stop to think, and realize that the four years at medical school were mostly wasted as far as taking care of the patients is concerned, and that I'm being exploited under the guise of learning, the psychological burden is too heavy. I just get furious at the system—the way medical school and internship and medical practice are interconnected—and at the society that supports it."

"Being furious is hardly the best attitude for a doctor to have," she added with coolness.

"I couldn't agree with you more, and I wish the establishment realized that, too. Eventually, you reach a point where you don't give a damn. Sometimes, after getting called on a cardiac arrest in the middle of the night, I suddenly realize that I wish the guy would die so I could go back to bed. I mean that's how tired and pissed off I get. In a sense, I've stopped thinking about patients as people, and of course that only adds to the guilt."

Looking over at her, I could see her ethics creaking under the strain of my words. But I went on blindly.

"I suppose this business of not thinking about patients as people is the hardest to explain. Maybe a few doctors can empathize indefinitely. But not me. I can't take it. To survive now, I want to know my patients only as gall bladders or hernias or ulcers. Of course, I include in that anything about them that directly affects their basic disease process, and I believe I am becoming a good doctor technically, but beyond that I don't want to get involved. My system is not geared for it. I had this one patient named Roso, and I got so tied up with him that when he was discharged I was more relieved he was gone than I was happy he was alive."

The silence was icy. I stared into the sky, purposely looking away from her. Then I went on.

"Another thing. Very important. As an intern, I'm exploited the same as an underdeveloped country operating under mercantilistic relations with a colonial power. For instance, all I do in the operating room ninety-nine per cent of the time is hold retractors, often for the sloppiest G.P., who shouldn't be doing surgery, anyway. I'm there to be used. Anything I learn is in spite of the system, not because of it. And if I don't do what I'm told, or make too many complaints about the medieval system—pouf!—out goes my chance to specialize in a good hospital. So when I say I'm scared about making a mistake, I'm worried not so much for the patient—although that's partly it—but because I might get the boot and end up in some hick town giving typhoid shots. That's medicine's equivalent of the living death.

"And besides, a lot of very real and serious problems come up, which no one tells us about or even offers any advice. Like the emergency-room question of when you should try to revive a patient and when you should just let him alone. As interns with no experience, we're totally vulnerable about such things. And this is not entirely a medical problem. What about the ethics involved? If the person is revived and becomes a brain-stem preparation—and that means he is taking up a sorely needed bed in the ICU—then you've deprived somebody else of that ICU bed, someone else who might have a better chance. That's a godlike decision. Medical school never taught me to play God. And then all—"

I had been rambling on, looking out through the dark trees, putting these thoughts together for the first time. In some ways I was talking only to myself, and when I turned and looked at Nancy she exploded, stopping me in the middle of a sentence.

"You're an unbelievable egotist!" she said.

"I don't think so. I just live in the real world."

"To me you're an egotist—cold, inhuman, unethical, immoral, and without empathy. And those are not traits I look for in a doctor." She could really lay it on when she wanted to.

"Look here, Nancy, what I've told you is the truth, and it's not just my truth. I'm a composite of most of the interns I know."

"Then the whole bunch of you ought to be thrown out."

"Right on, baby! If you feel so strongly about it, why don't you organize a sit-in at the ER? Compassion's a cheap commodity when you get eight hours of sleep a night. Most nights

I get less than half that much. The rest of the time I spend checking Mrs. Pushbottom's itchy hemorrhoids. Don't you moralize at me from your easy chair."

And so it went, ending with both of us steaming with anger. I left after a halfhearted promise to call her sometime.

Back in my geometric, all-white room, I lay fuming, all keyed up, with less than nine hours before the ER holocaust was to begin again. Sleep was clearly out of the question. I called the lab, and Joyce answered. Could she come by at eleven? She said she would, and I felt better.

Day 307

General Surgery: Private Teaching Service

To an intern in medical practice during the latter half of the twentieth century, Alexander Graham Bell is the arch villain of all time. The blame, of course, must be spread a bit wider, to include not only the man who invented the telephone, but also the sadist who designed the ring. And then all those fellows working for Ma Bell who perpetuate the jangle—they're in it, too. How did hospitals function before the invention of the telephone? I often thought of myself, nowadays, as a mere extension of that little piece of black plastic. It was every bit as terrifying as the ambulance, and a good bit more sudden—always somehow expected in the back of my mind, and yet at the same time coming on me unawares. In all the world, there is no sound like it for disturbing the peace.

My peace just then consisted of falling gently asleep beside Karen Christie in her apartment after, I trust, a mutually satisfying encounter. When the telephone rang at 2:00 A.M., we both reached. I let her have it—not because it was probably for her. Since I was on call, it would more likely be the hospital night operator extending me an invitation to return to those corridors. But it might have been Karen's so-called boyfriend.

Indeed it was the hospital operator, who put me through to a nurse. "Doctor, would you come immediately? One of Dr. Jarvis's private patients is having trouble breathing, and Dr. Jarvis wants you to handle it."

Rolling over on my back, I stared at the ceiling and cursed inwardly, holding the telephone away from my ear. Dr. Jarvis I knew all too well. He was none other than our old friend the Supercharger, famous for his OR butchery, especially on

128

breast biopsies. "Are you still there, Doctor?" the nurse intoned.

"Yes, Nurse, I'm still here. Does Dr. Jarvis plan to come in?"

"I don't know, Doctor."

Typical. Not only of the Supercharger, but of most private doctors affiliated with the hospital. The intern would go to see the patient, work up a recommendation, and phone the private doctor, who, of course, would tell the intern to do what he thought best. On most such occasions these guys didn't even bother with the amenities. One time I had spent about an hour going over one of the Supercharger's cases. When I called in my report, Supercharger had stepped out of his office and I had to leave a message with his secretary for him to ring me back. He rang back, all right, but to the floor nurse, not me. When she told him I wanted urgently to speak with him, he said he didn't have time to talk to every intern in the hospital. Rush, rush, for a few more bucks—that was the Supercharger's game.

Supercharger had another endearing habit. He admitted almost all his patients on the so-called teaching program. One might naturally think that a teaching program would in fact teach, at least a little. God knows, we interns were in need of it. In practice, the teaching program was a grim joke. It meant only that I or one of the other interns did the patient's whole admission history and physical—the "scut" work. As a reward, we might be allowed to do the discharge note as well. But in between we weren't allowed to fool with the orders, and in the operating room our contribution consisted of holding retractors, removing warts, and perhaps tying a few knots, if the doctor was in a condescending mood.

The ultimate in Supercharger's gall had occurred earlier, on that breast biopsy, the one he mauled so badly. On the admitting chart, giving the particulars of the case, he had written a little note saying that when the house staff—meaning the intern—worked the case up, he was *not* to examine the breasts. Now, how was I supposed to do an adequate history and physical on a breast-biopsy case without examining the breasts? Farcical. And now he wanted me to pop over at two in the morning to straighten out another of his messes.

The nurse was still waiting on the line.

"Has the patient had surgery?" I asked.

"Yes, this morning. A hernia repair," she replied. "And he's

not in good shape. The breathing difficulty has been going on
for several hours."

"All right, I'll be over to see him in a few minutes. Meanwhile, have a portable X-ray machine brought to the room and
get a chest film. And get me some blood for a complete blood
count, and be sure there's a positive-pressure breathing machine and an EKG machine on the floor."

I didn't want to wait the rest of the night for that stuff.
Maybe I wouldn't need it, but all the better if it was there anyway. When I got out of bed, Karen didn't budge. Not that it
mattered. As I put on my clothes, I thought again what a convenience she was. Her apartment was just across the street
from the hospital, even closer than my room in the quarters. It
held all the creature comforts—television set, record player, a
refrigerator well supplied with beer and cold cuts.

Karen and I had started seeing one another four months
earlier, just after I had looked at her unusual pelvic X-ray the
night she fell down the hospital stairs. Right after that she had
been moved to a day shift, where we met again and started
having coffee breaks together. One thing led to another, and
going to her apartment became a habit—just about the time
Joyce stopped being one.

Joyce, who'd been switched to the day shift, too, began
wanting to play the tourist, make all the night spots. With that
came some pressure to meet her parents and an increasing dis-
taste for those surreptitious leave-takings in the early-morning
hours. I tried to go along with her, but her roommate, the TV
addict, was still there, and our relationship, which hadn't been
very healthy to begin with, finally went completely sour. In
any case, Joyce and I decided to cool it a while, to give ourselves a chance to think.

Karen did have another boyfriend, who continued to puzzle
me. She saw him every now and again, perhaps two or three
times a week, when they would go to a movie or even to a
night club. She said that this fellow wanted to marry her, but
she couldn't make up her mind. I didn't know him, or much
about him, although we had talked once, briefly and quite by
accident, when he phoned Karen's place. On the whole, I was
not inclined to imperil a good thing by further investigation.

On my way over to see Supercharger's patient, I noticed
that the night was unusually quiet, with almost no wind, although a low bank of clouds hung over the island, obscuring
the sky. It had been raining hard all week. As I walked around
to the west end of the hospital I glanced over into the ER, and

the memory of my blind, exhausted bustle there came rushing back. I could see the usual clumps of activity, with people waiting and nurses appearing for fleeting moments in a seemingly disorganized jumble. It looked a little busier than usual for a Tuesday night, and I hoped that it would stay quiet enough not to require my presence. Whenever I got a night call from the ER, it usually meant an admission—probably surgery, and that could be bad.

The hall of the ward was deathly quiet and dark except for the little night lights that peeked out of the rooms as I walked briskly past them toward the nurses' station. The nurses' station was at the far end of the ward, and as I approached the light gradually grew brighter. It was a familiar sensation to me by now, walking down those dark corridors, the silence broken only by an undercurrent of hospital sounds—the light tinkle of an IV pole, an occasional sleepy moan—sounds that always made me feel I was alone in the world. Other doctors have told me of similar feelings. Actually, I had stopped analyzing the hospital and its effects on me as much as I used to, having become, in a sense, blind to my surroundings. Like a blind man, I took for granted the landmarks, the various doors and turns, and often reached my destination without noting my route or my thoughts along the way.

Some months ago the operator had called me in the early-morning hours for a cardiac arrest. I had gotten up, dressed, and run all the way over to the hospital before I realized that she had forgotten to tell me where the patient was, in which ward. Fortunately, I had guessed right about the location—through some sixth sense, you reached the point of being so routinized that when you were awakened you automatically plugged in the right information without being told.

This had its occasional disadvantages—as, for instance, on one of the frequent night calls to see a patient who had fallen out of bed. I made the automatic, insensate run to the ward and found him there, in good shape, of course. After calling his doctor, I left an order for an injection of Seconal, to be sure he'd sleep, and then plodded back to bed. All without ever coming fully awake. The same nurse called just a little later to say that the patient had fallen again, this time down a flight of stairs. So I got up again, plugged in the ward, and started off. In the middle of the journey, while climbing a flight of stairs, I stumbled across an inert mass lying on the landing. Standing there, dazed, I took fully ten seconds to re-program myself to the fact that lying before me was the pa-

tient I had come to see. He should have been on the floor
above! But, of course, he was where he was because he had
fallen downstairs. Being totally limp during the fall, he hadn't
hurt himself a bit. It turned out that all his shots—the painkiller, his antihistamine, his muscle relaxant, and my Seconal order—had been given simultaneously by the nurse and had tak-
en effect at the same time, just as he took the first downward
step.

I didn't always walk around in a fog. I simply developed an
uncanny ability to continue sleeping while on the way to do
some stupid job in the middle of the night. It was different
when I got called for something serious, or when I was angry.
But since our hospital suffered from an epidemic of patients
who habitually fell out of bed, I learned to carry out that mis-
sion only half-awake.

The nurses' station seemed as bright as a television studio
after that long walk in the dark. The nurse was effusively glad
to see me and ticked off what she had done. The blood had
been sent up and the X ray taken, and the EKG and positive-
pressure breathing machines were both standing ready in the patient's room. I took the chart from her hand and scanned the
work-up, which, of course, had been done by a fellow intern.
A box of chocolates beckoned from the nearby desk, and I
popped a couple in my mouth. Temperature was normal.
Blood pressure was up and pulse very high. The rum-cherry
centers were particularly good. I could find nothing to explain
the breathing trouble. All seemed more or less normal for a recent hernia operation.

I turned back down the hall and retraced my steps almost to
the end. Entering the room, I snapped on the light, illuminat-
ing a pale-looking man propped up in bed and forcibly inhal-
ing with each breath. As I got closer I could see that he was
quite diaphoretic, with beads of perspiration glistening on his
forehead. He glanced at me for a second and then looked off,
as if he had to concentrate on his breathing. Squinting, I realized I could see the apartment building next door, and Karen's
window, the second from the right on the third floor. I wondered if she knew I was gone.

With my stethoscope in my ears, I pushed the patient forward and listened to his lung fields. The breath sounds were
clear—no popping, no crackles, no rhonchi, no wheezing.
Nothing there. Perhaps his lung fields sounded a little high;
that seemed to go along with the fact that his abdomen was
swollen and rather firm. It was not tender, however. Listening

to his abdomen, I heard the familiar, reassuring gurgles. The heart sounds were normal; he had no signs of cardiac failure. About all that remained was to see if his stomach was full of air. Gastric dilatation was a frequent problem after general anesthesia. I told the nurse to get a nasogastric tube, and meanwhile I hooked up the EKG machine. These EKG contraptions were a source of irritation to me whenever I tried to use one at night, with no technicians around to help. Since I could never seem to get a good electrical ground, the tracing would wander all over the page. But I got this one going okay by hooking the ground wire to the drainpipe of the sink, and I took a tracing while the patient lay there still puffing hard. The nurse had returned with the nasogastric tube before I finished with the EKG. As I greased the tube, I couldn't help thinking of that doctor sleeping away at home while I was putting in his NG tube.

One thing had stayed with me, even grown stronger, over the past ten months—the satisfaction in achieving a quick, desired result—and I felt relieved when I evacuated a large quantity of fluid and air from the patient's stomach. My relief was minimal, however, compared to his. He was still having some troubles, but his breathing was much easier. When he thanked me very much, it took him two breaths to get the phrase out. I listened to his lungs again, just to make sure that there wasn't any fluid in them. They were clear. His legs were normal, too, showing neither edema nor any suggestion of thrombophlebitis. Peeking under the dressing, I thought his incision looked fine, without excessive drainage. I told the nurse to get a suction machine for the NG tube and hook it up, while I went back to the nurses' station with the EKG.

I was still pretty shaky at reading EKG's, but his looked okay to me. At least, there were no arrhythmias. Possibly there was some slight suggestion of right heart strain with the S wave, but nothing drastic. As a precautionary measure, I decided to call the medical resident for support on the EKG reading. After a rather awkward minute or so during which I explained the situation and the resident listened, he finally said he wouldn't come down to see the EKG because it involved a private surgical patient.

I could understand his reluctance. It resembled mine when the medical intern on duty called me at night for help with a cutdown or something else on a private medical patient. Had the attendings made us feel it was a matter of reciprocal co-operation, each fellow holding up his end, those nasty little jobs would have been easier to take. But in American medicine, much of the difference between an intern and a full-fledged doctor is literally the difference between night and day. They would let us do virtually anything at all after the sun went down, when teaching was nonexistent, but nothing during the day, when we might learn something. As always, a few pleasant exceptions proved the rule—but damn few.

Early in my internship, I had been rather naïve about this master-slave relationship, knowing nothing of my rights. Until it wore me out, I tried to see every patient, private or charity, on the teaching service or not, no matter how minor the complaint. Finally, however, it was a question of my survival. Nowadays, whenever I got called at night for some routine matter concerning a private patient—a temperature elevation, for instance—I always asked the name of the doctor. If he was on the wrong side of the answer—and most of them were—I told the nurse to call him back and say that interns are not required to see private cases except in emergencies. This was not true, of course, for private cases on the teaching service. Then I had to go no matter who the doctor was.

Doctors of middle age or older were fond of making invidious comparisons between our supposedly soft life and their Spartan days way back when. To hear them tell it, thirty years ago an intern lived well below the poverty line. Our sumptuous salaries, which I reckoned to be about half what was paid to a plumber's assistant, simply enraged them. What is the world coming to? they would say. Why, we had to do work-ups on every patient, no matter what his status, and we never slept, and we didn't have all these fancy machines, and so forth and so on. Their attitude toward us was a simple matter of venom: they had suffered, and so would we. Thus does medical education in this enlightened time creep from generation to generation; each takes its sweet revenge.

Where was the patient in all this? Caught right in the middle —a most uncomfortable place, with the shells and bombs of medical warfare landing all around him.

Curiously, most of the legislation coming out of Washington was only making the situation worse. The thrust was very strongly toward providing more and more private care at government expense, but without any attempt either to control the quality of the medical care or to educate the potential patient. Suddenly armed with dollar power, previously indigent patients were being thrust on the medical market with no notion whatsoever of how to choose a doctor, and somehow, as if by mischievous grand design, they seemed to flock toward those marginally competent M.D.'s whose practice depended on volume, not quality. The immediate result was that the kinds of patients whom the interns and residents used to care for were now appearing on the private floors under the tender care of doctors who, like the Supercharger, did not know how to treat, let alone teach. Even old Roso had appeared again, for some minor complaint, under the care of a private physician who didn't want the house staff nosing in the chart. Left stranded by the tide of money, the interns were forced into the clutches of these archaic doctors in order to gain experience in dealing with certain types of cases. Everybody suffered. In years past, when these patients were admitted on the staff service, they were taken care of with the help of the best specialists around. It would turn out, logically, that the most capable and knowledgeable attendings were also on the staff teaching service, because the hospital teaching committee and the house staff selected the best they could get. And the attendings who were most interested in teaching were almost invariably the most knowledgeable. If ever I was called at night to see one of their patients, I went, no matter what the reason.

But now, instead of being admitted on the staff service, where they were invaluable for teaching purposes and at the same time got better medical attention than anybody else in the hospital, these former staff patients were all flocking to the Neanderthals. How could something as vital as medical education and care get so screwed up? It seemed especially scary to me in respect to surgery, and it certainly made the English, the Swedes, and the Germans seem enlightened. They allow only specialists to operate in their hospitals. In the United States, any screwball with a medical diploma can perform any kind of surgery he wants to, as long as the hospital allows it. I knew how inadequate my medical-school training had been with respect to patient care; yet I also knew that I could get a license to practice medicine and surgery in any of the fifty states. What is it in the American psyche that allows us to spend billions policing the globe and yet makes us willing to put up with a criminally backward medical system? Like every other important question during my internship, this one was finally pushed aside by exhaustion. I began to accept the situation as if there were no alternative. In fact, there is no alternative at present. Now the problem only popped into my head when trouble was brewing, and I knew I would have plenty of trouble with the Supercharger over those X rays and other tests I had ordered on his hernia repair. I wondered again why I didn't go into research.

Before I called Supercharger and woke him up, I wanted a look at the X ray that had been taken on the portable machine. He'd probably explode when he found out about it in the morning, but I couldn't have cared less.

The hall got darker and darker as I retraced my steps and plodded through the hospital labyrinth on my way to X-ray. It was so silent and dark when I got there that I could not find the technician. Finally, in desperation, I picked up a telephone and dialed one of the numbers of the X-ray department. All around me, about a dozen phones came to life. Someplace, somebody answered one, silencing the others. I told the speaker that I was in his department and wanted to see a portable he had taken only an hour or so ago, whereupon he appeared through a door not ten feet away, blinking and tucking in his shirt. I followed him to a bunch of view boxes, waiting while he sifted through a stack of negatives.

One thing about the X-ray department—it never seemed to know where anything was. This X ray was less than an hour old, and still he couldn't find it. He said he couldn't understand it. They always said that, and I had to agree with them. The secretaries during the day were good at finding the blasted things, but they were the only ones. As the technician went through one stack of film after another, I leaned back against the counter and waited. It was like watching an endless replay of an incomplete pass. Finally he pulled one film from a bunch that were supposed to have already been read. Flicking it up into the X-ray view box, he turned on the light, which blinked a couple of times and then stayed on. The film was on backwards, so I turned it around.

It was a mess—the X ray, not the patient. Portable films were not, in fact, very good at all, and I was sure the radiologist would tell me that it had been ridiculous to order portables when the patient could have been sent upstairs to get a good film. I never tried to explain that a portable was justified because I could order it by phone from my room and then have it—provided it wasn't lost—by the time I reached the patient. Otherwise I would end up sitting on my ass for an hour in the middle of the night waiting while the patient had a regular shot. This type of reasoning didn't make much sense to someone—a radiologist, say—who slept all night long.

This X ray looked normal for a portable, which is to say that it was a blurred smudge except for the gas in the stomach and the fact that the diaphragm appeared elevated. Even that was misleading, because with the guy lying in bed you could never be sure from what angle the X-ray technician had taken the shot. Anyway, it looked all right.

Next I got the lab technician on the telephone and asked for the blood-count results. The blood lab was pretty good; usually they found test results right away. But tonight the technician there wanted my identification, because the hospital was not allowed to give out such information to unauthorized people. What a ridiculous question! Who else would be calling up about a stat blood count at three o'clock in the morning? I identified myself as Ringo Starr, which seemed to satisfy the girl. The blood count was normal, too.

Armed with all this information, I dialed the Supercharger. The sound of the phone ringing on the other end was a delight to my ears. Four, five, six times it rang. Supercharger, true to his reputation, was a deep sleeper. Finally he answered.

"This is Dr. Peters at the hospital. I've seen your patient, the hernia who was having trouble breathing."

"Well, how is he?"

"Much better, Doctor. His stomach was badly dilated, and I evacuated almost a pint of fluid and a bunch of gas by putting down a nasogastric tube."

"Yes, I thought that was the trouble."

What a fake, I thought, convinced that Supercharger hadn't had any notion about where the trouble might lie. I went on. "I thought it advisable to check out his other systems, too, so I have the results of a blood count, chest X ray, and EKG. They look acceptable. Everything but the diaphragm, which—"

A blast came through the telephone. "My God, boy, you don't need all those crutches. My patient isn't a millionaire, and this isn't the Mayo Clinic. What the hell are you doing? I could have told you what was wrong by using nothing more than a stethoscope and a little percussion. You kids think the world was made for machines. Back when I was doing your job, we didn't . . ." I could imagine his face getting red, the veins standing out on his neck. I sincerely hoped he would have insomnia for the rest of the night.

"And what have you done about the NG tube, Peters?"

"I put it on suction, Doctor, and left it in."

"Don't you know anything? He'll just get pneumonia, with that thing down him. Get it out of there right now."

"But, Doctor, the patient is still short of breath, and I'm afraid his stomach will dilate again right away."

"Don't argue with me. Get it out. None of my hernia patients are to have NG tubes. That's one of my basic rules, Peters, basic." Click. I was holding a dead telephone.

I went back to the ward and pulled the tube out. The patient was still struggling for breath, but not as badly as before. As I was leaving a nurse came in, obviously a little surprised and nervous to see me still there. She held a needle. Somewhat guiltily, she said that the Supercharger had called and ordered more sedative. I was so pissed off I didn't even ask her what it was; I just left.

Now I had to decide where to go, my room or Karen's apartment. The latter didn't make sense, because Karen was surely sound asleep. Besides, none of my shaving stuff was there—a policy we followed to avoid explanations to the other fellow. If I went back to my own room, I could shave when I got up in the morning, a few hours from now. It was after three. So I returned to my quarters and called the night operator to tell her I was not at the other number any more. She said she understood. I wondered how much she understood.

I was hardly down on the pillow when the phone rang again. Sweet Jesus, I thought, probably an ER admission. What a bitch of a Tuesday night! But it was the same nurse saying that the hernia patient was much worse again, and the private doctor wanted me to see him again immediately. I was getting tired of this routine—up, down, up, down, seeing patients for whom my responsibility was so muddled and indistinct that I never knew where I stood. The ironies of the situation were considerable. Here the Supercharger had no sooner finished bawling me out for ordering some laboratory tests and for leaving in the NG tube than he had called the nurse—not me—to give some medication; and now he wanted me to see the patient again. It didn't make any sense until you realized that you were just a convenient means of keeping the doctor up on his sleep. The patient obviously wasn't getting what he was paying for. And I? Well, I was getting less than zero teaching. Someday, if I was lucky, I could look forward to being a doctor like him and not giving a shit about the intern, the patient, or medical care in general.

So, for me, it was down the elevator again, through the long hall, into the dark blue light that enveloped the sleeping hospital, my footsteps making distinct clicking noises, as if in a vacuum. It was peaceful now, but come seven-thirty I would be in poor shape for surgery. I felt like checking myself into the hospital for a good going-over. I had lost fifteen pounds since the first day of internship.

Suddenly, from behind me, the world was shattered by frantic sounds of glass and metal hitting against each other. Turning around, I saw the ER intern coming at a run toward me in the blue light of the hall, clutching his laryngoscope and an endotracheal tube. A nurse behind him pushed the tinkling crash cart.

"Cardiac arrest," he panted, motioning for me to follow. We both ran now, and I wondered if it was the hernia patient.

"Which floor?" I asked.

"The private surgical ward, this floor." He went headlong through the swinging doors. A light shone from the room where I had been before, and we rushed in, filling it up. The patient was on the floor near the sink. He had pulled the IV out of his arm and gotten out of bed. Two nurses were there, one trying to give closed-chest massage. I grabbed the board brought in by the nurse and threw it on the bed to make a firm surface for the massage.

"Put him up here," I yelled, and the four of us lifted him onto the board. There was no pulse, no respiratory effort. His eyes were open, with widely dilated pupils, and his mouth was grotesquely agape. The ER intern slapped the chest very hard; no response. I pinched his nose, sealed my mouth over his, and blew in. There was no resistance, and the chest rose slightly. I breathed into him again and then motioned for the laryngoscope, while the ER intern began to give cardiac massage, getting up on the bed and kneeling beside the patient to do it. Every time he pushed on the chest, the patient's head bounced violently.

"Can you hold the head still?" I asked one of the nurses. She tried, but couldn't really. Between bounces, I slid the laryngoscope through his mouth and down into his throat. The epiglottis alternated in and out of view. Advancing the tip farther, I pulled up, and the 'scope clanked against his teeth. Nothing. I couldn't orient myself in the red folds of mucus membrane. Quickly taking out the 'scope, I blew in a few more breaths between compressions. The ER intern was getting nice sternal excursions; the breastbone was moving in and out about two inches, undoubtedly forcing blood through the heart quite well. I tried with the laryngoscope again, down to the epiglottis, tip of the 'scope up, then in farther, and down. There, I saw the cords for a second.

"The endotracheal tube." A nurse handed it to me. I didn't

take my eyes away from his throat. "Push on his larynx." I motioned to the neck. The nurse pushed. "Harder." Then I saw the cords again and pushed in the tube. "The Ambu bag." I hooked up the Ambu breathing bag and watched his chest as I compressed it. Instead of the chest rising, the stomach bulged a little. "Damn! Missed it." I pulled the tube out, put my mouth over the patient's again, and blew, twice more. Then the laryngoscope again. I *had* to get it this time. "Push again on his larynx." I pulled up very strongly, and then I could see the cords between each chest compression. "Hold it. Okay, stop the compression." The ER intern interrupted his rhythm for a second while I slid in the tube; then he immediately recommenced the massage. With the Ambu bag attached and compressed, the chest rose nicely. The ER nurse had put in the needle leads for the EKG, and we had a blip on the oscilloscope. It wasn't grounded very well.

"Put the EKG on lead two," the ER intern said. That was better. I was compressing the Ambu when a nurse-anesthetist arrived. She took over the Ambu.

"Medicut." The nurse gave me a catheter, and I put a piece of rubber very tightly around his left upper arm. Medicuts can be tricky, especially when you're in a hurry, but they're much faster than cutdowns, because you put the medicut into the vein by just pushing it through the skin rather than making an incision as with the cutdown. I pushed the medicut into the patient's arm and advanced it until I thought I was in the vein; fortunately blood came back into the syringe—but that was only half the battle. I pushed the plastic catheter forward on the needle, hoping it would remain within the lumen of the vein. Then, by wiggling the needle back and forth, I attempted to advance the catheter still farther into the vein. When I pulled out the needle, some dark brownish red blood flowed through the catheter over his arm and onto the bed. A nurse was still struggling with the plastic tubing from the IV bottle. I just let the blood flow; it didn't make any difference. After securing the end of the tubing to the catheter, I could see the blood disappear from the catheter, running back into the vein as the IV started up. Snapping off the rubber tourniquet, I watched the drip, and opened it all the way until it was running fine. "Tape." I secured the catheter to the arm. The EKG still showed rapid but coarse fibrillation. "Epinephrine," I barked. I thought a heart stimulant might smooth out the fibrillation, before we tried to change it electrically to a regular heartbeat.

"How about directly into the heart?" The ER intern suggested.

"Let's try just IV first." I wasn't very confident of that intracardiac method. The nurse gave me a syringe and said it was 1:1,000 diluted to 10 cc. I injected it rapidly into the new IV site through a small length of rubber tubing, being careful to compress the distal plastic tubing to keep the epinephrine from going back into the IV bottle. "Bicarbonate," I said to the nurse, holding out my free hand. The nurse gave me a syringe, saying it held 44 milliequivalents. "How are you doing with the pumping?" I asked the ER intern.

"I'm fine," he answered.

I injected the bicarbonate into the same IV site—and pricked my finger in the process by putting the needle all the way through the little rubber section. Sucking my index finger, I watched the EKG. Slowly it began to show stronger fibrillation.

"How about defibrillating now?" the ER intern suggested. The defibrillator was all charged up. A nurse held the paddles, with a smear of conductant on each one. Stopping his pumping, the ER intern took the paddles, placing one over the heart and one to the side of the chest. "Away from the bed!" The nurse-anesthetist let go of the Ambu. Wham! The patient jumped, his arms fluttered, and the EKG blip was gone. When it came back, it was just about the same. A medical resident arrived breathlessly and quickly got oriented.

"Hang up a 5-per-cent bicarbonate on the IV and give me some xylocaine." The nurse gave the medical resident 50 mg. of xylocaine. He handed it to me, and I injected it. We defibrillated him again. In fact, we tried about four times before the fibrillation disappeared. But instead of a normal cardiac rhythm taking over, all evidence of activity in the heart disappeared, as the electronic blip on the EKG screen became perfectly flat.

"Damn! Asystole," said the resident, watching the blip.

Epinephrine, isuprel, atropine, pacemaker: we tried all the stuff we had. Meanwhile, the man's pupils came down to about normal size from the widely dilated state they'd been in when we first started. At least that meant that oxygen was getting to his brain, that our cardiac massage was effective.

Another intern arrived, taking over the massage part so the ER intern could go back to his primary duty, poor fellow. Then I took a turn at the massage. "How about calcium?" the other intern suggested. The resident injected some calcium. I asked for another nasogastric tube, but didn't get to put it down until the intern could relieve me at the massage. There wasn't much in his stomach except some gas, and that was probably just what I had pushed in there earlier by mistake, through the misplaced endotracheal tube. I told the resident that this patient was the one whose EKG I had called him about earlier. I also told him that the portable X ray of the chest was generally clear.

Looking behind me, I was surprised to see the Supercharger standing there quietly watching our feverish activity. I guess the nurses had called him. He didn't say a word. The resident injected the heart several times with intracardiac epinephrine. Still we couldn't break the asystole, and we were running out of options. Pumping and breathing, pumping and breathing, for fifteen minutes more we watched the machine trace a straight line across the oscilloscope.

"All right, that's enough. Stop now." It was the Supercharger finally speaking, after standing by in silence for almost thirty minutes. His words surprised us and failed to penetrate our routine, so that we didn't stop right away, but kept on pumping and breathing as if he hadn't said anything.

"That's enough," he repeated. The nurse-anesthetist compressing the Ambu was the first to stop. Then the intern, who happened to be massaging at the time. All of us were tired by then, thinking about getting back to bed, and conscious of the fact that we might have stopped earlier if the man's pupils hadn't reduced so well. Constriction of the pupils is one of the signs of revival; that had kept us going. But clearly this time it had been a false sign. So we stopped, and the man was dead. The Supercharger walked out and disappeared down the corridor toward the nurses' station, where he did the paper-work chores and called the relatives. The nurses unhooked the EKG machine, while I got out a large intracardiac needle.

"How are you at hitting the heart?" I asked the other intern.

"I've hit it one hundred per cent, but only on two tries," he answered.

"I'm only doing about fifty per cent," I confessed. After attaching a 10-cc. syringe to the needle, I walked over to the patient and felt for the transverse ridge called the angle of Louis, about midway down the breastbone. This oriented me with respect to the rib cage. It was then a simple matter to find the fourth interspace on the left. The needle went in quite easily, and when I drew back on the plunger the needle filled with blood. Bull's-eye.

"I think my problem has been that I've been using the third interspace," I ventured. I tried it again, this time in the third interspace, and when I withdrew no blood appeared. "That's it. Okay, you have a go." I handed him the syringe, and he got the heart right away.

I pulled the endotracheal tube out of the dead man, wiping the rather thick mucus on the tip off onto the sheet, where it left a gray trail. "This guy was really hard to get an endotracheal tube into. Want to try?" Gingerly holding the tube between my thumb and index finger, I advanced it toward the other intern. I was pretty good at entubating now, because I had made it a point over the last few months to practice whenever we had an unsuccessful resuscitation like this one, which happened pretty often. He took the laryngoscope and slipped it in. He said he couldn't see anything. I looked over his shoulder and could tell he wasn't lifting enough with the point of the blade. "Lift until you think you're going to dislocate his jaw." His arm quivered as he strained. Still something wrong. "Let me try." I pulled up, and then with my right hand I pushed down on his larynx. The cords came into view. "He has a pretty oblique angle there. Try it again, but push a little on the larynx." The nurse stuck her head in, saying she needed the 'scope so she could return the crash car to the ER. With a wave of my hand, I staved her off for a few seconds, while I looked over the other intern's shoulder. A sound of satisfaction came out of him as he finally saw the vocal cords. Then, walking out, he handed the 'scope to the nurse, who clucked in disapproval.

Suddenly I was alone as the activity moved on, like some grim parade, to the living in other parts of the hospital. I wondered again whether to go to Karen's place or mine. It was a lonely time, especially because the man had died. I had been one of the last people to see him alive. But I had done everything I could—we all had—I guessed we had given it a good try. Besides, it was the Supercharger who had made me take the NG tube out and who had given him some sort of drug. So it wasn't my fault, though he probably thought it was. No doubt he would blame it on all those expensive tests. That was one of the troubles with the setup for private patients. I was available to see the patient but had no real responsibility, whereas the attending had the ultimate responsibility but was not on the scene. That made my position ambiguous, to say the least. It was too complicated for 4:00 A.M. Still, I was curious about Supercharger's last injection. The nurse had said it was a sedative. If I went back to look at the chart, I'd have to see the bastard again, and he'd probably have some timely comments about expensive blood counts. But, going up the hall, I decided it was worth the risk.

The Supercharger was gone already. That was a relief; it was also an indication of his interest in teaching. Seconal, the order sheet said. It added nothing to what I knew. Reading through the work-up again, I noted that the man did not have a history of heart trouble. The stomach and kidneys were normal, too. Then I read that the hernia had been a huge, basketball type of problem; yet that didn't seem to explain his course. Something had made him go into respiratory failure ultimately leading to heart failure. The gastric distention I had relieved must have added to the problem, but it had not caused it. What about the anesthesia? I wondered. Turning to the anesthesia record, I read that it had been pentothal induction, maintenance nitrous oxide, no complications. I vainly struggled to pull in all the loose pieces, but I couldn't work through the maze. I was too exhausted. Better hurry back to bed, I thought cynically, so as to be there when the operator calls to wake me up for the day. Very funny.

But it was a bad, bad Tuesday night. Tuesday nights were generally active, Like Monday nights, since both Monday and Tuesday always had full operating schedules, and that meant a lot of nighttime dressing, pain, and drain problems; still, I usually got *some* sleep. Not this time; hardly had I put my head against the pillow when the phone rang again. It was the OR; a case was coming up for amputation, and I was needed to assist.

There was something particularly upsetting to me about an amputation, especially of the leg. An appendectomy or a cholecystectomy or any of the other interior operations left the surface of the person intact. But lifting a foot and a lower leg from the table and carrying them away from the person they belonged to was an irreversible act of alteration. No matter how jaded I became, I was never able to look upon the removal of a human limb as just another medical procedure.

But it had to be done. So I got up again, with the most complete lack of motivation, and dragged myself over to the OR. On with the scrub suit, the hat, and the mask. Once the mask was on, I pulled it down off my face, leaving the strings tied, and studied myself in the mirror. I hardly recognized the wasted man who stared back at me.

Happily, when I got to the operating room proper I found

that it was not to be an amputation, after all, but, rather, an attempt to save a leg whose knee had been crushed by a truck. Only the nerve and vein were intact, spanning the gap where the knee had been. The artery, bones—everything else was gone. To my surprise, I found two private surgeons there, both excellent vascular men. I asked if I was needed, since there were two of them, and they answered, "Perhaps." That left me no choice but to scrub and put on a sterile gown and gloves.

My job was to stand at the end of the table facing the anesthesiologist and hold the foot rigid by cupping my hands together around it. Both surgeons, of course, had to be near my end of the table to work on the knee. But they had their backs to me, as usual—especially the surgeon on my left, who was leaning over the table. I couldn't see a damn thing. The clock to my right indicated that it was almost 5:00 A.M. by the time the operation really got under way. From their conversation, I gathered that they were putting in a graft for the main artery, which runs down behind the knee toward the foot. An hour passed as slowly as an hour can, the minute hand creeping around the face of the clock. They got the graft in, and a pulse appeared in the foot, only to fade and disappear after a few minutes. That meant the surgeons had to open the graft and take out a fresh blood clot. They got another pulse, which again faded. Another clot. Open again. Clot. This process went on and on and on. I was absolutely amazed by their cool persistence and patience.

With nothing to do and nothing to see except the clock, and standing there motionless with my hands in one position, I began to get uncontrollably sleepy. The sound of the surgeons' voices wandered in and out of my head, along with the image of the room. Only half-conscious, I fought hard to stay awake, and lost; I fell asleep still holding the foot. I did not fall down. Rather, my head sank slowly until my forehead bumped gently against the shoulder of the surgeon on my left. That brought me awake, so close to the fabric of his gown I could make out the cross weave of individual threads. The surgeon looked around and pushed me back into an upright position with the point of his elbow. Over his mask, cold blue eyes cut at me in clear disapproval. I was beyond caring, but the incident did serve to keep me in the ball game, because it brought back all my pent-up fury.

It was now eight in the morning and here I was, after a sleepless night, with a full schedule of surgery ahead of me, still standing and holding that foot like so much dead weight.

A job for a bunch of sandbags. In fact, sandbags would have done a better job; they do not sag or get angry. This was not the first time I had fallen asleep in the OR. Helping once on a thyroid case after a night without sleep, I had drifted away while holding the retractors. For only an instant, I think, because I had suddenly given one of those falling-asleep jerks, which startled the surgeon. He had asked, only partly in jest, if I was about to have an epileptic fit. But I don't think that surgeon knew I had fallen asleep. This one did, and he was irritated, although he and his sidekick continued to ignore me. Finally, when everything was finished and I was preparing to leave, the surgeon let me have it. "Well, Peters, if falling asleep during a case indicates your interest in surgery, I think the fact should be brought to the attention of the board." Rather than tell him to go to hell, I backed all the way down and pleaded lack of sleep and not being able to see the operative field. He was not impressed. "I'd advise you not to let it happen again." "No, sir." I walked out, harboring ineffectual, murderous thoughts.

The regular surgical schedule had begun more than an hour before. In fact, I had missed my first case, which didn't upset me much. It was a second assistant's spot on a cholecystectomy, totally routine. Besides, I was scheduled for two more of them that afternoon. Sneaking down to the surgeons' lounge, I scrounged a few slices of bread, my first food in about fifteen hours. As for sleep, I wasn't much better off—one hour during the last twenty-six. I felt a little weak. The thought of another full day in surgery was not cheering.

In the lounge I was bearded by an irritated chief resident who demanded to know where I had been during rounds. Early on, an intern learns the impossibility of pleasing everybody. Lately, however, I was striking out every time up and pleasing nobody, least of all myself. I reported to the chief resident on the few staff patients I had. Since I was on the private teaching service, I didn't have many staff patients—only those whose surgery I'd helped with. Both hernias were doing fine; the gastrectomy was already eating; the veins were okay and walking; and neither hemorrhoid had managed a BM. The disease paraded verbally out of me, unattached to personal names or thoughts.

I almost forgot to mention the aneurysm patient whom we had scheduled for aortography that day. He had been sent to us from one of the outer islands because his X ray showed a suspicious shadow in the left lung field. It was probably an aneurysm, a bulge in his major artery. Without surgery, such an aneurysm generally bursts in six months or so, and the patient quickly bleeds to death. So it was important to act quickly, and to be sure of the diagnosis, which we could do best by making an aortogram. This fairly simple procedure took place in X-ray, where radiopaque dye would be injected into the man's artery just above the heart. For a few moments, before the blood swept it away, the dye would outline the shape of the artery, and X rays taken in rapid sequence would pick up an imperfection. Only then would we know whether surgery was necessary. Since I had done the history and physical on the man, I wanted to be there, and I asked the chief resident about it. "Sure," he said. "If the surgical schedule permits."

That part of the system had not changed during the past nine months. We interns were still bounced back and forth between cases at the whim of the surgical schedule; too often, we had to miss seeing our own patients. If you work a patient up, you should stay with him and follow him through all his diagnostic procedures and his surgery. No one would care to argue against that, either from an academic point of view or from the standpoint of the patient's good. Nevertheless, whenever someone needed an extra pair of hands on a gall-bladder attempt (our *minds*, it seemed, were never in demand), we were sacrificed, without regard to the educational aspect or to the psychological effect on our own patients. It was another way to impress upon us how very dispensable we were.

The chief resident disappeared, and a few minutes later I got a call from the surgical desk telling me that he had assigned me to help on a gastrectomy that was already under way. Apparently those extra hands were needed. I finished my stale bread and plodded once more into the OR area, mentally mapping out the rest of my day in surgery. After the present gastrectomy, I was scheduled for a nephrectomy—a kidney removal—in Room 10, and then the two cholecystectomies. As I passed Room 10 I realized the nephrectomy was already under way and that I would miss it. Nakano, another intern, was scrubbing on the case. Lucky bastard. That nephrectomy was more interesting to me than all the other cases put together. The patient had a tumor on his kidney, and the tumor had to be removed, even though it was not malignant. Until very recently, the surgeon on such a case would have been forced to take out the whole kidney; now, with advanced radiology, such tumors could be "mapped" very accurately, so that only the involved portion need be cut away. Ah, well, another time. I continued down the corridor toward my gastrectomy assignment. Normally I would also have been dismayed at the prospect of back-to-back cholecystectomies. But today I was in for a bit of luck, because both were scheduled with a good teaching surgeon. This man was like an oasis in a desert of conservatism. Of course, there was always a chance that the gastrectomy I was joining now would run over into the first cholecystectomy with the teaching surgeon. I hoped not.

Hardly noticing the activity around me, I strolled slowly down toward Room 4, in no hurry, forcing myself all the way. A glance at the operating schedule posted on the bulletin board increased my dismay. Like the Supercharger, this G.P. was a man of advanced age, small skill, and no modesty. He was also given to interminable and egotistical stories about his travail in the early days. Apparently, he had for years carried most of the burden of American medical service on his shoulders, performing feats of skill and endurance that blew the mind. At least, they blew his mind. A puckish resident had once dubbed him Hercules, and the name stuck. Hercules was another who always admitted his patients on the teaching service, so that the house staff would do histories and physicals for him. If you ever ordered an X ray, or even an extra blood count, he'd hit the ceiling, bawling you out for extravagant utilization of costly laboratory tests. Apparently 99 per cent of the lab tests had been developed since he graduated from medical school about the time the Curies were beginning to play around with pitchblende. Moreover, he had a favorite habit of prescribing penicillin or tetracycline for every cold that appeared in the ER—a practice that virtually all medical authorities now agree is worse than doing nothing at all. That he was supposed to be one of our teachers was simply a bad joke.

I had scrubbed with Hercules several months earlier, on a kidney-stone removal. At the time, he'd just finished reading, so he said, an article in a recent surgical journal recommending a new way to remove kidney stones. I doubted that Hercules read deeply or often, but this article had intrigued him —although he could not seem to remember the name of either the author or the journal, or even where the experiment had been conducted. As he worked down to the kidney, fondling the notion of this new procedure, he had indulged his habit of slicing through arteries indiscriminately and then stepping back to say, "Get that bleeder, boy," hardly interrupting what he was talking about. The resident would scramble around in the wound, dabbing with gauze sponge and hemostats, while the surgeon pontificated.

This new kidney method of Hercules's involved putting a 2–0 chromic suture—a very large thread—through the kidney and then, by holding the suture at both ends and manipulating it somewhat like a blunt knife, sawing back up through the kidney. This was supposed to reduce bleeding. The procedure sounded a bit strange and oversimplified to me. As it turned out, mine was a healthy skepticism. Hercules had forgotten one vital point that the article repeatedly emphasized: before "sawing" with the suture, the surgeon must first gain control of the kidney pedicle—the source of blood to the kidney—so that the blood flow through the organ is essentially stopped. Well, our fearless innovator plunged ahead, making no provision to control the blood flow, but sawing nonchalantly up through the kidney "to minimize bleeding." The result was the worst uncontrolled hemorrhage I have ever seen in an operating room—except for the time the right atrial catheter of a heart-lung machine fell out of the patient. But that was a legitimate mistake. The kidney disaster was not. Blood from the kidney vessels filled the wound instantaneously, overflowing it and soaking the table and all the operating team. We began to pour blood into the man through the IV, as down a deep well. Eight pints later, we had finally clamped down on the kidney, sucked out the wound enough so that the stone could be removed, and put enormous sutures through the kidney cortex. Since the human body holds only about twelve pints of blood, we had practically drained the poor man and filled him up again. It scared hell out of everybody. Even the anesthesiologist—normally in another world up behind the ether screen, with one eye on the automatic breather and both hands on his newspaper—was upset.

Naturally, then, I wasn't looking forward to this gastrectomy with Hercules, whom I could see inside working away as I scrubbed. I hoped he hadn't read any more current literature. A resident named O'Toole was there, too, but no intern was in evidence. As I backed in, surrendering, I could tell the atmosphere was anything but congenial.

"I want a decent clamp," yelled Hercules to the scrub nurse as he threw one over his shoulder against the white tile wall. "Peters, get the hell in here. How is a man supposed to do surgery without any help?" Some of these surgeons took a bit of getting used to. Much of the time they behaved like petulant children, especially when it came to the instruments, which they tended to throw around rather indiscriminately and to use in unexpected ways—such as cutting wire with dissecting scissors. Yet the next time they were handed one of these instruments that they might have damaged themselves, they'd stomp and rage, blaming all their recent bungles on a lack of proper equipment. No one ever said anything about these outbursts. You got used to them after a while.

As I moved in next to Hercules, he clamped my hands around a couple of retractors and said to lift up, not pull back. A familiar line. Actually, I was able to fake it, because there was nothing to retract at the moment. The stomach, which Hercules was working on, sat right on top of the incision in full view. He would need retraction later, while making the connection between the stomach pouch and the beginning of the intestine called the duodenum. I fervently hoped he had already cut the nerves to the stomach that are partially responsible for the secretion of acid. Those vagus nerves wind around the esophagus, and in order for the surgeon to cut them the intern has to hold up the rib cage; I hated that retraction.

Here I was again at my post in the OR watching a minute hand that appeared to be glued in place. As I fought to stay awake, my eyes blurred after each yawn, and my nose itched uncontrollably on the left side, a little below my eye, as if I were being attacked by a subtle, sadistic insect.

The position of my mask was another subtle torture. Each time I yawned it moved a little down my nose, perhaps half an inch. After five yawns it fell completely off my nose and was just covering my mouth. This called into play the circulating nurse. She hopped around to my side and lifted the mask up, touching it ever so carefully to avoid my skin, almost as if my whole face were infectious. Wishing to relieve the itch, I tried several times to push my nose against her hand as she adjusted the mask. But she was too quick for me, and pulled away each time before hand and nose could meet.

Hercules was even more nervous and erratic than usual. None of us around the table could anticipate what his next move might be. Fortunately I was immobilized by the retractors and not expected to contribute otherwise, but poor O'Toole was like a rat in an uncharted maze being called upon to perform impossible feats of anticipation.

"O'Toole, are you with me or against me? Hold that stomach still!" While delivering this rhetorical question, Hercules gave O'Toole's left hand a sharp swat with the Mayo scissors. O'Toole gritted his teeth and adjusted his grip on the stomach.

"For Christ's sake, Peters, haven't you learned how to retract?" He grabbed my wrist for about the sixth time to readjust the retractors, even though retracting had nothing to do with what was going on at the moment. In fact, I wasn't needed; yet he wanted me there. He was like a lot of surgeons, who felt slighted if they weren't assisted by both a resident and an intern, regardless of need. I was a status symbol.

Hercules had rotated in front of me so that I was staring at his back as he began putting in the second layer of sutures on the stomach pouch. I could see neither the operative field nor my own hands.

The anesthesiologist spoke up rather suddenly. "Peters, please don't lean on the patient's chest. You're compromising his ventilation." He pushed my lower back through the ether screen to keep me from crowding the intravenous line. But I had no place to go, being already mashed up against Hercules.

Just then O'Toole stepped abruptly back with a startled expression on his face, holding up his right hand. I could see a few drops of blood dripping out of a neat slice through the rubber glove into the side of his index finger.

"If you had your finger where it was supposed to be it wouldn't have happened, O'Toole. Let's wake up," boomed Hercules.

O'Toole said nothing as he turned to the scrub nurse, who slipped on another glove. I guess he was thankful to be still in possession of the finger.

Despite all, the surgeon somehow finished, and we began to close. One of my jobs was to irrigate with the bulb syringe after the strong, fibrous fascial layer of the abdominal wall had been closed with silk sutures about a quarter of an inch apart. O'Toole and I were feeling frisky by then, and as Hercules was rinsing his hand I raised the syringe up over the wound, over the patient, and shot a stream of warm saline across the table, hitting O'Toole in the gut. Our eyes met in understanding; we were partners in an unhappy situation.

Rejoining us at the table, Hercules turned suddenly jovial. Obviously, he thought he had accomplished the impossible once again. "It's too bad that my art gets covered up under the skin instead of being visible to the patient. All he has to show is this little incision." O'Toole's eyes rolled up into his head in mock dismay.

Since both O'Toole and Hercules were on hand to finish up, I marshaled my courage for the exit. "I have several other operations coming up, Doctor. Will you excuse me, please?" That irritated the old boy a little, but he waved me free with a gesture of *noblesse oblige*.

First I scratched my nose, long and hard, a sensual experience. Then I urinated, which was equally satisfying. It was eleven-twenty-five, and since the nephrectomy patient was just coming out of Room 10, I had a few minutes while it was being made ready for the first of my cholecystectomies. Nearby, at the door of the recovery room, I saw Karen, my angel of mercy and sex, pristine in her white uniform. She had come to take a patient down to the ward, and when she saw me she smiled broadly, asking with a trace of sarcasm if I had slept well last night. I told her to be pleasant or one of these nights I would roll her out of bed. Glancing around, she shushed me, adding that she had told her boyfriend she didn't want to go out that evening; she would be in, probably from eleven on, in case I was free. I filed the fact away, but I didn't think I'd be up to doing anything about it.

My aneurysm had been scheduled for his aortogram at eleven-fifteen, and I went down to see what was happening. Stepping into the fluoroscopy room, I saw that the chief resident was in the final preparations for the study. "You're ten minutes late, Peters. I could have used you to help get the catheter into the aortic bulb."

"And I would have been here, but I had to scrub for another case." I consciously withheld a "thanks to you."

"Well, here's the catheter position. Put on a lead-lined apron first. This fluoroscopy puts out a lot of radiation. Gotta protect the old gonads."

Following his advice, I took one of the heavy leaded aprons and put it on. By stepping behind him I could see the fluoro screen. As the lights went out, the fluoroscope came on automatically with a low resonant click. The image was extremely faint, as usual. In order to see a fluoroscopy well, you ought to adapt your eyes by wearing red goggles for thirty minutes or so beforehand. I couldn't tell very much about the aneurysm patient on the fluoro screen, because I hadn't had the chance to dark-adapt my eyes, but I could distinguish the heavy radiopaque stripe on the catheter.

"Here's the end of the catheter." The chief resident's pointing finger was silhouetted by the light from the screen. "It's in the aorta just above the heart. See it jump with each heart contraction?" I could see that with no difficulty. "Now, we went to inject enough radiopaque dye into the artery to get an image, and to do that we have to use the pressure injector." He indicated a small machine that looked something like a bicycle pump turned on its side. It had three or four stopcocks positioned on the end—I thought one or two should have been sufficient to prevent a mishap. "All we do is push this handle, which shoots the dye very rapidly into the heart, at about 400 psi. At the same time the Schonander camera will be shooting X rays at a rate of one every half second for ten seconds. We'll watch on the fluoro screen."

The chief resident swung into the final preparations, calling to make sure the X-ray technicians were ready and positioning himself behind the arm of the pressure injector. Desiring all the protection I could get, I squeezed in behind the lead screen with the X-ray technician, who was a solid little thing. We watched through the quartz window.

At a yell from the chief resident, the X-ray technician started the Schonander camera, which cranked and pounded, taking X ray after X ray in rapid succession, while the chief resident plunged the pressure injector all the way down. The dye shot from the injector into the stopcocks, and then, instead of being propelled into the patient's heart, rose in a graceful geyser to the ceiling, splattering there and running a little way along before dripping down onto the chief resident, the patient, and the mass of machinery. The chief resident had forgotten to open the last stopcock. As for the patient, he just lay there blinking and looking around, trying to figure out what sort of strange test this was. The chief resident was in a state of shock blending rapidly into exasperation. Since the whole procedure would now have to start over and I was already a little late for the cholecystectomy, I took the opportunity to make an unobtrusive exit and hurried back to the OR.

Working with a real professional is different in every way from assisting a Hercules or a Supercharger, and Dr. Simpson was the best the hospital had. With the resident on one side of him and me on the other, we scrubbed together, talking and joking. Simpson told us the one about a Columbia professor who discovered a way to create life in the laboratory. Everything went well until his wife caught him.

A simple joke—perhaps, on reflection, not even a very good one. But in the context of my hours with Hercules, the image of dye all over the fluoro-room ceiling, and my tiredness, that joke plunged me into hysterical laughter. We were still chuckling as the three of us entered the operating room, where the atmosphere changed immediately to one of congenial concentration. Ready to go, we were still light toned, but nevertheless intensely interested in the task ahead.

The nurse handed Simpson a scalpel. Interesting how he started an operation. There was no pause. The knife shot in to the hilt and zoomed cleanly, diagonally down the abdomen. He didn't pause to catch bleeders with hemostats. "Why scratch around like a chicken?" he would say, completing the incision rapidly, with the same sharp, purposeful dissection, as the tissue fell apart. The resident would then pick up the tissue on his side, the surgeon on the other, both using tooth forceps, and with a final flash of the knife they were into the abdomen. Only then were a few bleeders caught and tied. No more than three minutes from skin to peritoneal cavity. Perfection.

This time, however, Simpson didn't make the first cut. He surprised us by handing the knife to the resident instead. "Your gall bladder," he said. "One false move and you'll be doing enemas for a month." Under his expert eye, the same kind of incision was made, at just about the same speed. The surgeon explored rapidly inside, then the resident, then me. Stomach, duodenum, liver, gall bladder (I could feel the stones), spleen, intestines. The examination was gingerly but thorough; with your arm elbow deep in someone's abdomen, you tend to be gingerly. I told Simpson I was having trouble feeling the pancreas. He explained a landmark and a bulge. Then I felt it.

Using Simpson's technique, the resident carefully placed the saline-soaked white towels that are used to separate the gall bladder from the mass of intestines. I was given the usual retractors. At a suggestion from Simpson, the resident moved down a little, enabling me to see into the wound. It all went rapidly, with encouragement but no manual assistance from Simpson. The gall bladder came out cleanly, the base was closed, and then the skin, all within thirty minutes. Feeling good now, I congratulated the resident on our way to the recovery room. He *had* done a professional job.

With thirty minutes between cases, Simpson and I went down to see several of his patients, one of whom, a gastrectomy, I was following closely after having helped with the surgery. I had been given total responsibility for writing orders on the case, although I tried to follow Simpson's preferences, which, I knew by now, were sound and sensible. When he changed one of my orders, as occasionally happened, he invariably wrote out a short explanation, an opinion on some drug or procedure. He was a born teacher.

After our trip to the ward, we put on another set of clean scrub suits and began to scrub again, in the same bantering way, this time without hysteria on my part. I decided, on reflection, to switch to Betadine for this scrub; its pale yellow color offered a bit of variety, after the colorless pHisoHex we usually used. Entering the OR, we observed the usual hierarchic routine. A towel went first to Simpson, then one to the resident, and then one to me. It was the same with gloves.

As we huddled around the patient, the nurse handed Simpson a scalpel, and to my utter confusion he handed it on to me. "Okay, Peters. Get the gall bladder, and get it right the first time or I'll remove yours without anesthesia." Obviously, I had never done a cholecystectomy before, though I had seen a hundred or more, and this development was definitely not in my imagined scenario. I had looked forward to another session as interested spectator, watching two professionals (the resident had come of age) work together. Now, however, I was to be not a spectator, but a participant—indeed, the chief actor. Suddenly the man on the table and the scalpel in my hand took on new reality. Inwardly awash with uncertainty, I knew that if I hesitated now, I might be too scared ever to try again. I somehow conquered a tremor that threatened to develop in my right hand, grasped the knife firmly, and tried to duplicate Simpson's first slice into the top of the abdomen, going straight in, up to the hilt, then coming diagonally down the abdomen just below the ribs on the right, trying to keep the blade at a ninety-degree angle with the skin. I wanted to please Simpson as a son wants to please his father.

"By golly, there's hope for you yet," he said in jest, not knowing how sweet the words were to me. As I repeated the maneuver, muscles and fat parted and retracted. Some bleeding followed, but not much.

"Forceps." The nurse gave them to me, and a pair to the surgeon. I lifted one side of the incision, he the other. At this point we were very close to the thin, peritoneal membrane that forms the lining of the abdominal cavity. We were lifting now to protect the underlying organs as I pushed in the blade of the scalpel. Pop! A hole appeared in the abdomen, and I let go of the forceps.

"Keep the forceps," Simpson suggested, "and cut while you can see." I tried, going carefully because the liver and intestines were clearly visible in the widening incision. It worked fine. Then, for the lower end of the incision, I had to change the technique. Dropping the forceps, I slid my hand into the

wound and opened the rest of the peritoneum by cutting between my fingers. My heart was racing. I didn't feel tired now,
nor did I notice the clock, the radio, or the anesthesiologist. I
was scared but determined. Simpson felt around, then I did,
then the resident, and the resident took the retractors as I
moved down to give him an open view if he wanted it. I also
tried to follow Simpson's technique with the abdominal tapes.
He helped me with the last one, and then with his hand he
rolled the duodenum far enough that I could see a smooth
curve of tissue stretching from the top of the duodenum to the
gall bladder. After clamping the gall bladder and pulling up, I
used the Metzenbaum scissors to push down the delicate tissue.
An artery was in there somewhere, the cystic artery, which
carried blood to the gall bladder. Mustn't cut it.

The muscles of my neck were hard as rocks as I bent far
over, trying to see clearly. Simpson told me to straighten up or
I wouldn't last fifteen minutes. The artery appeared—about
the usual size for a cystic artery—and I isolated it with a gall-
bladder clamp. A tie went around, and I took the ends. First
throw. I ran it down with my right index finger. Good. Second
throw. Down. How much tension should I put on the thread?
That was enough; I didn't want it to break. One more throw,
just to be sure. With the help of the gall-bladder clamp, another suture went around the cystic artery. This time I had to
make the tie way down, close to the hepatic artery going to the
liver. The cystic artery branched from the hepatic artery, and
by pulling slightly on the suture already tied around the cystic
artery I could see the wall of the hepatic artery. In fact, I
could even see the branch going to the right side of the liver.
That made me feel better, because there was always the danger of confusing that bugger with the cystic artery and tying it
off.

I was quite concerned about this second knot on the cystic
artery. It was the single most important tie of the whole operation. If it fell off some days later, the patient could bleed to
death internally. With this in mind, I ran down the first throw
and then peered into the hole. It looked okay. Involuntarily, I
glanced at Simpson, who didn't complain. So I finished it, and
then cut through the artery between the ties, beginning the isolation of the gall bladder.

Next came the cystic duct, through which the bile normally
flows. I handled it the same way, tying it with two sutures and
then cutting between the knots. Once the gall bladder was isolated, I tensely ran a scalpel lightly around its bed so that just

the outside layer of glistening tissues parted. With the scissors, I began to lift the gall bladder away from the liver.

"He's making this look difficult," kidded Simpson. "If he takes much longer, the thing will develop gangrene." I hardly heard him. The whole operation was only twenty-five minutes old.

With one more gentle cut and a tug, the gall bladder came free. I plopped it in the pan proffered by the nurse. With her other hand she gave me a needle holder with 3-0 chromic suture. Picking up the tissue from the edge of the gall-bladder bed and pulling it over the exposed hepatic duct and right hepatic artery, I took a stitch and tied it down firmly. Too firmly. The suture broke. Another, same place, tied this time with more care, less tension. Then with a running stitch I closed the gall-bladder bed.

After removing the towels used to separate the gall-bladder area from the other internal organs, I began to close. The nurses started their sponge and instrument count to make sure I hadn't left anything behind. All was in order. Carefully I identified all the levels of the abdominal wall, especially the tough fascial layer, which had retracted back out of sight. Stitch after stitch went into the wound, with both the surgeon and the resident helping me tie. I dug the curved needle into the lower side, took it out through the incision, repositioned it with my left hand, then through the upper side. Layer by layer I closed the incision, as if shuttling a deck of cards, watching them snap together and overlap. Finally the skin. When it was over a soaring confidence came over me, like the feeling you get at the end of a good wave when your board breaks out of the white water. As I snapped off my gloves, the resident returned my earlier compliment. The world was mine.

Accompanying the patient down the hall to the recovery room, I was still on a high. Two nurses took charge of the patient while I wrote postoperative orders and dictated the operative note. Then the fatigue came back, hard. I was hungry, too, and I decided to eat, because I hadn't had anything but those two slices of bread since supper the night before, nineteen hours ago; it was 2:00 P.M.

Outside the hospital it was pouring rain; had been all day, I guessed, since water was standing in the low spots. The sky swirled with gray clouds chased in over the island by strong kona winds. It was raining so hard I could barely see the coffee shop a hundred yards away. As I ran the breeze ruffled the puddles of water collected under the overhang. I felt my luck go off a little when I saw Joyce across the room, and, sure enough, she immediately came over to join me. With plenty of other people near us busily talking about the rain, the Hula Bowl, and what not, Joyce said little at first, which suited me. Then, as if by signal, everyone else left and Joyce started in.

"Have you been thinking a lot?" she asked.

"About what?" I was curious.

"You know, about us, like you said you'd do."

"Oh, about us. Yeah, I've been giving it some thought," I said.

"Well, I have, too," she added, sitting up a little. "And I think we should be more open with each other."

"You do, huh?" I was slightly sarcastic, but not enough for her to notice.

"We just haven't been telling each other enough about our feelings and our thoughts," she added.

She was wrong there. She had been telling me too much, especially about how terrible it was sneaking down those back stairs. Uneasily, I realized she was only a step from proposing an instant cure to sneaking around—marriage. She was slightly out of control.

"You had been telling me what was on your mind pretty well," I said. "You never stopped talking about those stairs and how lousy everything was."

"Well, that was getting very uncomfortable," she said righteously.

"Uncomfortable. Well, that's true. Why don't you do something about your Miss-Apples-and-TV so we can go to your apartment like normal people?"

"My roommate has nothing to do with it."

"Your roommate has a lot to do with it. If it weren't for your roommate, we could stay over there at your apartment, and you wouldn't have to sneak down the stairs."

"You don't care about me at all," she said petulantly.

"Of course I do, but that's not the point. If you—"

"It is the point," she interrupted.

"You're changing the subject," I protested.

"Well, it's the only subject I'm interested in," she said staidly, standing up and scraping back her chair. "Anyway, I've decided you can stop thinking about us, and drop dead." She strode out indignantly.

Drop dead. A great suggestion. Actually, the idea held a kind of morbid appeal. It was that tired. With Joyce gone, the room moved away from me suddenly. A lot of people were still sitting around other tables, but not a soul was there with me. The sounds of a hundred voices mingled, all distant and incomprehensible. Staring through the window at the rain and the gray scudding clouds, I chewed absent-mindedly, overcome by loneliness. Nothing remained of that good feeling after the gall bladder; in its wake, I was simply drained of all emotion. Looking at the clock, I realized I had been going full steam for thirty hours. I thought about the clinic, and that I should go over there. Interns are supposed to help with outpatients in their "free time." But in my state I wouldn't be of any use. To hell with the clinic.

Raindrops danced around the overhang as the wind whipped them into sheltered areas. It was surprisingly cold. When tired, the body cannot tolerate much in the way of temperature variation. So the chills I felt coursing through me were probably more a product of my physical condition than of the weather. I hurried along, concentrating totally on my bed, anticipating the pleasure. All interns develop an extraordinary appreciation for simple things others take for granted —free muscular movement, the right to relieve an itch, void one's bladder, or empty one's bowels, more or less regular meals, a decent amount of sleep. In bed, I felt my body sinking, growing tremendous and filling the room, until my huge body and the room gradually merged, became one, and I slept.

The abscess was small when I began, no more than a pimple. Now it was enormous, covering most of the left arm and growing. No matter how much I cut, more appeared; now it crept toward the shoulder. Behind me, Hercules was whispering to the Supercharger, "He'll never make it. Neither will the patient." For encouragement, I looked toward Simpson, who said, "Get it right the first time, Peters, or it's Hicksville for you." In one final, desperate effort, I slashed to the bone through tissue, and to my horror I severed the ulnar nerve, immobilizing the hand forever. Time's up, I thought, as the bell rang; failure! It was, of course, the telephone. I leaped to answer it, still half in the dream and confused by the light. Had I missed rounds? No, they weren't until five o'clock, and my watch indicated three. It was surgery. I had been put on a case scheduled to start in fifteen minutes.

Hanging up, I slowly regained orientation. Why should I have waked up in such a state of terror? Then I connected the dream with the incision and drainage I had done yesterday on a huge elbow abscess. After opening the abscess with a sharp blade, causing a spontaneous flow of pus, I had pushed in the tip of a hemostat clamp to insure good drainage. But the abscess was much deeper than I had expected; it seemed to extend to the area of the ulnar nerve. So I had cut down and down, never truly getting to the bottom of the abscess and finally quitting for fear I would cut the ulnar nerve, if I hadn't already. Anyway, I decided to stop by now and check the case on the way to surgery.

The fright reflex had gotten me out of bed, but then my state of physical disintegration began to finger its way back. After having been up for so long, sleeping less than an hour just made everything worse. Nothing about me seemed to work right; I felt dizzy and slightly nauseous when I stood up after putting on my shoes. Unfortunately, I looked into the mirror—a serious mistake, because I realized I would have to shave to join the living. My hand was shaky, and, as usual, I cut myself a couple of times, not badly, but enough so that the blood kept running despite tissue, cold water, and a heavy, stinging application of styptic pencil.

I hurried over to the ward. It had stopped raining, although clouds still hung thick and heavy over the hills. My abscess patient was probably a bit startled when I ran into the room and asked him to hold up his hands and spread his fingers. As he did so, I tried to compress all the fingers together and got good resistance; that indicated his ulnar nerve was all right. I didn't have time to see anybody else except my waterlogged edema patient, whose bed was right next to that of the abscess. He had a question about his diuretic pills that I felt I couldn't ignore.

I had developed a great respect for serious edema cases of the sort that requires a lessening of body fluids by one kind of diuretic or another. My awakening had been sudden and brutal—a carcinoma patient, transferred from a medical ward, who had swelled up through total body edema, a condition called anasarca. I decided that she was in that state because the medical department had missed the boat; there was always a little friction between those who cut—the surgeons—and those who treated with drugs—the medicine guys. This patient had cancer, diagnosed from a lymph-node biopsy. Although the primary site had never been found or the exact type of cancer determined, somebody decided to zap her with radiotherapy, which did nothing to the cancer, and then with chemotherapy, which was equally useless. Meanwhile, the patient was on IV's, and the medical boys allowed her to gather so much water that her sodium and chloride levels dropped to the point where she was practically delirious. And they ignored her plasma proteins, which dropped as well. When I got the patient, I was determined to get rid of all that water. By giving her some albumin and a diuretic, I achieved some diuresis, and hence a slight improvement in the edema. But I wanted more. When I tried to get some advice, nobody was much interested, including the attending. Since her urine was alkaline, I decided to give her a good dose of ammonium chloride with the diuretic, and this time the results were spectacular. What a diuresis! Water poured out of her as her urinary output soared. It was terrific, amazing—except that it would not stop, and overnight she dried up like a prune. Bronchopneumonia set in immediately, and she was dead in a day and a half. I had never said anything more to the medical guys about the case, but I was wary now of those diuretic agents. I was being very careful with this man next to the abscess. He was taking only pills.

Actually, I had learned to respect abscesses as well. There had been one patient—not mine, although I had seen him on rounds every day—who was admitted because of spreading cellulitis in his right leg from an abscessed area. When he came to us, most of his calf muscles had already liquefied. We cultured a number of different organisms out of that abscess; they all seemed to be working together against the patient. One day, when the intern handling the case was sick, I had to drain it. The smell was indescribable; once again I resorted to my three-mask ploy to keep from retching. As I attempted to open the abscess cavity, I realized that it went in every direction, as far as the hemostat would reach. An argument had raged off and on during rounds about whether his leg should come off, but advocates of a new method of continuous antibiotic perfusion won out—at least, they won the argument—and dripped gallons of antibiotic into his leg, seeming to stabilize him for a few days. But suddenly, one day while we were looking at him on morning rounds, the man died. We had just walked up to the bed, and another intern had started to say that the patient was "essentially unchanged." Odd, how often that word "essentially" was used on rounds. This man had been in liver failure, heart failure, kidney failure—in fact, total body failure. But just as the intern was mouthing his neutral status report the patient gasped, and it was over. It seemed an act of enormous bad taste. We stood there dumfounded. No one tried to resuscitate him, because all of us had become used to the hopelessness of his condition. Our insignificant drugs had only supported him precariously for a while, until the bottom fell out, as it had with those Gram-negative sepsis cases in medical school. It was as if he had absolutely no defense against the infection. Thus I came to respect abscesses. In fact, as time went on, I was learning to respect every illness, no matter how innocuous it appeared to be.

Now I was hurrying on to surgery, already late. There was a lot of activity on the medical floor. I passed interns, residents, and doctors standing around beds talking, as they always were —unless they were sitting around talking in the lounge. Most discussions centered on treatment, on which drugs to use. As a point of agreement would near on some medication, one of the participants would bring up a side effect, whereupon a drug would be suggested to counter the side effect, which drug could, in turn, have its own side effect. Which was worse, the question now became, the second side effect or the original condition? Would the second drug make the original symptoms worse than they were before the first drug made them better? On and on it went, around and around, until usually the discussion got so complicated it seemed best to start again, on the next patient. Or that's what the medical wards looked like to me. Talk, talk, talk. At least, in surgery we did something. But the medical guys pointed out, with some truth, that we just cut it out when we couldn't cure it. We countered that cutting it out did, in fact, often cure it. The argument went inconclusively back and forth, always conducted in an entirely friendly, even jovial, style, but its roots sank deep.

Climbing into another clean scrub suit was a compounded *déjà vu.* I was beginning to live in those things. Since no medium sizes were left, I had to wear a large, and the strings of the pants went around me twice. Through the swinging doors into the OR area. While I was putting on my canvas shoes, I glanced at the board to see who was doing the operation. Zap! It was none other than El Almighty Cardiac Surgeon. But what was he doing here? The procedure was listed as "Abdominal abscess, dirty," and obviously El Almighty usually worked in the chest. Strange things had ceased to surprise me, however. As I looked up, he saw me and greeted me by name, being very friendly, but I knew better than to lower my guard. It was just the first move, a condescending act early in the show —especially since he had to shout the greeting from halfway down the corridor to make sure everyone noted his good cheer and camaraderie.

I remembered wryly one time when a resident and I were

assigned to a cardiac case with not one, but two such surgeons. These men, completely alike in manner and hidden behind masks, could be distinguished only by their girth, one being much fatter than the other. That case had begun smoothly enough, with affability and backslapping all around. Suddenly, with no warning whatever, one of the surgeons began to harangue the resident for giving blood to a patient dying of lung cancer. True, the decision was debatable, but not serious enough to warrant such a tirade in front of all assembled. He was just puffing himself up, improving his self-image. So it went throughout the operation, praise and then blame, each overdone, until we reached a kind of frantic crescendo of invective that gradually ebbed away, back into good humor. It had been like a madhouse.

There is something of this in many surgeons—a kind of unpredictable passive-aggressive approach to life. One minute you are a close and valued friend; the next, who knows? It was almost as if they lay waiting in ambush for you to cross some invisible line, and when you did—*wham!*—you got a fireworks of verbal abuse.

Perhaps this is a natural effect of the system, the final result of too much intensity and repression through too many years of training. I had begun to feel it in myself. If he wants to get ahead, an intern learns to keep his mouth shut. Later, as a resident, he learns the lesson so well that it becomes internalized. Underneath, however, he is angry much of the time. No matter how cleansing it might have been to tell some guy to stuff it, I never did, and neither did anybody else. Being at the bottom of the totem pole, we naturally aspired to rise higher, and that meant playing the game.

In this game, fear was symbiotic with anger. If anything, the fear portion of it was more complicated. As an intern, you were scared most of the time; at least, I was. At first, like any good little humanist, you were afraid to make a mistake, because it might harm a patient, even take his life. About six months along, however, the patient began to recede, becoming less important as your career went forward. You had by then come to believe that no intern was likely to suffer a setback because of official disapproval of his practice of medicine, however sloppy or incompetent. What would not be tolerated was criticism of the system. No matter that you were exhausted, or were learning at a snail's pace, if at all, and being exploited in the meantime. If you wanted a good residency—and I wanted one desperately—you just took it without a murmur.

Plenty of hopefuls were lined up to take your place back there in the big leagues. So I held feet and retractors, and took the other shit. And all the time the anger ate at me.

Most of us didn't believe in the devil theory of history, or in an extreme notion of original sin, and so we knew that these older men we hated so much must have once been like us. At first idealistic, then angry, and then resigned, they had finally come to be mean as hell. At last the anger and frustration, held in so long, were gushing out in a gorgeous display of self-indulgence. And at whose expense? Who else? The sins of the fathers and grandfathers were visited on us, the sons of the system. Would it happen to me? I thought it would. Indeed, it had already started, because I had advanced beyond my period of medical-school idealism. I was no longer surprised that there were so few gentlemen among surgeons; in fact, the wonder of it to me was that any doctors at all came out as whole human beings. Apparently, few did. Not among them was El Almighty, whom I was about to face.

He slapped me on the back, wanting to know how every little thing was. It was as if he were going to give me candy or kiss my baby like a corrupt big-city politician gathering votes. Actually, he was gathering ego points. I was so tired I didn't care what he said or did. I kept my head down, scrubbing away, taking one step at a time. I put on the gown, and then the gloves. The scene around me was unreal. The surgeon's voice boomed on about nothing and everything, several decibels above everyone else. The anesthesiologist seemed to have either a special immunity or effective earplugs; oblivious to the surgeon, he went quietly about his business. Even the nurse ignored El Almighty. Whether he asked politely for a clamp or thundered for one, she would hand it to him in the same reserved efficient way and go on adjusting the instruments. I hoped he was listening closely to himself, because he apparently was his only audience.

The case turned out to be a reoperation for inflammation of the little pockets older people sometimes get in the lower colon. This unlucky patient had been operated on for his diverticulitis, as the condition is called, about a month before. Normally, a three-stage operation is recommended, but the first surgeon to operate on the fellow had tried to do it all at once. The result was a large abscess, which we were about to drain, and a fecal fistula, leading through the previous incision down into the colon, that was draining pus and feces.

Mercifully, the procedure was short. I tied a few knots, all unsatisfactory to the surgeon. Otherwise, I remained silent and immobile as he went on about the vicissitudes of his life when he was an intern. "Really tough in those days . . . do histories and physicals . . . every patient . . . through the door . . . and besides . . . quarter of the salary . . . and you crooks get . . ." I hardly heard it. My exhaustion really made me immune, bouncing all his comments off my brain.

At the end I wandered out and changed into my regular clothes. It was almost four. A little afternoon sun had dodged the thick clouds and was sneaking in the window. The rays refracted and sparkled off the raindrops clinging to the window. It made me think of going surfing. But afternoon rounds were still to come; I wasn't free yet.

Descending to one of the private surgical wards, I saw my gall-bladder patient, who was doing fine. Blood pressure, pulse, urine output—all normal. The IV was going well, and orders were adequate for the night. I wrote in the chart and walked down to the other gall bladder, although I was sure the resident had seen her. And he had.

Stopping by X-ray, I asked a secretary to locate the aortogram taken on my aneurysm that morning, so I could have a quick look. The chief resident had apparently accomplished the job after his mighty struggle. The secretary found the films right away, and I began to put them up on the viewer. There were so many they would not all fit on the screen. Thank goodness the numbers allowed me to get them up in sequence. Now to find the problem—usually an educated guess for me. But this time even I could make out a sizable bulge in the aorta, just beyond the left subclavian artery. Catching sight of me in front of the X rays, the radiologist called me over to give me the usual pitch on portable films, with special reference to the hernia man of the night before. But this time I got the last word. The radiologist was subdued to learn that the patient had died. Perhaps he believed now that I couldn't have sent him up for a regular shot. I relished the victory, although of course I didn't think the X ray, good or bad, could have made any difference.

Everybody on ward service was under control. Both hernias were in good condition, already walking; the gastrectomy had taken a full meal; the veins were ready to go home in the morning; one of the hemorrhoids had had a bowel movement. My abscess patient, not unreasonably, wanted to know why I had squeezed his fingers, and the edema man asked again about his pills, wondering how they made him lose water. I humored both patients with overly simplistic answers.

Only one problem—a new patient, or, rather, a new-old patient, for me to work up. This man, a big decubitus ulcer, had a history of at least twenty-five previous admissions. One was for swallowing razor blades, others for attempted suicide by more traditional methods and for psychoneurotic-conversion reactions, convulsions, alcoholism, abdominal pain, gastric ulcer, appendicitis, liver incompetence—his chart was a check list of primary and secondary diseases. He had also been in and out of the state mental hospital for ten years. Just the sort of patient I needed, in my freshness and good humor. Talking with him was impossible, because he was so intoxicated he could remember only wild, sketchy details about the previous few hours. Trying to examine him and go through the charts took over an hour. Then I had to clean out his ulcer, a process known by the romantic-sounding French word *débridement*.

Bent over his buttocks and staring into the black and oozing necrotic ulcer that he had contracted from lying in the same position too long, I wished I had studied law. With a law degree, I would already have been out earning a living for two years. A full wardrobe, an impressive office, crisp, clean papers, a secretary, long, full nights of sleep—all would have been mine. Not one of them was mine now. Instead, I was crouching over an alcoholic's smelly posterior snipping out dead tissue, trying to avoid the stench and discourage nausea. It had been exciting the first time in medical school, putting on that white coat and pretending I was a part of the seething, mysterious hospital complex. And how I'd envied the senior students and interns, with their stethoscopes and little black books and purposeful, knowledgeable ways. I had made it, slowly climbing the ladder of medicine and jumping the specific hurdles—until reality yawned before my eyes. Those buttocks were reality, the rear end of life, where I lived.

As I cut, the ulcer started to bleed a little at the edges. When the patient's knuckles turned white where he was gripping the sheets, and when he started to swear and pound the pillow, I decided that I had reached viable tissue. I squirted in some Elase, which was supposed to continue cleaning the wound by enzymatically breaking down the dead tissue; then I packed it with iodoform gauze. That iodoform gauze was not Chanel No. 5, but at least it dominated the other smells, changing them from sickly dirty to unpleasantly chemical. I preferred the chemical smell. The Elase? I didn't know whether it would work, but I put it in because of an article I'd read recently; it made me feel I was doing something scientific.

Before me now was the joy of afternoon rounds. No one liked these rounds, and few felt it was necessary for all of us to be there, because all essential arrangements were made by committee, so to speak. Nevertheless, we had afternoon rounds as if they were one of the Ten Commandments. Standing for long dreary minutes on one foot, then the other, we talked and gestured, indicating here a hemorrhoid, there a gastrectomy. We looked into all the wounds to make sure they were closed and not fiery red. The dressings were replaced rapidly, haphazardly, while the patients submitted like silent sacrifices on an altar. When one of them ventured a question, it was usually ignored, lost in the patter—"How many days since the operation?" "Should we switch to a soft diet or stay with full fluids?" Like the others, I presented my cases in a terse monotone. "Hemorrhoids, two days postoperative, wick out, no bleeding, no BM yet, normal diet."

We shuffled to the next bed; a couple of doctors seemed to become interested in a crack in the ceiling plaster near one of the lights. "Gastrectomy, six days postoperative, soft diet, has passed flatus but no BM, wound healing well, sutures out tomorrow, discharge anticipated." Somebody asked if the operation had been a Billroth I or II. Of course, he didn't give a damn; it was just one of those questions you always asked about a gastrectomy. "Billroth II."

Somebody else asked if there had been a vagotomy. "Yes, there was a vagotomy, and final path report was positive for neural tissue." The patient suddenly got interested and asked what a vagotomy was, but no one paid any attention. Instead, a resident asked if the vagotomy had been selective—another timely query that would lead into a maze. "No, it was not selective. The path report on the ulcer substantiated a preop diagnosis of peptic disease." By suddenly injecting concrete information not directly associated with the trend of the conversation, I had effectively changed the subject, and we shuffled on to the next bed.

Somnolently we went, growing tired and fidgety, and messing up all the dressings. The attending said that everything seemed to be under control and that he'd see us at the same time the following day. As in the sixth grade, in a game of spud, everybody scattered in all directions, except me. Apparently I had the ball, because I simply stood there, not thinking about anything in particular, just staring at the corner of a table that was tilted somehow and made the perspective look a little strange.

When I broke out of my semitrance, I was undecided about what to do. I could check on the private cases again, or I could sit around the ward and wait for new admissions, or I could go back and take a nap. The last option was immediately ruled out on superstitious grounds. If I went to sleep, I was sure to be called about some admissions, whereas if I stayed on the ward perhaps none would come in. A very scientific point of view. Anyway, I parked myself at the nurses' station and leafed through some back issues of *Glamour* one of the girls had left behind. I wasn't recording anything I saw. Flipping the pages and watching the patterns of colors as pictures mingled with print, I was lost in my own closed world, taking account of the sounds and motions around me but indifferent to them. One external event did penetrate my wall: it had started to rain again. Curiously, the sound of rain made me want to go surfing; a good wave or two might rinse away my depressing thoughts. I was overtired, and I knew that I'd be restless if I went directly to bed. Besides, there was a good hour of daylight left.

The rain fell cold on my bare back as I tied the board to the roof of the VW. Once in the car, I turned on the heater and strained to see out the window. It was raining quite hard, and the wipers were having trouble, as usual, keeping up with the water. I had great faith in VW's, except for the wipers. They never kept the window clear without distortion—curiously bad engineering on an otherwise reliable car.

As I drove toward the beach the rain increased, breaking my image of the road into blurs of gray and black. From time to time I strained my head out the side window to regain perspective. The passenger-side wiper was working a little better now, and I found I could see pretty well by leaning over that way. Somehow the rain began to comfort me, closing in the world a little and heavily dominating my awareness.

The rain felt even colder on my back as I struggled to get the surfboard off the rack. The heater in the car had not been a good idea. Once the board was off the car and on my head, however, I was protected from the icy drops. Eager to see the waves, I trotted across the street and onto the beach, but, of course, I could not see more than a few yards into the gray of air and sky. For the first time in my experience, the beach was completely deserted. Plopping the board in the water, I jumped on in a kneeling position and began to paddle out furiously, trying to generate some heat in my cold bones. The rain pelted down hard enough to hurt my nose, forcing me to put my head down and peer ahead from under my eyebrows. The water was choppy and disorganized as I headed out. The farther I went, the more difficult it became to maintain speed and direction in the face of the strong onshore kona wind. Paddle, paddle, looking down, most of the time, at my board just in front of my knees. The water swept by in swirls. When the front of the board came out of the water, it would appear to be dry because of the wax, but then the board would go awash again as I leaned into another stroke.

Out in the surf, the beach, and the whole island, vanished in a misty wall of rain. This was storm surf, choppy, windy, and completely unpredictable. When I caught a wave, I couldn't tell how it would go, whether it would break or just disappear. Gone were the usual harmonic motions and familiar landmarks. I could have been a thousand miles at sea. The only sounds were those of wind, rain, and waves. My mind began to see fantastic shapes in the waves and in the unvarying gray curtain that hung over me. Imagining sharks patrolling under the disturbed surface of the water, I pulled my arms and legs up and lay flat on the board. A wave suddenly reared, broke, and turned me over. In a panic, I scrambled back on the board like a cat with his ears flattened, afraid to look back. I let the wave action and the wind push me toward shore as I searched for signs of the island, reassurance that I was not adrift on a lonely sea. Relief flooded over me as the hazy outline of a building took shape. My skeg scraped coral. Then the deserted beach appeared, its texture beaten by the rain into millions of miniature craters. A few people hurried along, grotesque and faceless blobs trying to shield themselves from the rain and wind.

Once in the car, I turned the heater back on, with wrinkled fingers, and felt its welcome heat rush out of the vent. I was blue and shivering by the time I headed back to the hospital, again leaning over to the passenger side to see out. It was still raining very hard, and the lights of the other cars shot off the wet pavement in broken, scattered paths.

Happiness is a hot shower. Billows of warm vapor filled the stall, washing away the salt and the cold and the stupid little fears my tired mind had conjured up. I stayed there for almost twenty minutes, letting the warm water splash onto the top of my head and run down all the crevices and bumps of my body. As I relaxed, I began to think about how to pass the evening. Sleep. I should sleep. I knew that. But I also had a compulsion to get away from the hospital, to see someone. Karen had said she was not going out, after all. Karen. That was it: I'd park in front of her TV set, drink beer, and let my mind vegetate. Every other night I was off duty the telephone stayed quiet. It was a pleasure to know it wouldn't ring. Tonight was going to be one of the quiet nights. Ahhhh.

I dried myself, slowly and luxuriously, and then padded back to my room with a towel wrapped around my middle. The bed looked tempting, but I was afraid that if I slept for six hours or so and then got up, I wouldn't be able to drop off again. It was better to stay up and sleep later. Then the phone rang. In all innocence, I answered it. I shouldn't have, because it was the intern who was on call. He was in a jam and had to go home for an hour, maybe two at the most. It was a problem that couldn't wait.

"I'm sorry, Peters, but I've got to do it. Would you cover for me?"

"Is there any surgery scheduled?"

"No, none at all. Everything's quiet."

Though the idea of covering made me weak, I couldn't refuse. It's a part of the code to help, and who knew?—I might want the favor returned sometime.

"Okay, I'll cover for you."

"God, thanks, Peters. I'll let the operator know you're covering, and I'll be back as soon as possible. Thanks again."

Hanging up, I thought wearily that if I had to go to surgery I'd pass out. I was sure to go to pieces either mentally or physically if faced with a long session of any sort, especially a scrub with somebody like the Supercharger or Hercules of El Almighty Cardiac Surgeon.

In anticipation, I put on my whites, again hoping to ward off evil by excessive preparation. When I called Karen I got no answer, and I vaguely remembered her saying something about eleven, but I couldn't remember exactly. For lack of anything else to do, I lay down and opened a surgical textbook, propping it on my chest. Its weight made breathing a little difficult. Not really concentrating on the book, my mind wandered to Karen. What was she doing at seven o'clock if she wasn't out with her boyfriend? I couldn't say I had much reason to trust her. Still, what did I mean by trust? Why should the word enter into it at all? It was a bit adolescent to speak of trust when we were just a convenience to each other.

I had been lulled to sleep by my reveries when the phone

woke me up. The blasted surgical text was still on top of my chest, and I was breathing with my abdominal muscles. It was the emergency room.

"Dr. Peters, this is Nurse Shippen. The operator says you're covering for Dr. Greer."

"That's right." I reluctantly agreed.

"The intern on duty here is really behind. Would you come down and help out?"

"How many charts are waiting in the basket?"

"Nine. No, ten," she answered.

"Did the intern actually ask for help?" Hell, I'd been ten charts behind every Friday and Saturday night during my months on the emergency service.

"No, but he's quite slow, and—"

"If he gets behind about fifteen or so, and if the intern himself asks for me, then call back."

I hung up, stuffed to the eyeballs with those ER nurses, always pretending to run the show and make the decisions. The ER was that intern's territory; perhaps he would be angry if I suddenly appeared. There was a grain of truth and a pound of rationalization in that, I suppose. Still, during my two months in the emergency room, not once had I asked for help from the on-call intern. I couldn't imagine its being uncontrollably crowded and busy on a Wednesday night. I tried to read a little more, making no headway and growing more nervous and upset. My hands shook slightly—something new—as I balanced the book on my chest. My thoughts raced around disconnectedly from surgery to Karen to the lousy time I had had surfing and back to surgery. Getting up, I went to the toilet, indulging a slight diarrhea—not unusual with me these days.

When the phone rang again, it was the same officious ER nurse saying with satisfaction that the intern had requested help. It so pissed me off that I didn't say anything, just hung up. Before I could even get out of the room, the phone rang once more. It was the nurse asking huffily whether I was coming or not. I summoned as much acid as possible and said that I'd be there if they could possibly handle things while I put on my shoes. It had no effect. She was beyond insult, and I was almost beyond caring, in no hurry to rush over; perhaps by the time I got there things would be quiet. I wouldn't have minded doing a quiet suture or two, something like that. But I was sure to get slugged with a freeway wreck or convulsion.

The rain had passed overhead, and a star or two twinkled between the black violet hulks of heavy clouds. The wind had

shifted again, back to the trades, blowing away the kona
weather.

Upon reaching the ER, I had to admit that things were far
from calm. A medical intern and two residents were working
away. In addition, four or five attendings were there seeing
their own patients. One of the nurses handed me a chart and
said that this fellow had been waiting for some time; they
hadn't been able to reach his private physician. I took the
chart and headed for the examining room, reading as I went.
Chief complaint was "Nervousness; ran out of pills." Christ! I
stopped and looked closer at the chart. The private doctor was
a psychiatrist; no wonder they couldn't locate him. And the
patient, a thirty-one-year-old male, was in the psych room.
That was back the other way, to the right. Just my luck, I
thought, a psych patient. Why not a simple scalp laceration—
something I could fix—instead of an inside-the-head job?

As I walked into the psych room and sat down, I faced a
youngish-looking man sitting on the bed. The bed and the
straight-backed chair I was in were the only two pieces of furniture in an otherwise plain, white-walled room. Both bed and
chair were securely fastened to the floor. It was spotlessly
clean in there, and quite bright from a bank of white fluorescent lights built into the ceiling. After glancing at the chart
again, I looked at him. He was a reasonably good-looking fellow with brown hair, brown eyes, and neatly combed hair. His
hands were clasped in front of him, giving the only hint of his
nervousness; they worked against one another as if he were
molding clay in the palms of his hands.

"Not feeling well?" I asked.

"No. Or, yes, I'm not feeling too well," he replied, putting
his hands on his knees and looking away from me. "I suppose
you're an intern. Isn't my doctor coming?"

I looked at him for a few seconds. I had learned that letting
them talk was the best thing, but it became apparent he wanted me to answer his questions. "Yes, I'm an intern," I said, a
bit defensively. "And no, we can't reach your doctor. However, I believe we can help you now, and you can see your own
doctor later, perhaps tomorrow."

"But I need him now," he insisted, taking out a cigarette,
which I allowed him to light. Psych patients could smoke if
they wanted to; there was no oxygen in this room.

"Why don't you tell me something about what's bothering
you, and either I or the psychiatry resident will be able to

help." I was certain I couldn't get the psychiatry resident to come in, but I could probably get him on the phone.

"I'm nervous," he said. "I'm nervous all over, my whole body, and I can't sit still. I'm afraid I'm going to do something."

There was a pause. He was looking at me again, steadily. Although he had lit the cigarette, he did not raise it to his mouth, but held it between his second and third fingers, with its trail of smoke snaking up past his face. His eyes, wide open, showed relatively dilated pupils. Moisture glistened at the hairline above his forehead.

"What kind of thing are you afraid you'll do?" I wanted to give him all the rope he'd take. Besides, I didn't really care whether I sat there for a long time or not. The other ER problems, out in the pandemonium, would get solved without me. Served them right for giving me a psych patient.

"I don't know what I might do. That's half the problem. I just know that when I get this way I don't have too much control over what I think . . . over what I think. Think." He was looking straight ahead at the white wall, staring without blinking. Then he made a sudden grimace, his mouth forming a tight slit.

"How long have you been having this type of problem?" I asked, trying to break the trance, to keep him talking. "How long have you been under the care of a psychiatrist?"

At first he seemed not to hear me at all, and I was about to repeat my question when he turned toward me once more. "About eight years. I have been diagnosed as a schizophrenic, paranoid type, and I've been hospitalized twice. I have been under a psychiatrist's care ever since the first hospitalization, and doing well, especially over the last year or so. But tonight I feel like I did a number of years ago. The only difference is that now I know what is happening. That's why I need more Librium, and why I must see my doctor. I have to stop this before it gets out of control."

His insight surprised me. I surmised that he had been under quite intensive care, maybe even psychoanalysis. He was intelligent, without a doubt. Although I was a novice at this sort of thing, I knew enough to try to keep him talking and communicating. It would have been easy just to give him some more Librium and wait for it to take effect or not. But I was interested now, partly in him and partly in his ability to keep me out of the rest of the ER. In the background I picked up the wail of a screaming child. "What necessitated your hospitalization?" I asked.

He responded eagerly. "I was in college, in New York, and having some mild difficulties with my studies. I was living at home with my mother. My father died when I was a baby. Then, during my second year of college, my mother started having an affair with this man, which bothered me, although at first I didn't know why. He was very gentlemanly, handsome and pleasant and all that. I suppose I should have liked him. But I didn't. I know that now. In fact, I hated him. At first I kept telling myself I liked him. I mean I was attracted to him. I know that now, too."

I was beginning to get the picture—the same one that psychiatry had given him, a framework for his anxieties. Now that I had him started, he kept going.

"And my mother, well, I began to hate her, too, for several reasons. It was hate on an unconscious level, of course. One reason was for starting up with this man and leaving me out in the cold, and the other for keeping him to herself. I think I had latent homosexual tendencies. But I loved my mother. She was the only person I was close to at all. I didn't have many friends—never had—nor did I find much enjoyment in dating. Well, then President Kennedy was killed, and I heard it was some young guy. I was riding in the subway coming home from school at the time, and I could see the newspapers all around me: KENNEDY ASSASSINATED BY YOUNG MAN. I was nervous, had been for days, and all of a sudden, since I was a young man, I decided, don't ask me how, that I had been the one who killed Kennedy. The next couple of days were just hell, as much as I can remember about them. I didn't go home. I was terrified that everybody was out to get me. What made it worse, people were crying everywhere. I was worried that they would find out about me being the murderer, so I just kept running, for two days, apparently, afraid of every person I saw, and, believe me, it's hard to get away from people in New York. Luckily, I ended up in a hospital. It took me almost a year to calm down, and another year of intensive care to understand what had happened to me. Then things went . . ."

Suddenly he stopped dead in the middle of the sentence and stared at the wall again. Then he looked at me and asked, "Would you take my blood pressure? I'm worried it's too high."

I didn't mind taking his blood pressure, but the room held

no equipment. I went out for a pressure cuff, slightly dazed by the sudden, concise, and overwhelming history of a paranoid schizophrenic. On my way back, a nurse tried to give me another chart, but I waved her off, saying that I wasn't finished with my present patient.

Back in the room, my patient had his sleeve rolled up in anticipation. He was intensely interested as I put the cuff around his arm, and he tried to see the gauge when I pumped it up. His pressure was 142/96. I told him it was slightly elevated, but consistent with his agitation. Actually, I was a little surprised at its height. Then I asked him what had happened after he got out of the hospital.

"Which time?" he asked.

"You were hospitalized more than once?"

"Twice. I told you."

"What happened after the first hospitalization?"

"Everything went fine. I saw my psychiatrist regularly. Then, out of the clear blue sky, I started getting nervous, like now, and it got worse and worse, until I had to go back in the hospital for another four months."

"How long was the interval between hospitalization?" I asked.

"About a year and a half. The real problem was that we could never figure out why it happened the second time. I wasn't paranoid, just nervous. I had what they call all-pervading anxiety. Then my psychiatrist started to talk about pseudoneurotic schizophrenia, but I didn't understand that so well, even though I read a lot about it. That's why this situation worries me so much. I'm nervous now, really nervous. I have that same anxiety like before I went into the hospital the second time, and I can't stand it. I don't want things to go crazy again. I don't know why I should be feeling like this now. Everything has been going fine lately. Even my business is good."

I realized that he must have been psychologically well compensated. He had been able to make a new home in Hawaii and even to start a business. Oddly, I felt nervous, too, but, of course, for different reasons and to a different degree. I was exhausted, but my trouble could be cured with a little sleep and relaxation. His was long-term, and, besides, he was worried that he might go suddenly out of control. A nurse opened the door, started to say something, and then closed it when she saw us talking.

"Do you have many friends here?" I asked.

"No, not really. I've never had very many friends. I prefer to stay home and read. I just don't enjoy going out and sittin' in bars and drinking. It seems like such a waste of time. I guess I don't have very much in common with other people. I like to surf now and then, and I have a couple of guys I go surfing with, but not always. Most of the time I surf by myself."

That amused me for a moment. A schizophrenic surfer. But in some ways his style was a little like mine. "How about your mother? Where is she these days?"

"She's back in New York. She married that fellow she had been going with. My psychiatrist suggested I go away for a while. That's why I came to Hawaii. It certainly has changed my life for the better."

I got up and walked over toward the door. One of my legs had begun to go to sleep, and my foot was tingling. "What kind of business are you in?"

"Photography," he answered. "I'm a photographer, a free lance, but I also do some industrial work. That's what keeps me busy." He got up to stretch and walked toward the other end of the room, near the chair. I turned around, put my hands behind my back, and leaned on the door. He seemed a little calmer, slightly relieved of his anxiety.

"What about women?" I asked, a little hesitantly, wondering what had become of those latent homosexual tendencies he mentioned earlier.

He looked at me briefly after the words left my mouth, and then he sat down in the chair, looking at the floor. "Fine, just fine. Never better. In fact, I'm getting married very soon to a fine girl. That's why I want to be sure everything is all right with me. I don't want to spend any more time in the damn hospital. Not now."

I could understand his concern. By voicing it, he had suddenly moved the conversation to a more personal plane. Not that we hadn't been talking very personally already; but the fact that he connected a desire to get married with his mental difficulties made it easier for me to understand and empathize with him. After all, if he could pull it off and establish a real relationship with his fiancée, she might be the means to a permanent compensation. At least, it was a chance. Unlike many mentally disturbed people, this guy was really trying. I liked that. I sat down on the bed, near the chair he was in.

"That's good," I said. "You're overcoming your basic problem."

"Yeah, it's wonderful," he repeated, without much emotion. The fact that schizophrenics display blunted affects appeared in my mind from some dim psychiatry lecture. It gave me a momentary feeling of understanding and academic pleasure.

"When are you getting married?" I asked, to see if I could get any emotional response from him.

"Well, that's one of the problems," he said. "She hasn't really set a date yet."

That comment set me back somewhat. "But she has agreed to marry you, hasn't she?"

"Certainly she has. But she just hasn't decided exactly when we should get married. In fact, I was planning to ask her again tonight if we could get married during the summer. I'd like to get married this summer."

"Well, why don't you?" I asked. I began to formulate a definite impression of a case of a schizophrenic's hypersensitivity toward any sign of rejection. Perhaps his anxiety had risen because he was afraid of being rejected by the girl. All signs led to it.

"I can't tonight," he said.

"Why not?" This was a crucial point. If things went smoothly, he could be golden; but if she rejected him, it could be devastating. He knew it, too.

"Because she called this morning and said she couldn't see me tonight. When I asked her why not, she just said she had something important to do. She does that every so often."

I knew he was in a difficult position. The more he pushed, the more he came to depend on his fiancée for mental stability. I didn't know what to say. We had reached a sort of impasse, and I thought now might be the time to give him some Librium or something. Then he started talking again.

"Maybe you know her," he said. "She's a nurse in this hospital."

"What's her name?" I was curious.

"Karen Christie," he said. "She lives very close to the hospital, just across the street."

His words smashed into my brain, tearing down carefully constructed walls of defense and carrying everything away. I felt my jaw drop open involuntarily and a glaze cover my eyes, reflecting the confusion and disbelief inside. I struggled hard to regain my outward composure. He was sunk too deep in his own troubles to notice my discomfort. He went on, describing his relationship with Karen. Now, twenty seconds after the revelation, I was outwardly calm again, and listening, but inside, my own urgent messages robbed his words of all meaning. We were like two men discussing the same subject, but in different languages.

So here was the "boyfriend," the "fiancé." I was sharing Karen with a schizophrenic who depended totally on her for mental equilibrium, whose world fell apart when that compensation was denied him, as it had been by Karen's decision to stay home with me tonight. In a grotesque but very real way, we had exchanged roles: he was now the therapist and I the patient. How fitting that I sat on the bed and he was in the chair. About a half hour earlier, I had felt rejected because Karen could only see me late at night, after eleven. At the same time, I had illogically blessed my luck that she had another man willing to take her out, but bringing her home in time for beer and sex with me. The fact that I had been sharing a role with a schizophrenic made it tempting to identify with him, to see myself in the same light. I wondered how much of my own personality was schizophrenic. But surely I wasn't schizophrenic; my grasp of reality was too good. I couldn't believe I had any delusions, because, if anything, I was the realist, especially about my role as an intern. Besides, I never hallucinated. I would have known, I thought. Wouldn't I have known?

It suddenly got through that he was looking at me as if expecting an answer. With my eyes, I asked him to say it again.

"Do you know her?" he was repeating.

"Yes," I said mechanically. "She works days."

We began to speak and think in different languages once more, as he went on drawing out the story of his half life with Karen and I retreated into my speculations. No, I most certainly was not schizophrenic, but perhaps was tending toward schizoid. Searching back through lectures and pages of textbooks, I tried to remember the characteristics of schizoid personality. Most such cases, I remembered, avoided close or prolonged relationships. Did that fit me? Yes, most definitely, of late. Certainly no one would describe my associations with Karen, Joyce, or even Jan as close, or characterized by respect and affection. They were more in the realm of reciprocating conveniences in which I—and perhaps the girls, too—hadn't invested much genuine emotion or attachment. I had to admit that to me they were more like walking vaginas than whole people, serving not as a means to move close, but as a method of escape and further withdrawal. It was the same with my patients. Over the months my attitude toward them had changed. Each case had become an organ, a specific disease, or a procedure. Since Roso, I had avoided all close contact, intimacy, and involvement. Even that seemed schizoid now. Suddenly, vile, sick thoughts flooded through my brain, poisoning me, and I realized that I had to leave this room quickly and get away from the hospital, to some place where I could breathe. Mustering my thoughts, I concentrated on the reality in front of me. "What kind of tranquilizer have you been taking?" I asked hurriedly.

"Librium, 25 mg. size," he answered, a little confused. Evidently I had interrupted him.

"Fine," I said. "I'll give you a supply, but I recommend that you contact your doctor tonight or tomorrow. Meanwhile, I'll prescribe an injection of Librium to give you an immediate effect."

Before he could say anything else, I rose quickly from the bed, opened the door, and stepped out into the fluorescence and bustle of the ER. Mechanically, I wrote a prescription for "Librium 25 mg., sig: T tab P.O., QID, disp. 10 tabs," my mind going back over the absurdity of patient becoming therapist. That in itself seemed an almost schizophrenic delusion. A nurse tried to give me another chart, but I waved it away. I told another nurse to give the patient in the psych room 50 mg. of Librium intramuscularly. I was only half aware of the activity around me. Then, before leaving, I just had to go back and look in on that schizophrenic once more, to make sure he wasn't a hallucination. I opened the door. He was there, all right, staring out at me.

I closed the door and started down the long passageway to my room. It was all too true—all the things I had thought about myself in those seconds after he said Karen's name. I was a cold, detached son of a bitch and getting more so. Everything I thought about confirmed it. My initial relationship with Carno, for instance; it had just disappeared in a disguise of inconvenience. In fact, I had been too selfish and lazy to keep it going. Surfing was probably the biggest cop-out of all, especially since I apparently was using it to cover and relieve my progressively isolated life. And Karen herself—a vacant and meaningless relationship if ever there was one. Feelings I had vaguely noticed, the emptiness and undirected yearning—I had sought vainly to repress them by encounters with Karen and Joyce, even Jan. Much of this became horribly clear to me as I sat in the chair in my dark room, searching for answers.

I hadn't always been like this. Not in college, where friends had come easily and stayed. And the lonely yearning so much a part of me now? Perhaps a little during the first year of college, but not after that. Medical school had come next. Had the seeds of change been planted there? Yes. After all, it was during medical school that friends had drifted away, and attitudes and practices with women had changed, out of necessity, driven as I was by hard economics and limited time. But not until internship had the seeds of change germinated. Now I was sexually and socially little more than a cruiser, except that I operated in a hospital rather than the real world. How different it had all turned out. The phone rang, but I ignored it. Taking off my whites, I put on some wheat-colored jeans and a black turtleneck.

Why had this happened to me? Was it only the schedule? Or that combined with the fear and anger always inside me? Was it basically my self-disgust at not speaking up when I believed the system was rotten, at letting myself be carried along nevertheless, holding it all in? Was my brain so warped by exhaustion it was no longer logical? I didn't know. The more I thought, the more confused and depressed I became. Confused about causes, not effects. In perspective, the effects were clear: I had become a real bastard.

Suddenly, I thought of Nancy Shepard, of how I had pushed her out of my mind, rejected her questions and accusations. That night we argued, she had been trying to tell me what I had just learned from my therapist—my therapist, the schizophrenic. What a triangle, I thought: a double-dealing nurse, a barely compensated schizophrenic, and a screwed-up intern. Nancy Shepard had called me an unbelievable egotist, a selfish blob working toward a point at which love would be impossible. And she had been right. What did it matter that there was more to it; that it was not innate in my personality, but developed; that I had been encouraged, day in and day out, to avoid genuine emotional involvement because to do so was the only natural defense I could conjure up to deal with the anger, hostility, and exhaustion? What did it matter that an intern's routine was senseless monotony, or that the medical system was designed to use and harass him? To a Nancy Shepard—to anyone—the end personality result was all that mattered. She had brushed me lightly with some truth, and I had kicked her out of my life for her pains.

Lying down on the bed, I wondered what to do now. For the moment, sleep. How many bridges did I still have standing? And Karen? I didn't know. Maybe I'd see her, maybe not. I hoped I wouldn't, but I knew I probably would.

Leaving

The appendix lay to one side in a steel dish, where I had put it a moment earlier before turning back to the operating table. The surgeon was finishing sewing up the stump where the appendix had been. Our concentration was so intense that neither of us saw the hand until it crept into the operative field and began groping aimlessly around, palpating the fleshy, moist intestines. The hand was ungloved—most definitely out of place in our previously sterile operative field. It seemed to be a foreign thing from the twilight zone beneath the surgical drapes. The surgeon and I looked up at each other in alarm, and then at Straus, the newly arrived intern, but Straus couldn't take his eyes off the hand. The next few seconds whirled in mental confusion as the three of us strove to connect the intruder with one of the operating team. Just as I dropped my needle and thread and was reaching to pull the hand away from the incision, the surgeon figured it out. "For Christ's sake, George, the guy's got his hand in his belly!"

Awakened from his reverie, George, the anesthesiologist, poked his nose over the ether screen and commented, "Well, I'll be damned," in a noncommittal sort of way, before dropping back on his stool. With a deftness that belied his apparent torpor, he injected a potent muscle-paralyzing drug, succinylcholine, into the IV tubing. Only then did the patient's hand relax and fall back onto the surgical drapes.

"When you said you'd keep the patient light, I never thought I'd be wrestling with him," said the surgeon.

Instead of answering, George eased off on the succinylcholine IV with his right hand while his left opened the tank of nitrous oxide a few more turns. After several forceful compressions of the ventilation bag, to speed the nitrous oxide into the patient's lungs, George looked up to join the fray.

"You know, George, this epidural anesthesia of yours is good fun. Puts the challenge back in surgery. In fact, this case is exactly like a sixteenth-century appendectomy."

"Oh, I don't know," George retorted. "Back then the patients not only attacked with their hands; they kicked, too. Have you noticed how quiet his feet have been? We're making a lot of progress in anesthesia."

As such sallies went, this was a pretty heavy barrage, and the surgeon decided not to return fire. Instead, he directed his attention toward salvaging what he could of the operative field. While he kept a precautionary hold on the patient's troublesome hand, I covered the incision with a sterile towel soaked in saline. Straus and the scrub nurse and I were still sterile, as the OR terminology put it.

Breaking the sterility of the operative field was a serious problem, because it greatly increased the probability of postoperative infection with something like a staph. Some surgeons are quite maniacal about sterility—but never, it seems, in a consistently rational way. For instance, one professor in medical school required interns, residents, and students to scrub for exactly ten minutes by the clock. Anyone trying to get into the OR after a scrub of less than ten minutes had to start over from the beginning. These strictures did not extend, however, to his own scrub, which lasted, by generous estimate, no more than three or four minutes. Apparently the others were more contaminated, or his bacteria less tenacious.

His fastidiousness about sterility had been responsible for one memorable episode. The case was an interesting one, involving a bullet wound of the right lung, and residents and interns were three deep around the OR table. One resourceful medical student, a rather short fellow, was intent on seeing every detail. He piled several footstools on top of each other, stood on them, and by holding on to the overhead light for support, could lean over and gaze directly down into the operative field. This ingenious vantage point worked well until his glasses slid off and fell with an innocent plop directly into the incision. This had so unnerved the professor that he directed the resident to continue the case.

Luckily, Gallagher, the surgeon for the appendectomy, had a firmer grip on his emotions than the medical-school professor had. Though obviously upset, he was still functioning.

"George, see if you can pull this arm out from under the drapes and hold it securely," Gallagher said, looking over at me and rolling his eyes at the absurdity of it all as the anesthesiologist burrowed headfirst under the sheets.

"And, Straus, you just back away from the table," I said.

Poor Straus was obviously confused. His eyes moved back and forth from the surgeon, still grasping the patient's hand, to the trembling mass of drapes that indicated the anesthesiologist's progress, or lack of it. "Just fold your hands, Straus, and keep them about chest level." Straus backed away, grateful for the instruction.

With some difficulty, the anesthesiologist worked the patient's hand back into its proper position and attempted to secure it flat on the operating table. Then the surgeon stepped back and allowed the circulating nurse to remove his gown and gloves, while the scrub nurse descended from her footstool with a new, and sterile, replacement set.

What a way to end my internship, I thought. This was my last scheduled scrub as an intern—perhaps my last time in the OR as an intern, although I was scheduled to be on call that night and could get some after-hours surgery. Anyway, this case had been a circus right from the start. For one thing, the patient had been given breakfast because I had forgotten to write "nothing by mouth" in the chart, and the nurses, who should have known better, what with all his other preoperative orders, had missed it, too.

"Straus, help me with the sterile drapes." I leaned across the patient and held one end of a fresh sterile drape toward the new intern. We were overlapping by one day—his first and my last. I was still officially an intern, although I suppose I had been acting more like a resident since all the new interns arrived. They seemed a good group, as eager and green as we had been. Straus and I had been scheduled together so I could help him get acquainted. In fact, we were on joint call that night.

"Hold it up high," I directed, raising my end of the drape to about eye level and letting the edge cover the old drape. "Good. Now let the upper portion fall over the ether screen." He seemed to catch on easily, and I gave him the lower drape. But the surgeon, now freshly gowned and gloved, was impatient, and he took the drape from Straus, helping me to complete the redraping rapidly and without another word.

It was two-fifteen by the large clock with its familiar institutional face. I could not comprehend that within twenty-four hours I would be leaving my internship behind. How rapidly the year had passed. Yet some memories seemed older than a year. Roso, for instance. Hadn't he always been a part of me? And . . .

"How about a little help, Peters?" Gallagher was already brandishing a needle holder that trailed a fine filament of thread from the tip. But he couldn't begin because the sterile towel I had draped over the incision was still in place.

"Large clamp and a basin." I reached toward the scrub nurse, and she crashed a clamp into the palm of my hand. She was a demon when it came to OR procedure. Apparently she had been watching a lot of television, because she cracked the instruments into your hand almost to the point of pain, and when she gloved you it was as though she was attempting to stretch the glove all the way to your armpit. Using the clamp, I removed the sterile towel without otherwise touching it and plopped it into the basin. The concept of OR sterility baffled me to the point that I always erred on the safe side. I didn't know if Gallagher thought the towel was contaminated, but, to be sure, I didn't touch it. Of course, with the patient rummaging around in the wound with his bare hand, all this procedure was nonsense.

The towel out of the way, Gallagher returned to the appendix stump. Luckily, the patient had chosen a good time for his antics; not only had the appendix been removed, but the stump had also been inverted. Gallagher had been nearly ready to put in his second-layer closure over the area when the mysterious hand appeared.

George, the anesthesiologist, had made a fantastic recovery. Things were already back to normal over his way—the sound level of his portable Panasonic was competing with the automatic breather that had been brought in after the succinylcholine. This was not a mere precaution. Succinylcholine is so powerful that the patient was totally paralyzed now, and the machine was breathing for him. As Gallagher took the first stitch after his arm wrestle, the general atmosphere returned to precrisis level. We even paused to listen when the surf report drifted out of George's radio over the ether screen—"Ala Moana three-four and smooth." But my board had already been sold. Gallagher was one of a couple of the younger attending surgeons who occasionally surfed. I had seen him a few times at "number 3's" off Waikiki, and he was definitely a better surgeon than surfer, being rather dainty at heart. He had a telltale habit of picking up surgical instruments with his little finger stuck out, the way a flower-club lady holds a teacup.

That was the way he took the next stitch—extending his pinky as far as possible from the rest of his fingers and deftly trailing the silk out of the needle holder into my waiting hand. Since I was the first assisting, it was up to me to tie. Straus was holding the retractors. The first throw was formed and run down extremely rapidly, as happens when an act has become reflexive. The opposing walls of the large intestine came together over the inverted appendicial stump. As I tightened the suture, Gallagher pretended not to watch, but I was sure he had an eye cocked. Since he didn't say anything, I guess he approved the degree of tightness I placed on the first throw. Then he took the freshly loaded needle holder from the scrub nurse as I started the second throw.

"Hey, Straus, how about lifting up a little on those retractors so I can see my knot?" It bugged me that Straus was staring off into space just then. I held up running down the second throw while he looked into the wound and lifted with his right hand, opening the wound wider. That made it possible for my right index finger to carry the fold of thread down until it mated with the first throw, where I tightened it with a precision that seemed to me exactly right. Another throw, but with my other hand leading, so the knot was sure to be a square knot, not a slippery granny.

Five such sutures completely covered the appendicial-stump area, and we were ready to close.

"Straus, you did a fantastic job," said Gallagher, winking at me, as he took the retractors from the new intern. "Couldn't have done without you." Not really knowing if Gallagher was putting him on, Straus wisely elected to remain silent. "Where'd you learn to retract like that, Straus?"

"I scrubbed a few times in medical school," he said quietly.

"I was sure of it," returned Gallagher, a supercilious smile creeping from the sides of his mask. "Peters, can you and our young surgeon here close the wound?"

"Yes, I think so, Dr. Gallagher."

Gallagher hesitated, looking at the incision. "On second thought, maybe I'd better stay. If the patient gets a postop infection, I want as few people to blame as possible—just George. George, you hear that?"

"What's that?" George looked up from his anesthesia record, but Gallagher ignored him and stepped back to rinse his hands in the basin.

"Straus, how are you at tying knots?"

"Not too good, I'm afraid."

"Well, ready to try a few?"

"I think so."

"Okay, when we get to the skin, you tie."

The facial sutures went in quickly. My tying now was nearly as rapid as the surgeon's suturing, and the scrub nurse had to hustle to keep up with us. The smiling wound came together as the subcutaneous sutures were placed and tied.

"Okay, Straus, let's see what you can do," said Gallagher, after placing the first skin suture in the center of the wound and trailing the silk thread out over the patient's abdomen. The first skin suture, in the center of a wound, is the hardest, because until the adjacent sutures are placed it bears a lot of stress, and the stress makes it hard to tie with the correct tension. Gallagher winked at me again as Straus picked up the two ends of the thread. Straus didn't even have his gloves on tightly, and there were wrinkled bunches of rubber at the tips of his fingers. He didn't look up, though—which was a good thing, because I knew what was coming and my face was contorted in a broad smile of anticipation.

Poor Straus. By the time he got the second throw down, he was perspiring, and the skin edges were still almost half an inch apart. Moreover, he had gotten his fingers all bunched up in the suture in a fashion that suggested he was going through a comic routine. But he still didn't look up, a good sign. He would be all right.

"Straus, you've got the theory right. Skin sutures should not be too tight." Gallagher chuckled. "But half an inch is pushing a good thing too far."

"You guys can take all the time you want. The patient is going to be paralyzed for quite a while with that succinylcholine," added George.

I cut the gaping suture, pulled it out, and dropped it on the floor. Gallagher flipped in another in its place, detaching the thread from the needle with an almost imperceptible twist of his hand. Straus silently picked up the ends and started fumbling again.

"This isn't the first time I've seen a bare hand in a stomach wound," I said, looking over at Gallagher. "Once in medical school about eight of us students were in the OR trying to see a case, and the surgeon said, 'Feel this mass. Tell me what you think.' The residents all took a feel, nodding in agreement, and then an ungloved hand sneaked between two residents and felt around, too."

"Was it one of the medical students?" asked the anesthesiologist.

"Probably. We never knew for a fact, because we were all

thrown out by the chief resident, who was trying to calm the surgeon."

Straus was still fussing with the second suture, dropping the ends, getting his fingers caught, and leaning this way and that in a kind of hopeful body English. I'm not sure how he expected body English to help, but I recognized the same tendency in myself.

"Did the patient get a postop infection?" asked Gallagher.

"Nope. Sailed through without a complication," I said.

"Let's hope we're traveling the same path."

Without saying anything, I untangled the silk from Straus's hands and rapidly placed a knot, pulling it over to the side so that it was away from the incision. Straus doggedly kept his head down while Gallagher whipped in another suture.

"How about that one, promising surgeon?" said Gallagher, stretching his arms out with his hands inverted and his fingers intertwined. One or two knuckles cracked.

This Straus certainly was a silent fellow; not a sound came out of him as he concentrated on the skin suture. Actually, I was already tired of the game, of watching him fumble around. It was getting pretty close to three; and I had a lot to do, last-minute packing and other details. After a reassuring glance at Gallagher, I again untangled the suture from Straus and laid a rapid square knot, bringing the skin edges together without any tension.

"Well, I think you two can finish this up. Remember, I want only a piece of paper tape for a dressing." With that, Gallagher swaggered over to the door, snapped off his gloves, and disappeared. Straus looked up for the first time since starting the skin sutures.

"Do you want to tie or stitch?" I asked, looking at his drawn, sweating face. Actually, I couldn't decide which would be worse, his tying or his stitching. I wanted to get out of there.

"I'll stitch," he returned, reaching toward the nurse, who, true to form, slammed the needle holder into his palm. The sharp sound of metal on tense rubber glove surged and echoed around the blank walls of the OR. Straus literally jumped, startled by the impact. Then he winced and, after pulling himself together with another quick glance at me, bent over the wound and tried to dig the needle into the skin on the upper side of the incision.

"Straus."

"Yeah?" His face tilted up from his hunched position.

"Hold the needle so that the point is perpendicular to the skin, and then roll your wrist—in other words, follow the curve of the needle."

He tried, but when he rolled his wrist he pivoted the needle holder without taking account of the distance from the end of the needle holder to the tip of the curved needle. The result was a faint metallic snap as the needle broke off right at the skin. His hand froze, while his eyes, filled with disbelief and anxiety, darted from the broken needle point back to me.

Screw, I thought. "Okay, Straus, don't touch anything." "Big Ben" said five after three. Needle points—in fact, whole needles—were almost impossible to find once you lost them. Luckily, I could see the upper part of this one flush with the surface of the skin. "Mosquito clamp." Without taking my eyes off the almost invisible needle point, I reached toward the scrub nurse. Wham. The force of the delicate instrument sent a shock wave up my arm, vibrating my field of vision. The broken needle vanished. I scowled at the scrub nurse. She was a hulk, practically spherical, who surely outweighed me by a good twenty pounds, and her glare at that moment held such unexpected malice that I declined the opportunity of saying anything.

Instead, I concentrated on the delicate mosquito clamp, which was, at any rate, still in one piece in my tingling hand. By placing my left index finger in the incision and pulling up slightly under the broken needle, I was able to get some resistance before I attempted to grasp the embedded piece of steel. Still, the first attempt only succeeded in pushing the damn thing a little farther in. That was when I decided to finish both the suturing and the tying myself. The second attempt was more successful; withdrawing the clamp, I was relieved to see the gleaming needle point firmly caught on the end of it, and with a watchmaker's care I deposited the broken point on the corner of the instrument tray, matching the piece with its base to be absolutely sure there were no missing segments. Satisfied, I asked for a suture, avoiding a look at Straus.

The skin indented under the perpendicular needle as I raised the pressure until, with a pop, the needle broke through the skin. Rolling my wrist in an arc whose center shifted to eliminate torque on the needle point—the force Straus had ignored—I brought the needle point to the undersurface of the skin on the opposite side of the incision. Against the counterpressure exerted by the index and middle fingers of my left hand, I gave a decisive, crisp final twist of my right hand, and the needle point burst forth. Plucking the needle out with the needle holder completed the stitch. I detached the thread by lifting the needle holder so that the eye of the needle pointed upward; the drag on the end of the thread looping through the skin pulled the thread from the instrument.

Following the accepted routine, I dropped the empty needle holder into the draped area between the patient's legs. The scrub nurse would automatically retrieve the instrument and rethread it. Meanwhile, I snatched up the end of the thread, laid four throws of a square knot, and finished with the two ends on a stretch. Only then did I look at Straus.

"How about cutting, Straus?" I said.

He moved without answering, cut the thread, and continued looking at the incision. Ten more sutures were placed in like manner, rapidly and without conversation. After cutting a piece of paper tape and placing it over the closed incision, I turned to Straus. "Why don't you write the postoperative orders? You've got to start sometime. I'll look them over after I change. Then I'll introduce you to your patients. Okay?"

"Okay," he said finally, in a flat tone.

"Also," I continued, "I'll show you what I know about suturing and tying if you want." Straus didn't say another word.

What a drag, I thought. If he's tired already, he'll have a long, long year. But that was his problem, and his attitude didn't bother me for long; I had too much to do. Dropping my gloves in the bag by the door, I left the OR for the last time as an intern without the slightest feeling of nostalgia. In fact, I was euphoric. I felt I had done my time and was ready to be a resident—very ready. Medical practice was at last within sight. As I walked down the OR corridor, I wondered whether to buy a Mercedes or a Porsche. I'd always wanted a Porsche, but they were, after all, a little impractical. A Cadillac? I'd never own a Cadillac. What an obscene automobile!—although it was a favorite with surgeons. Hercules had one, and Supercharger, too. Anyway, a Mercedes sounded better to me.

The menu called them veal croquettes, but to us they were mystery mounds; ketchup was the antidote. Like that of most hospital cafeterias, the food here required a vivid and willing imagination on the part of the diner. If the menu said veal, it was best to cling tenaciously to the notion of veal, despite evidence to the contrary in taste, texture, and appearance. It was also helpful to suppress any knowledge of slaughterhouse malpractices, to be very hungry, and to be blessed with good conversation.

In fairness, I suppose the cafeteria cuisine in Hawaii was *cordon bleu* compared to hospital cafeterias I had seen during medical school in New York. Yet even in Hawaii the food service occasionally resorted to mysterious patties of ground meat, and, as if helping me celebrate, they picked this night to serve the veal, one of my favorite conversation pieces. Also, I was still on call. Even so, the meal was like a banquet. It was my last night as an intern, and yet I was already a step removed from the battleground. Straus would undoubtedly be the first line of defense if and when trouble started.

The climate in the dining room was pleasant. Crisp, thin shafts of sunlight cut through cracks in and around the blinds on the windows facing the southwest. Specks of dust danced in and out of the golden beams of light, like bacteria under a microscope. Leave it to a doctor to think of such a comparison. One of the drawbacks of concentrated technical training, such as medicine, is that your mind eventually reduces everything to a technical experience. The dust could just as easily have looked like fish in the ocean or birds in the sky. But to me it looked like bacteria in a urinalysis sample.

A group of us were sprawled around one of the large round tables near the window. Straus was on my left, just beyond Jan, who sat next to me. In a social context, away from the terrors of the OR, Straus was anything but quiet and withdrawn, as I had typed him. In fact, he was extremely animated, vocal, and, you'd have to say, contentious. He seemed to disagree with every point I made, whether it concerned automobiles, the drug scene, or medicine.

As frequently happened, the conversation had drifted inexorably toward the subject of medical care in the United States. There were six or seven others at the table, besides Straus, Jan, and me, but for one reason or another they had elected early in the meal to listen, rather than participate, and they ate their food and drank their coffee silently, leaving us to jabber on. Their only input involved an occasional incredulous laugh, accompanied by much eye rolling and headshaking, to demonstrate the ridiculousness of what had just been said. Obviously, they weren't going to add anything concrete or relevant. I began to tune them out, concentrating on Straus, who was plunging volubly onward.

"The only way medical care can be equitably distributed so that everybody enjoys the benefits is to restructure the whole delivery system," Straus was saying, alternately lifting his opened palm from the table and lowering it in time with the points he wanted to stress.

"You mean just junk the present system of doctors, hospitals, et cetera, and try something new?" I asked.

"You're damn right. Scrap it. Let's face it. Medicine is behind the times in the way it organizes and distributes care. Think how much technology has changed over the last fifteen or twenty years. And has medicine changed? No. Sure, we know more science, but that doesn't help the man in the street. The fat cats get the benefit of the newly developed isoenzyme test, round-the-clock handholding, everything and anything new. What about the poor guy in the ghetto? He gets nothing. Did you know that forty million Americans have never even seen a doctor?"

Straus didn't wait for an answer, but kept up his attack, moving closer to the table. It was a good thing he didn't pause, because forty million seemed like a hell of a lot of people, and I wanted to question the figure. Besides, what did the figure mean, anyway, since it was common knowledge that plenty of Americans were literally starving for food? What good was sophisticated medical care when people didn't get enough to eat? But the statistic got lost in the conversation as Straus continued.

"What we have is a bunch of street-vending doctors pushing around handcarts in the space age. And it's the doctors' fault!"

"Now, wait a second," I said. I couldn't let that generality go by. "Things might not be in the best possible shape, but there are a lot of fingers in the pie."

"Right, a lot of rich, greedy fingers. I mean when health care, as lousy as it is, takes seven per cent of your gross national product—that's about seventy billion dollars a year— there are bound to be a lot of interested parties. But the fact remains that in the United States doctors have made the system, and they run it. They run the hospitals, the med schools, and most of the research. Most important, doctors control the supply of doctors."

"What about the medical-insurance companies and drug firms?"

"Insurance companies? Well, their hands are not so clean, but, at any rate, they haven't interfered in the doctor-patient relationship—I suppose out of fear of the AMA. I mean if one company pushed too hard, the AMA could conceivably refuse to honor and treat that company's patients."

"Oh, be reasonable, Straus." I looked for support and got no commitment except from Jan, who nodded her head vigorously.

"So you don't think the AMA would do such a thing?" asked Straus.

"I can't imagine it."

"Ho-ho, my friend. Are you aware of the glorious history of the AMA?"

"What do you have in mind? I know some things about the organization." Actually, I was far from being an authority on the subject, both because it had been ignored in medical school and because—well, I just hadn't been very interested in it.

"What do you mean, some things about the AMA? Are you a member?"

"Well, sort of. You know interns and residents can join at a reduced rate. So I did. But I haven't done anything. I mean I haven't gone to any meetings, or voted, or participated in any way."

"There, that's one of the problems. You are a member. You're one of their statistics. They like to think that everybody is a member, only some are more active than others. The AMA claims it represents some two hundred thousand M.D.'s in the country, but do you know what?"

"What?" Straus definitely gave the impression of knowing what he was talking about.

"Their figures are out of whack. In lots of states, it's rigged that in order to get hospital privileges a doctor must join the local medical society, and with it comes automatic and compulsory membership in the AMA. And do you think most of those doctors care or even think about what's going on in the AMA? Well, dream on, because they don't. They say to themselves, I'm too busy; I don't have time. Or perhaps they have a feeling, although they don't examine it very carefully, that the AMA is dirty politics. In that they are correct. But through their apathy the sweet old AMA stands up in Washington and says that it speaks for some two hundred thousand M.D.'s, who never contradict the allegation. To make matters worse, it not only speaks for them, but throws their money around as well. Do you realize the AMA budget is over twenty-five million dollars a year, paid in dues by the doctors who say they haven't the time to find out what's going on?"

"Okay, okay." I had to interrupt him; he was getting too excited. Two of the residents on the other side of the table stood up and left, dropping their napkins onto their trays. It was after six, and I had to get to my packing. Yet I couldn't ignore Straus. By now he was leaning toward me, literally in front of Jan, who had to sit bolt upright to accommodate him. I could see his eyes. He was a skinny, intense guy, anyway, and his eyes were burning.

"Straus, I'm not going to defend the AMA, but it is common knowledge that they've lifted the art of medicine out of the chaos it was in the nineteenth century. Before the Flexner report, around 1910, medical training was a joke, and it was the AMA that took on the burden of altering that."

"Yeah, sure they did. But let me ask you, for what end?"

"What do you mean, what end? To rectify a sorry situation."

"Perhaps, but also for their own ends."

"What do you mean by that?"

"Just that they cut the number of medical schools and made them better—that I'll agree to. But at the same time they locked up their control over the accreditation of medical schools. Translated, that means they have control over the supply of M.D.'s and control over the curriculum. In other words, they have determined the social path through which potential doctors must pass, and they make damn sure that the students are nicely molded into the system."

"Straus, you are a romantic. Are you sure you want to start an internship?"

"I want to be a doctor, and if there were any other way of getting there, I'd do it. But to change the subject, tell me, Peters, are you aware of the burden of history you're assuming in entering the medical profession in America?"

"What are you driving at?" The last two doctors who had been sitting silently opposite us scraped back their chairs and departed. Only Straus, Jan, and I remained, leaning on a table littered with dirty dishes and soiled trays.

Undaunted, Straus continued. "The AMA has an almost unblemished record of failure in supporting, much less initiating, progressive social changes. For instance, the AMA was against the Public Health Service giving diphtheria shots and setting up V.D. clinics. And against Social Security, voluntary health insurance, and group practice. In fact, in the thirties the AMA labeled medical groups as soviets!"

I sputtered, trying to say something, but I couldn't get it out.

"A couple more points. Did you know the AMA fought

against full-time salaried hospital chiefs, and, closer to home, even against federal low-interest loans to medical students?"

"What was that?" I had started tuning Straus out when he lapsed into his list of grievances, until the words "loans" and "students" connected in my head. I still owed quite a bit of money from my medical-school days. "They were against loans to medical students?"

"You better believe it."

"Why?" That really did surprise me.

"Lord only knows! I guess it opened medicine up to the nonrich. But one of the most pathetic aspects of this scene is that after such reforms have been accepted by society and forced on the AMA, the AMA later tries to take credit for them. Makes you think of Orwell's newspeak in *1984*. I mean the whole crummy scene has got to change. I think the government has to do it."

"Okay, Straus. Are you trying to tell me that after going all through those years of study, and all the years you still face, you're going to be willing to work for the federal government? That's what you seem to be suggesting."

"Not necessarily. All I'm saying is that doctors have had the control, and they've screwed it up. Their responsibility is a lot broader than their solitary practices, treating a succession of individual patients. They've got to consider the totality of health care, including the treatment of the man in Harlem and the family in Appalachia—they're as important as treating a chairman of the board in Harkness Pavilion. If doctors fail again, the government will have to take control and order the medical profession to accomplish what is needed. After all, adequate health care is the right of every citizen."

"That's easy enough to say, but I'm not so sure. After all, when someone is bothered by a headache at 4:30 A.M., and he gets a doctor out of bed because health care is his right, what about the rights of that doctor? I mean how much can you impose on one person for the rights of another? Surely the doctor has rights, too.

"And besides, if somebody's kidneys give out, but all the artificial-kidney machines are in use, whom does the patient sue? Society can't have an artificial-kidney machine sitting in the corner for every citizen. The fact of the matter is, health care is a service industry provided by highly trained people and sophisticated equipment, both of which are always in short supply. You can't promise health care to all when you have limited resources."

"I'm not going to argue that point, Peters. The federal government has clearly defined health care as a right of its citizens by passage of the Medicare and Medicaid laws."

"Well, Straus, I'd like to talk to you again after you finish your internship. Up until now you've been a student, and let's face it, if things got too bad you could just walk out and leave somebody else with the responsibility. I wonder if you'll feel the same after this year is over."

Jan had been listening quietly, more, or less on my side, I thought. Now she chimed in. "There might be some problems with health-care distribution, but we do have the best medicine in the world, Straus. Everybody knows that."

"Nonsense," retorted Straus. "Take infant mortality. The United States ranks fourteenth in prevention of infant mortality, eighteenth in projected male life span, and twelfth—"

"Hold on a minute, Straus," I said, refusing to listen to another statistic.

"Only fourteenth in infant mortality?" asked Jan. Straus had really gotten to her.

"Jan, dear, don't be misled by statistics. You can prove almost anything with statistics if you deal with different sample populations. It can be a kind of mathematical gerrymandering. Straus, being fourteenth or whatever we are in infant mortality probably has more to do with the fact that we keep such accurate records in this country. Lots of countries record only the births in hospitals. All others go unrecorded."

"They're pretty good at record keeping in Sweden," returned Straus with a smile.

"Well, then, there are differences in records according to what time during the pregnancy the kid came out—whether it was a stillbirth, dead *in utero,* or whether it was a case where the kid died when it was really a viable being. It makes a big difference where a country draws the line in amassing statistics on infant mortality."

Straus put up his hands, palms toward me, and slowly lowered them as he continued. "Again, I won't argue about the technical details of the statistics. But the fact remains that the United States is not at the top. And fourteenth is a pretty low position when you consider where we are in most other technological and service fields. Frankly, Sweden makes us look pretty sick."

"Sweden doesn't have our problems," I said sharply. "They deal with a relatively small, homogeneous population, whereas the United States is a pluralistic society. Do you mean to say you feel that a socialistic welfare state like Sweden is the answer to all social ills, and the solution for us?"

"It seems to be better for infant mortality, and children's dental care, and longevity. But I'm not saying that the United States should adopt the Swedish system of government or health care. All I'm trying to say is that there are places where health care in general is better than here. That, translated, means that better health care *is* possible, and we have to make it happen."

"Well, you can't create a service industry like medicine out of a vacuum, nor can you abruptly legislate it. Changes in social structure occur only through changes in the attitudes of people. These changes are slow, and related to the educational forces organized to deal with them. People are used to the current doctor-patient relationship. I don't think they want it to change."

"For Christ's sake, Peters, forty million people have never even seen a doctor! How can they develop an attitude? Man, that's a vacuous excuse. Yet it's typical, too. You and your buddies can think of a million little irrelevant reasons why the present system should stand without change. That's why the whole structure has to be scrapped. Otherwise, we'll water down the problem by compromises like Medicare and Medicaid."

"So even Medicare and Medicaid are bad. Straus, you're a real bomb thrower. Everything is black from where you sit. I think Medicare and Medicaid are pretty good laws. The only problem I can see with them is that they screw up the graduate teaching system by making it possible for many of the patients we'd been handling to go to private M.D.'s, who don't let the interns and residents in on the case. As a result, we have effectively lost a large population of patients for learning."

"Well, that's pretty important," said Straus. "And it's indicative of the Band-Aid solution to gigantic social ills. Yet the biggest problem of Medicare and Medicaid is that they have just thrown more money into the hopper, creating more demand. If the demand goes up and the supply stays the same, prices soar."

"Sure, sure." I was getting a little angry now. "What you want is another monolithic government bureaucracy, with millions of file cabinets and typewriters. But this is going to cost a lot of money. Health-care cost would probably go up, not down, with such a bureaucracy. And I suppose you envision all doctors on government salary. That would be interesting!

Society is going to be in for a little shock when it finds out how much money it needs to pay those doctors. Financial return would have to go up, as the doctor rapidly learned to compare himself to someone like a unionized airline pilot, who can get about fifty thousand dollars a year for a sixty-five-hour month. How many doctors would it take to man the health-care system if each one worked sixty-five hours a month? Plus they'll want retirement benefits—"

"That is a—"

"Just let me finish, Straus. Putting all the doctors on salary would have other, more subtle effects. If you are on salary, no matter what you do, it has an effect on your motivation in marginal situations. Look, Straus, when you drag yourself out of bed at 4:00 A.M., you want something for it, something more than the satisfaction it gives you. Lots of times it doesn't give you any satisfaction at all. Quite the reverse.

"After all, the garbage man, the airline pilot, everybody else gets overtime. Well, the doctor is going to want that, too, or he won't crawl out of bed. Let me put it another way. When you work for a salary, you have specific hours. Come five o'clock, and the salaried doctor washes his hands and goes home. I happen to know that, stripped of a lot of mythology, a doctor is a pretty ordinary human being."

"Can I talk now?" asked Straus.

"Please."

"Several things. Number one: a national health service is not the only answer. You're jumping to conclusions. Private pre-paid health plans, for instance, work well, plus improving the productivity of individual doctors for a number of reasons. The government's role could be merely to guarantee that everyone is covered, one way or another, with at least a good-quality, basic health-care package. And number two: I don't agree with your views about the sleeping doctor. At the same time, I do believe the doctor will have to be paid in relation to some rational scale that compares favorably with airline pilots, or plumbers, or anybody else, keeping in mind the duration and investment of his training, as well as the long hours he must work. But, on top of that, I believe that the professional pleasure of practicing medicine will carry the doctor over the bumps in his day—especially if he is relieved of the burden of paper work and other piddling tasks that absorb twenty-five per cent of the solo practitioner's time. Besides—"

"Dr. Peters, Dr. Peters." My name suddenly shot out of the page speakers near the ceiling and echoed around the room.

Straus went on talking as I moved toward the phone in the corner.

"Besides, in group practice," continued Straus, "there is more chance for peer review. The doctors can keep a good eye on each other and offer advice and criticism when needed. And records. Patients' records would be far better, because they'd be organized and complete whether the patient saw the G.P. or a specialist." Straus was literally shouting by the time I got to the phone and dialed the operator. Then, thank God, he finally shut up.

The operator connected me to the private surgical floor, and then I had to wait while they looked for a particular nurse.

"Dr. Peters."

"Yes."

"We have a patient of Dr. Moda's who's having some breathing difficulty. He wants the intern to see her. Also, I need an order for a laxative on one of Dr. Henry's patients."

"How bad is the breathing problem?"

"Not too bad. She feels okay when she's sitting up."

"Dr. Straus will be up right away."

"Thank you."

Turning around and retracing my steps, I noticed the whole cafeteria was empty except for us. The sun had disappeared, and the illumination in the room had changed from sharp, contrasting light and shadow to a soft, suffused glow. It was a peaceful scene, made more so by my inner joy at knowing that I could send Straus to see the lady with the breathing problem and to handle the constipation case.

"Peters."

"Yeah?" The voice on the other end of the line was familiar.

"This is Straus."

"I couldn't have guessed. You certainly do seem to be busy."

"I can't help it. Everybody's going sour," he said. I glanced at my watch. Ten-thirty.

"Well, what's the current crisis?" I asked.

"An old lady died. About eighty-five years old. A private patient on Ward F, second floor."

There was a pause. I didn't say anything, expecting to be told more about the problem. Straus's breathing could be heard on the other end of the line, but he apparently had nothing to add. Eventually I spoke.

"Okay, so an old lady died. What's the problem?"

"No problem, really. But would you mind coming over and taking a look?"

"Look, Straus, she's dead, right?"

"Right."

"Well, what do you expect me to do? Perform a miracle?"

There was another brief silence. "I just thought you'd want to see her."

"Thanks a million, old boy. But I think I'll pass it up."

"Peters?"

"I'm still here."

"What do I do about the family and the paper work?"

"Just ask the nurses. They're old hands at this stuff. All you have to do is sign some papers, notify the family, and get an autopsy."

"An autopsy?" He was genuinely surprised.

"Sure, an autopsy."

"Do you think the private doctor wants an autopsy?"

"Well, he ought to, that's for sure. If he doesn't, he can turn it down. But we should get autopsies on everybody who dies here. It might not be easy, but get the family to agree."

"All right, I'll try, but I'm not guaranteeing anything. I'm not sure I'll be able to communicate much enthusiasm for an autopsy."

"I'm sure you can handle it. *Ciao*."

"*Ciao*."

He hung up and so did I, thinking once again about the yellow woman in the autopsy room in medical school. Jan interrupted me.

"Something wrong?" she asked.

"No. Someone died, and Straus wants to know what to do."

"Are you going over to the hospital?"

"Are you kidding?"

Jan was helping me pack. Actually, she was just there. We certainly didn't need any excuse to be together; we'd been spending a lot of time with each other. So much, in fact, that my imminent departure cast a shadow over the evening, although we had stopped discussing it.

The point at issue was whether I loved her enough—her wording—to ask her to follow me to my residency. I had implied as much many times, yet something kept me from asking straight out. What I had tried to tell her was that I wanted her to make the decision, without my direct interference. I didn't want the responsibility of forcing her to come with me. That was how I viewed it. I mean what if we didn't make it after we got to my residency? If I had forced her to leave Hawaii, then I'd undoubtedly feel bound by some sort of guarantee, and I just couldn't do that. I wanted her to come, all right, but on her own.

Jan and I had had a ball. It had been a relief to build a significant relationship with her after the debacle with Karen Christie and her screwed-up fiancé. Although I had gone over to Karen's a few times after the confrontation with her boyfriend, I eventually realized that I couldn't keep seeing her. So I stopped.

The phone rang again. "City morgue," I answered, in a loud and cheerful voice.

"Peters, is that you?"

"At your cervix, Straus, old boy."

"You really threw me for a second. Don't do that," said Straus.

"All right, I'll try to be more civil. What's up?"

"I got a call from the ICU, and there's a patient having difficulty breathing. The nurse said it was probably pulmonary edema. Apparently the private doctor is worried about heart failure."

"Pretty good nurses in there, huh, Straus? Diagnosis and all. That's real service. Do you agree with them?"

"I haven't seen the patient yet. I'm just on my way up there. I wanted to call you in case you care to be in on the action from the start."

"Straus, your courtesy warms my heart. But why don't you hustle up there, check it out, and then give me a buzz, okay?"

"Okay. I'll call you right back."

"Fine."

Jan was absorbed in trying to fit my medical library into several trunks. It was obviously a problem of Gordian complexity requiring an equally drastic solution. I had to decide which books to leave behind—a terrible tragedy to a doctor. A lot of people appreciate books, but doctors worship them and communicate with them almost sensuously. If a doctor is at all realistic, he quickly grasps the fact that he can never match wits with his library. Consequently, he surrounds himself with books, greedily searching for reasons to buy a new text, whether he will ever read it or not. Books are a doctor's security blanket, and they were mine.

The mere thought of discarding any of my texts smacked of sacrilege—even that psychiatry text, or the one on urology. Urology wasn't my favorite specialty, by any means. I frequently wondered how anyone could spend the rest of his life fooling around with the waterworks—although the field couldn't be too bad, because urologists seemed a pretty happy group, on the average. Undoubtedly they had the best repertoire of dirty jokes.

"You're never going to get all these books in here," said Jan.

"Will, let's take them all out and start over. In fact, let's try to stand them up rather than lay them flat." I showed her by propping up approximately forty-eight pounds of *Comprehensive Textbook of Psychiatry* in the corner of the trunk. Then the phone rang again. It was Straus; his voice carried a sense of urgency.

"Peters?"

"What's wrong now, Straus?"

"You know the patient I told you about before, the one the nurses thought had pulmonary edema?"

"What about him?"

"Well, I think he does have pulmonary edema. I can hear bubbling rales with my stethoscope up both lung fields almost to the apices."

"Okay, Straus. Calm down. Did you telephone the resident on call?"

"Yeah."

"What'd he say?"

"He said to call you."

"Oh, fine." I hesitated, collecting my thoughts. "Is it a private patient?"

"Yes. Dr. Narru, or something like that."

"Is it a teaching case?"

"I don't know."

"Well, check, Straus." I played with the bell of my stethoscope while Straus left the line. Jan was making good headway with the books; it began to appear that she would get them all in.

"Yeah, it's a teaching case, Peters," said Straus.

"Did you call Dr. Narru?"

"Sure. I did that first."

"What'd he say?"

"He said to go ahead and do whatever was necessary, that he'd stop by later and check on things when he made his evening rounds."

With my index finger, I tipped my watch over so I could see the dial. Five after eleven. Either Narru was putting Straus on or he really did make late-evening rounds—very late. Somehow I couldn't imagine that.

"Jan, why don't you put Christopher's surgical text in before those little books? Just a minute, Straus. Christopher's is that big red one. That's it." It was going to be close. "All right, Straus, what kind of surgery did this fellow have?"

"I'm not sure. Some sort of abdominal surgery. He has an abdominal dressing."

"Does he have a fever?"

"A fever? I don't know."

"Is he on digitalis?"

"I don't know. Look, all I've done is listen to his chest."

"Did you listen to his heart?"

"Sort of."

"Was there a gallop rhythm?"

"I'm not sure," he said evasively.

Good God, this guy is really eager, I thought sarcastically. "Straus," I said, "I want you to examine the patient, keeping in mind three possible diagnoses—pulmonary edema, which he probably has, pulmonary embolism, and pneumonia. Read the chart and find out about his cardiac history. Meanwhile, get a chest film, a complete blood count, a urinalysis, an EKG, and anything else you think you want. Is he very stuporous?"

"No, he's quite alert."

"Okay, then give him 10 mg. of morphine and put him on oxygen with a mask. But be sure to watch him carefully when you first give the oxygen. Then, when you get everything organized, call me back."

I was about to hang up when I thought of something else. "One other thing. If he's never had digitalis—at least, not during the last two weeks—give him 1 mg. of digitoxin IV. But do it slowly. Straus, are you still there?"

"I'm here," he said.

"We probably should give him some diuretic as well, to get rid of some of his excess fluid. Try about 25 mg. of ethacrynic acid." I knew that stuff was so powerful it would wring pee from a stone. Powerful—my inner fear of diuretics made me think twice, and I changed my mind.

"On second thought, hold the diuretic until we're sure of the diagnosis of pulmonary edema. If he has pneumonia, it wouldn't help too much." The old lady with cancer whom I had killed with the diuretic haunted me for a moment; she had died of pneumonia. Finally I hung up the phone.

"Hey, Jan, that's great." She'd been able to squeeze in all

but one small book. The remaining volume was what we called a throwaway—one given out by a drug firm hoping to convince somebody that one of its drugs was the answer to all pathological evil. I'd never read it, nor did I intend to. Nevertheless, I jammed it into one of my already full suitcases.

Except for my shaving equipment and other toilet articles, the clothes I was going to wear in the morning, and the dirty set of whites I was now wearing, all my junk was packed. The shippers were scheduled to take my trunks in the morning; the suitcases were going with me, along with an array of hand luggage that included a large piece of coral. Finally all was ready. I could relax and enjoy what remained of my year in Hawaii.

Jan chose that moment to drop her bomb by abruptly informing me she was going home. Just when we could forget all the packing and be together, she decided she was leaving. Obviously, it came as a complete surprise, since I had blithely assumed we would sleep together, as usual.

"Jan, why in heaven's name do you have to leave? Please stay. It's my last night."

"You need a good night's sleep before your trip," she said evasively.

"Well, how about that!" I gazed into her tanned face. She looked at me with her head tilted slightly forward and to one side, flirting expertly and suggesting that her sudden coyness was based on complicated female reasons. Yet I wasn't sure. I could understand her desire to leave if it sprang from a disdain for the artificial last-night routine, from not wanting to reduce our love-making to a sort of ritual to celebrate a passing era. The closeness we normally enjoyed probably wouldn't have been there, anyhow, since we were both preoccupied with other thoughts.

She kissed me lightly, said she'd see me in the morning, and noiselessly floated out the door. It all happened too rapidly for mental digestion.

Fleetingly, I thought of going to the ICU, even though I didn't really want to, but ultimately I shrugged off the thought with the rationalization that Straus needed to stand on his own two feet.

So I decided to take a shower—and no sooner had I stepped in than the jangle of the telephone sounded. The only way I could drown out the ring was by putting my head directly under the nozzle. I shouldn't have left the bathroom door ajar. But habit won out. On the fourth ring I sprinted back to my room and picked up the phone, while a puddle at my feet rapidly expanded its periphery.

"Peters, this is Straus."

"What a surprise!"

"Guess what? Good news!"

"I'm certainly ready for a little of that."

"The pulmonary-edema patient I talked to you about turns out to be on the medical service, not surgical, and the medical intern has assumed control."

"What about his surgery?" I asked, quite surprised.

"He hasn't had any surgery. At least, nothing recent. The dressing was covering a colostomy he'd had put in years ago."

"Congratulations, Straus. Your first clinical success as an intern. But why don't you hang in there just the same? Unless, of course, you have something else cooking."

"Sorry, can't stay. I got a call from surgery. They've scheduled a kneecap removal. Automobile accident, I think. Unless you want to go, I'll head up there."

A patellectomy, an orthopedic case! It was becoming very clear to me how much I would treasure being a resident rather than an intern. Imagine being able to send someone else on a midnight patellectomy! That was true happiness.

"I wouldn't deprive you of the pleasure, Straus. You go ahead and scrub."

Orthopedic surgery really freaked me. Before med school, I had labored under the delusion that surgery was an accurate and delicate science. Then had come the holocaust of my first orthopedic scrub, where I witnessed the grossest nail pounding, drilling, and bone crunching I could possibly have imagined. Not only that—the mayhem had also been accompanied by comments like "Get X-ray in here so I can see where the hell that nail went"; then, after looking at the X ray, "Damn, missed the hip fragment completely. Let's pound in another one, but this time aim at the belly button instead."

Such experiences had quickly eliminated orthopedic surgery as a specialty for me. Neurosurgery had fallen away soon after, when I saw the best neurosurgeon in New York pause during a case and peer into the hole he'd dug in a patient's brain to ask, "What is that light gray thing?" No one answered—after all, he was only talking to himself—but that was the end of neurosurgery for me. If he didn't know where he was after twenty years, there was no hope that I'd ever learn.

With all my medical books packed, I didn't have anything to read to put me to sleep. Then I remembered the drug-firm throwaway I'd crammed into my suitcase. I pulled it out and settled back into the cool white pillow. Appropriately enough, it was titled *The Anatomy of Sleep*. Flipping to the back of the book, I learned it was a hard sell for a sleeping pill. I cracked open the volume haphazardly and began reading. With so much on my mind, I managed to finish a whole page before my eyes began to droop.

The harsh ring of the phone came at me even before I had a chance to start a decent dream. In customary panic, I snatched up the receiver as if my life depended on it. By the time the operator connected me to the nurse who had paged me, I was well oriented as to time, place, and person.

"Dr. Peters, this is Nurse Cranston of F-2. Sorry to wake you, but Mrs. Kimble has fallen out of bed. Would you come over and check her, please?"

The luminous radium dial of my alarm clock told me I'd been asleep for about an hour.

"Miss Cranston, we have a new intern tonight. Name's Straus. How about giving him a call on this problem?"

"The operator already tried," she said. "But Dr. Straus is scrubbed in surgery."

"Piss."

"What did you say, Doctor?"

"Is the patient all right?" I was stalling.

"Yes, she seems to be. Are you coming, Doctor?"

I growled something implying the affirmative and hung up. Clearly, I hadn't graduated from internship yet. Until I actually hauled my body out of range, there would always be one more patient to fall out of bed. Lying there thinking about it was a mistake. I drifted back to sleep.

When the phone rang again, I responded with the usual panic, wondering how long I'd been asleep. The operator enlightened me—twenty minutes, she said—and, canny as she was, saved me the effort of making an excuse by suggesting I might have fallen back to sleep. After all, it happened to everyone, even on emergencies. If I didn't put my feet out on the cold floor immediately, my chances of getting up fell precipitously. For a while, my trick had been to place the phone several yards from the bed, out of reach, so that I had to climb out of the warm nest just to answer it. However, with so many laxative calls that I could handle while horizontal, I eventually abolished that ploy and returned the phone next to the bed.

After the second call, I hauled myself out straightaway and

dressed rapidly. With luck, I could be back in bed in twenty minutes. My record was still seventeen.

The fluorescent lights in the hall, the elevator doors, the stars in the sky—in fact, the whole trip over to Ward F escaped record in my brain. I functioned as an aware creature only when I found myself face to face with Mrs. Kimble.

"How are you, Mrs. Kimble?" I asked, trying to judge her age by the meager light of the lamp on the night table. I guessed about fifty-five. She was neat and tidy, and gave the impression of being a particularly meticulous individual. Her hair was drawn back in a tight bun that had streaks of gray.

"I feel terrible, Doctor, just terrible," she said.

"Where did you hurt yourself? Did you hit your head when you fell?"

"Heavens, no. I didn't hurt myself at all. I didn't even fall, really. I sat down."

"You didn't fall out of bed?"

"No, not at all. I came back from the bathroom, and I was squatting down right there." She pointed to the floor by my feet. "I was trying to get my notebook out of my night table when I lost my balance."

"Well, now try to get some sleep, Mrs. Kimble."

"Doctor?"

"Yes?" I looked back over my shoulder, having already turned toward the door.

"Could you please give me something for my bowels? I haven't had a decent movement in five days. Here, let me show you."

With great effort, she reached over and pulled out the night-table drawer, withdrawing a four-inch black notebook. She had to reach so far for the book that I was sure she would topple over, after all. I moved closer to the bed and held my arms under her extended torso.

"Look here, Doctor." She opened the notebook and ran her finger down a neatly written list of days. Each day was followed by a graphic and complete description of her bowel activity—form, color, and effort expended. Abruptly her finger halted at one of the days.

"There, five days ago was the last normal movement I had. Even that wasn't completely normal, because it wasn't brown. It was olive-green, and only this big around." She held up her left hand, with the thumb and index finger defining a circle about a half inch in diameter.

What could I say to her that would indicate competence and

concern, and, most important, would extricate me immediately? I looked from the notebook to her face, groping for a reply and finding none. I passed the buck.

"I'm sure your private doctor would know far better than I what would be best for you, Mrs. Kimble. Just try to get some sleep for now."

Back at the nurses' station, I wrote something in her chart about the alleged fall; an entry in the chart was required after all such "falls." Then I set out on my return journey to my waiting bed.

"Well, Straus," I ruminated. "What would that little episode be worth under your new system? Professional pleasure, bull!"

My faith in airplanes is not unlimited. In fact, I don't truly believe in the aeronautical principle. But I had to admit that the Pratt and Whitney engines sounded sturdy and reliable. I could hear them smoothly whining as they did their thing, and the huge, ungainly hulk of the 747 lifted off the ground, leaving Hawaii and my internship behind. I had a window seat on the left side of the aircraft, next to a middle-aged couple dressed in matching flower-print Hawaiian shirts. My carry-on luggage had been a bit of a problem—where to put it all—and I sat now holding my piece of coral, which was not designed by nature to fit neatly into a modern public conveyance.

The final good-byes had been rather subdued, after all. At the airport, Jan had "leied" me four times, as Hawaiian terminology puts it. Two of the leis were made of pekaki, and their delicate aroma floated in the air around me. There had been no more talk of Jan and me and the future. We would write.

I had mixed emotions about leaving Hawaii, but no ambivalence about the termination of my internship. Already, though, I was noticing a curious tendency in myself to remember and magnify the high spots, the fun of the year, and to forget the hassle and the hurt that actually had been dominant at the time. The body has a short memory.

As the plane banked to the left, I looked out the window at the island of Oahu for the last time. Its beauty was undeniable. Rugged ribbed mountains jutted toward the sky, covered by velvetlike vegetation and surrounded by a shining dark blue sea. By pressing my nose against the glass, I could see straight down to where the waves were breaking on the outer reef of Waikiki, forming long ripples of white foam. I would miss those.

I thought of Straus just starting his internship, with the

whole year ahead of him. Right now, he was having one of the experiences I had had. Life was repeating itself. Straus and Hercules—that would be quite a confrontation. I imagined that the sharp edges of Straus's idealism would round off soon enough, after four or five cholecystectomies with Hercules.

Like a big bird in slow motion, the plane rolled back to a level position on its path toward California. The only evidence that we were moving was an almost imperceptible vibration. The island was gone now, replaced by an indistinct horizon where the broad expanse of ocean merged with the sky. I thought of Mrs. Takura, the baby born in the VW, Roso, and then Straus again. I didn't agree with everything Straus had said, but he had made me realize how little I knew, how little I cared about the system, except, of course, when it affected me directly. Imagine the AMA trying to block my federal low-interest loan for medical school! Impulsively, I rolled slightly to my right, clutching the coral, and extracted my wallet from my pocket. Settling back into the seat, I sorted through my cards and licenses until I came to it. "The physician whose name and signature appear on this card is a member in good standing of the American Medical Association." The words were impressive. They suggested an allegiance with a powerful institution. I had worked for five long years, and now I was there.

Just then I felt the first jolt, and then another one, sharper, more forceful, as the sign flashed on. "Ladies and gentlemen, please fasten your seat belts. We are expecting some local turbulence," the stewardess droned reassuringly.

I sat there next to the couple in the flowered shirts, holding my piece of coral and folding the AMA card nervously back and forth, back and forth, until the ragged fold parted and the card tore in half.

The Last Word

Dr. Peters has made the troubled journey from medical student through internship to the point at which society will recognize him as a full-fledged doctor. He can apply for, and undoubtedly receive, a license to practice medicine and surgery in any state of the Union. That will signal his readiness to be entrusted with all the responsibilities a medical license confers.

Thanks to his rigorous training, it can be assumed that he is ready academically. But is Dr. Peters equipped psychologically to practice medicine as a modern humane society has a right to expect?

"Old-line" doctors will be satisfied that he is. To the greater number of them, his personality aberrations are merely assurance that the "hazing" he got during his internship initiated him into the fraternity. Internship was rugged for them, and it should be just as rugged for the next generation. Toughen them up—these youngsters are too soft. Does such logic suggest that the older men may possibly be suffering from the same psychological problems as Dr. Peters, and for the same reasons? And what happens to the patient during these juvenile exercises?

The physician's traditional—indeed, antique—lofty standing on the world's scale of social values and, in the United States, the current awe of technological achievement have led to an attitude of increased veneration for the medical practitioner. As a direct corollary of this worship of all things medical, it has become unthinkable to question the medical profession's control over the education of the embryonic physician. Medical schools and medical training programs have been relatively free to do as they please. No one asks why.

Yet it has not always been so. The training of doctors in the United States was seriously challenged once, early in this century, when an extramedical group was appointed to study American medical education. This group—in the landmark

Flexner report—mercilessly exposed the abominable conditions that then existed. Most medical schools, it said, were mere diploma mills totally lacking in academic controls. Indirectly, the report indicted the medical profession itself for having made such poor use of the carte-blanche charter given it by an adoring public.

This document had far-reaching effects. It began a gradual and relentless improvement in academic standards at medical schools. But its effects were not wholly beneficial. For one thing, the report made it possible for the medical profession—in the person of the American Medical Association—further to tighten its grip on medical education by actually decreasing the number of medical schools and training facilities—a move that was necessary, it was alleged, in order to raise the quality of instruction.

And the improvement and standardization of the curriculum that the report instigated caused the pendulum to swing toward the inclusion of more laboratory and science courses in the study of medicine. But the pendulum did not stop swinging until it had reached the point of infringing on clinical medicine. (Did anyone stop to think about the patient?) One result is that today's medical graduates are amply equipped with the latest hypotheses on the more bizarre diseases and rare metabolic processes, but they often do not know the simple clinical facts necessary to treat the common cold or how to deal humanely with a dying man who is beyond strictly medical help.

A feeling grows in America that another "Flexner report" may be needed to bring about reforms in medical training. There has never been an objective examination of the psychological education of physicians. Any mature, honest, and forward-looking analysis would have to consider it with the same seriousness given to academic excellence.

The public is distantly aware that some physicians are prone to personal peculiarities—the surgeon's childish tantrums, for example. Most people are more likely to be aware that when a student enters medical school his head is usually full of idealistic visions about relieving suffering, aiding the poor, and doing good for society. However, few have noted the discrepancy between the number of idealists who enter and the tiny percentage who come out on the other side with their ideals still intact. And hardly anyone makes the connection between lost ideals and the surgeon's silly antics. Or between lost ideals and the preoccupation of many emerging doctors, at the end of their long training, with "staking out a claim" to a financially and socially rewarding group of patients, and with buying luxury houses and cars to repay themselves for the deprivations of their years of preparation.

Obviously, the possibility that a doctor's ideals could change between medical school and medical practice is diametrically opposed to what people want to believe—and to what is presented to them in the mass media. Movies, television, and "doctor" novels have all tended to reinforce the myth of the inherent psychological health and goodness of doctors—especially young doctors.

Thus we return to the credibility of Dr. Peters as the representative of interns in general. Once more I state my belief that he *is* representative. He is not one of a few aberrant individuals. He *is* the typical young fledgling who began with relatively idealistic goals. He *is* the typical student and intern, whose personality gradually undergoes certain modifications that turn him into the whining, complaining, and selfish person we have come to know—understandable, but not admirable.

The contention that the medical world is full of Dr. Peterses is a large mouthful to swallow. If, in addition, it can be accepted that almost everyone who goes through medical school will suffer similar personality wounds, the suspicion might arise that the fault rests with the system, not the people entering it. And doesn't this, in turn, suggest that the system needs to be studied for its psychological effects, and altered toward a direction that would nourish, rather than extinguish, the idealism and sensitivity of its students?

Change is inevitable, and it is the hope of men and woman of good will that change will be for the better—better for society and for each individual. Voluntary reform is a saner and healthier form of change than explosive measures taken as a result of abuse. It is time for analysis and reform in our medical schools and in the medical centers where interns and residents are trained if medicine—as both a science and an art—is to meet the needs of our time. Even the most thoughtful and probing analysis will be imperfect. Even the most earnestly pursued remedies will not be wholly successful. But if we cannot reach the ideal, we can move toward it. At the very least we will have had the sense and courage to try.